M000303266

*Advance Praise for*

# MURDER
## *on the*
# PRECIPICE

Penny Goetjen has that rare ability to quickly capture the reader's attention and keep their interest from scene to glorious scene. In *Murder on the Precipice*, she draws the reader into the raw beauty of the rugged coast of Maine, taking you down the paths with her captivating characters, capturing the local charm of a quaint inn beset by the disappearance of a young female guest. There is elegance to her writings. She is a gifted storyteller and never disappoints.

—Martin Herman
*Author of the Will James Mysteries*

# MURDER
## *on the*
# PRECIPICE

## PENNY GOETJEN

SECRET
HARBOR
PRESS

Murder on the Precipice
Copyright © 2017 by Penny Goetjen
All Rights Reserved. First Edition, 2012; Second Edition, 2017.

For information about this title or to order other books and/or electronic media, contact the publisher:
Secret Harbor Press, LLC
www.secretharborpress.com
secretharborpress@gmail.com

Library of Congress Control Number: 2017950841
ISBN: 978-0-9976235-3-6
Printed in the United States of America

Publisher's Cataloging-In-Publication Data
(Prepared by The Donohue Group, Inc.)


Names: Goetjen, Penny.

Title: Murder on the precipice / Penny Goetjen.

Description: [Charleston, South Carolina] : Secret Harbor Press, [2017]

Identifiers: ISBN 978-0-9976235-3-6 | ISBN 978-0-9976235-4-3 (ebook)

Subjects: LCSH: Women interior decorators--Maine--Fiction. | Missing persons--Maine--Fiction. | Murder--Investigation--Maine--Fiction. | Bed and breakfast accommodations--Maine--Fiction. | Families--Maine--Fiction. | LCGFT: Detective and mystery fiction.

Classification: LCC PS3607.O3355 M87 2017 (print) | LCC PS3607.O3355 (ebook) | DDC 813/.6--dc23

*To Kent, who has always supported
me through all my endeavors,
including this one.*

# CHAPTER ONE

Grasping *tightly onto the cold*, brass railing that traveled waist-high along the inside wall, Elizabeth gazed out the windows through heavy sheets of rain, watching tumultuous ocean waves crash against the rocky breakwater below. The thunderstorm was particularly violent, remnants of a hurricane that had worked its way up the East Coast, thrashing parts of Maine before exiting out to the open sea. Tiny bits of sleet pitted against the windows and were blown away just as quickly by gusts of wind.

She loved climbing the tall, spiral staircase to the old Pennington Point Lighthouse, counting each step as she went, lingering on the treads that creaked. The only thing she loved more was watching a storm roll in from the sea from within the solid, hundred-year-old walls. As a child, she would steal away from her family's home and head for the beacon at the first sign of an impending storm, feeling secure once inside.

Wind rattled the panes, threatening to loosen them from the casings. Larger sleet pellets knocked on the glass before sliding down, etching a trail on the wet surface. With the late afternoon light melting into the grayness of the rain clouds, Elizabeth became mesmerized by the rhythm of the storm.

Movement at a distance caught her eye. Something dark on the breakwater. An animal? Squinting to discern, she stepped closer, swiping the fogged-up glass with her palm and drying it on her pants leg. Was it a person? Someone drawn to the tempest of the sea? An unfortunate soul who'd been caught too far out on the over-sized, jagged boulders when the storm arrived? The shape shifted, appearing to stand more upright. Just as a second figure emerged, a wave rose up and swatted them both down against the rocks. Elizabeth pulled away at the sight and her back stiffened. Biting her lip, she crept closer again. Only one shape remained, flattened against the breakwater.

Entranced by the storm's fury, Elizabeth didn't hear anyone approaching from behind but felt a hand on her shoulder. Pivoting on her heels away from the windows, she over-rotated her turn, teetering in a suspended moment with arms flailing, flopping awkwardly into the conference room chair. She grabbed the arms to steady herself, squinting at the glare from the overhead fluorescent lights that ran the length of the table.

"Sorry, Liz. Didn't mean to startle you." Clearly amused to have caught Elizabeth off guard, her boss' voice was rough and raspy from decades of smoking cigarettes. She preferred the long, skinny brown type that looked more like cigars.

Trying to gather her composure after drifting away from work, Elizabeth felt her cheeks burning. She hated it when that happened. Her boss seemed to have a knack for catching her in uncomfortable situations, or rather putting her in them.

"No, n-no. It's all right. I just—I got lost in my thoughts. Quite a proposition, wasn't it?" She switched the focus back to the excitement at hand.

One of their major clients had just become dramatically larger. During her brief career to date in interior design and her college years at NYU, she'd only dreamed of the opportunity Jack Drescher had just presented. A fairly good-looking man in his mid-forties, Jack was stocky with piercing blue eyes, complete with laugh lines and wavy, dirty blond hair. He usually used too much aftershave, but he probably couldn't tell he overdid it. It reminded Elizabeth of Pig Pen in the *Peanuts* comic strip—as if he had his own cloud of scent that billowed around him as he walked. It wasn't entirely terrible. In fact, she found the fragrance intriguing—from a distance. There were times she wondered if she found *him* intriguing in some distorted sort of way but couldn't allow herself the indulgence to think very long about it. He was so much older than she was. But it was hard to know if he was even her type. Her shy nature seemed to preclude her from meeting guys she found interesting. In the years since college that were approaching a decade, she'd only been in a couple of relationships that fizzled long before turning serious.

During his visit, Drescher had looked uncomfortable in his dark blue Armani suit that belied his humble beginnings. He was a self-starter who had made a name for himself and a fortune to match in New York City real estate. Beginning in the Bronx where he grew up, Jack purchased neglected properties or buildings in foreclosure and renovated them before putting them back up for sale. Soon he had amassed an impressive net worth and moved on to Manhattan. Most recently, he'd been acquiring properties throughout New England, particularly in Connecticut and Massachusetts.

A powerful and well-connected man, he seemed to enjoy a life of luxury, yet never tired of the pursuit of the next acquisition, traveling in impressive circles of politicians, wealthy investors, and dignitaries. Known for his business savvy, Drescher knew the right people in the right places who could make annoying complications go away. Given his tenacity to get whatever he went after and a temper to go along with it, he'd made his share of adversaries over the years as well.

Drescher's latest acquisition was near Battery Park, a block west of Ground Zero, an empty twenty-four-story foreclosed commercial building. Previously used for office space, the front of the property gazed across the Hudson River to the sprawling expanse of New Jersey and offered a view to the southwest of the Statue of Liberty, still standing, unwavering after the dust settled from 9/11. Confident the resurgence of construction currently underway in the area would mean a rebirth in lower Manhattan, Drescher's plans were to be a part of this growth by reconfiguring his building into a luxury downtown hotel. He planned to gut the first three stories and, enlisting the help of Elizabeth and her boss, Vera Loran, transform it into the lobby, creating an exquisite, unforgettable focal point that would be the trademark of this and future Drescher hotels. Accommodations would be luxury suites, complete with fine furnishings and amenities.

Rumors had circulated recently that Drescher was leveraged beyond his means and showing signs of serious financial problems, but Elizabeth didn't see how that was possible if he was actively pursuing this new hotel project. She hoped when she was finally brave enough to open her own design studio one day that she was able to acquire powerful, successful clients like Drescher.

Vera leaned her backside against the end of the table next to Elizabeth's chair and folded her arms as if keeping a measured distance. Elizabeth took it as a sign she should stay seated. She played her part and looked up submissively. Plastic wrapping from a package of smokes poked out of a pocket on the lower right side of Vera's teal-blue linen suit jacket. Elizabeth didn't have a visual on the lighter, but a bulge in the other pocket told her it was tucked there.

"Drescher has big plans for the future and he wants Loran Design to be a big part of it—*you* to be a big part of it." She seemed to add the last part for clarification and emphasis. Gazing upon Elizabeth more like a jealous big sister than her boss, Vera appeared to be contemplating her subordinate's role in the new project.

A petite woman with a slender, almost fragile build, Vera usually wore six-inch spiked heels, presumably to compensate for her lack of height. She was somewhat of an overly stylish woman with short, masculine, coarse blonde hair, the color of which originated from a bottle. Although the years had taken their toll and the lines on her face gave away her late fifty-something age, she was always dressed as if the next person through the door was going to be from *Cosmopolitan* magazine. The design studio had been engaged by its share of high-visibility clients over the years, but *Cosmo* hadn't been one of them.

Loran Design had grown with its clients, both residential and commercial, but it had been a long, hard fight for Vera to transform her company into one of the top design firms in the city. The battle came with a price. While her friends were marrying and raising children, Vera was burning the midnight oil preparing presentations for prospective clients, trying to build a name for herself and a business to sustain her. Men had come and gone in her life, having different priorities than her at the time. Eventually men stopped showing up on a personal level, so she was simply grateful when they became clients. Her work had become her life. But how far would she go to maintain her success? Would she break the law? Commit murder? Elizabeth pushed the thought away.

Vera barely stifled a sinister chuckle as she regarded Elizabeth, perhaps scoffing at her conservative dark blue Brooks Brothers suit she'd once teased her for wearing, claiming it made her appear matronly. Reaching into her pocket, she pulled out the small package wrapped in clear plastic. Her hand with its pale, withered skin, protruding blue veins, and gnarled fingers, looked like a vulture's claw grasping its latest kill. Vera skillfully tapped the package against the side of her fist. A single smoke emerged. Raising the package to her mouth, she pursed her lips around the lone cigarette, accentuating the creases encircling her mouth, and pulled it out. By the time she had returned the rest to her pocket, she'd already retrieved the lighter with her other hand. In a single, flawless motion that came from years of repetition, Vera pressed the red tab, took a long drag on the end while her eyes found a random spot on the ceiling, and then released the tab, shoving the lighter back into its secure spot. Turning to her staff designer, she exhaled.

As on many occasions, Elizabeth held her breath as long as she could, all the while despising her boss' filthy habit, albeit fitting with Vera's personality. It was agonizingly tiresome to have her clothes reek of cigarettes at the end of each workday. Unable to hold it any longer, Elizabeth let out a long, deliberate exhale, wishing she didn't have to inhale again. She blinked and fought to keep from coughing as she took a shallow breath.

"Sometimes I wonder about you, Elizabeth Pennington." Vera glared. Turning away, she walked half the length of the table before pivoting to face Liz again, motioning with her left hand while grasping the cigarette. "Are you really that naïve?" Her tone dripped with condescendence.

Elizabeth tried to control her reaction but inadvertently furrowed her brow. Never having felt such strong, negative feelings, she feared a deep-rooted hatred festered inside.

Her boss' voice became quieter as she leaned over and pressed her forearms against the back of a padded chair. "You do realize Jack finds you attractive, don't you?"

Clearly, it wasn't lost on Vera that Drescher had a glimmer in his eye when he gazed at Elizabeth, fifteen years his junior. So if her biggest client kept coming back for more and her top staffer was part of the reason, apparently she could live with that. It was good for business, even if Liz shuddered every time he spoke her name or caught her eye during a meeting.

Shifting uncomfortably in her chair, Elizabeth could feel her face turning red again.

Vera's hands slid fluidly to her hips, the cigarette sticking out like an extension from her side. Feathery, gray ash hung precariously. She appeared to be carefully choosing her words. "You need to be more aware of what's going on around you." Sashaying back toward the end of the table, she stopped at the last chair, leaning her right side against it.

Elizabeth watched in horror as a large clump of ash fell to the floor, landing on the black floral Oriental rug next to the pointed tips of Vera's shoes. Her boss was unaware of her transgression, but Elizabeth couldn't tear her eyes away from the glowing ember until it died out. She returned her gaze to her boss who stepped closer and continued.

"For a young woman who's talented and shows a lot of potential, you sure lack street smarts." Vera hovered uncomfortably close at the end of the table. "But you need to figure out how to do everything in your power to make sure Jack is happy. He's a major client and we need to cater to him, to his needs. Whatever they might be."

Elizabeth withdrew from the confrontation and sat back in the chair, unsure of what Vera had meant. Her boss' bloodshot eyes had the look of someone desperate enough to do almost anything to avoid becoming a has-been, certainly to hang onto a client that represented a major portion of Loran Design's revenues.

As Vera leaned closer, Elizabeth fought to keep her nostrils from flaring at the stench of her ashtray breath. A throat clearing startled them. Fortuitously they were interrupted by Sara, the office receptionist, a young perky woman with a blonde page boy hairstyle, who had stepped into the conference room far enough to tell Elizabeth her grandmother was on line one. Liz did her best to stifle a gasp at the announcement. Her grandmother usually only called when something was amiss. Elizabeth switched her gaze to Vera to catch her reaction, knowing she vehemently opposed personal calls on the company clock. Her eyes widened as she cocked her head with nicotine-stained teeth visibly clenched. Turning away from Elizabeth, she flicked her cigarette over her shoulder before striding toward the door. Elizabeth watched in horror again as a lump of glowing gray mass fell—this time into her lap. She jumped to her feet to allow the ashes to roll off her skirt and fall to the floor.

Reaching the door, Vera turned back, striking an authoritative pose with a hand on her hip and the other poised with palm open to the ceiling, her cigarette caught securely in the "v" between two fingers. She instructed Elizabeth to stop into her office before she left for the weekend.

Elizabeth cringed, knowing what that meant—Vera wanted to get started on developing ideas and making preliminary sketches for Jack's project. *No time to waste!* Instead, she was anxious to head out and start enjoying the long weekend away from the office. She didn't have any particular plans but ached for a break from the grind. The whole office had been working hard lately. That never seemed to bother her boss. It was as if Vera had nowhere else to go and nothing else to do.

Arching her back in defiance, Elizabeth reached for the receiver to speak to her grandmother, Amelia Pennington, spinning her chair around toward the wall of windows behind her, high above the busy streets of Manhattan. Rain gently spattered the glass. Florescent lights from neighboring office buildings glistened through the raindrops.

# CHAPTER TWO

Elizabeth rode down in the elevator with two middle-aged men in dark suits she recognized as attorneys from the firm of Mendelson, Jenkins, and Leate. They had entered on the nineteenth floor and stood next to her, self-absorbed in their own conversation, without so much as a nod or a word. She was entertained by their chatter, though, as they tossed client names around like confetti, bantering about this judge and that judge. *Amazing how unprofessional two guys can be.*

As the doors opened to the lobby, the two men pushed forward to exit before Elizabeth. She stood back. A smirk spread across her face as she watched them enter the bustling lobby and stride swiftly across the broad room, their egos in tow. "Jerks." Her voice barely audible, she stepped out into the flurry of activity.

A grand room with a high ceiling, the lobby had antique brass chandeliers and dark marble pillars spaced evenly throughout. A warm burgundy carpet with a stylized geometric pattern anchored the large space. It was furnished with traditional mahogany coffee tables paired with stately wingback chairs set in small groupings. Since the location was a popular meeting place after work, particularly on Friday afternoons, many of the chairs were occupied by young professionals with glasses in hand. Located on the far left side of the lobby was a large, European-style bistro that catered to lunch and dinner crowds. Happy hour was in full swing with noisy young urban movers and shakers. On the opposite side of the lobby were a newspaper stand, a shoe shine booth, and a quaint flower shop.

Noticing a small group of men in suits gathered just ahead and to the left of her path to the exit, Elizabeth recognized the one gesturing with the flair of an orchestra conductor as the mayor of their fair city. The rest were probably aides and a handful of the city's well-connected. Elizabeth had only made it halfway across the lobby when someone stepped out from behind one of the grand pillars, startling her.

"Elizabeth, so good to see you again." Drescher lunged uncomfortably close, leering at her. She wasn't surprised he was among the mayor's entourage at happy hour.

"Mr. Drescher." She took a step back to put more space between them, examining his eyes to discern what was going on behind them. The overwhelming smell of cologne made her nose wrinkle. She rubbed the tip of it to stifle a sneeze.

"Elizabeth, please call me Jack." His voice was sickeningly sweet. Stepping closer to her, he gently touched her forearm. She could feel his stale breath. "Elizabeth, why don't we go grab a drink?" He nodded toward the lively bistro. "Then we can talk further about this new project."

Desperately wanting to back farther away, she could hear Vera's voice reminding her to keep Drescher happy. His happiness was going to have to wait.

"It's the weekend," he implored. He seemed to be able to tell she wasn't going to acquiesce.

"Mr. Drescher, I'm sorry. I'm on my way out of town. I can't stay." She was polite, but firm. "I'm sorry."

The two stood looking at each other in the awkwardness of the situation gone sour. Elizabeth pushed past him and strode for the revolving doors, leaving him standing alone by the pillar. Her stomach twisted. Too many times over the past couple of years Jack had gotten too close for comfort. She'd turned him down on several occasions when he asked her out for drinks or dinner. Although she had to admit to herself there was something about his self-confidence and powerful presence that was attractive, she had no intention of jeopardizing her career by making a mistake like that. It concerned her, though, that his obvious frustration bordered on anger each time she declined his offer. Clearly, he wasn't used to having to take "no" for an answer. Sensing his eyes following her out, she tried to shake off her uneasiness and lengthened her strides.

When she reached the sidewalk in front of the building along Lexington Avenue, the rain had slowed to a fine mist. Delayed by the encounter with Drescher and worried about the phone call from her grandmother, she had some things she was anxious to sort through. Nana, as Elizabeth referred to her, hadn't gone into a lot of details but obviously was concerned about recent events at the inn that had been in the family for several generations in Pennington Point, Maine. It was originally built not long after the conclusion of World War II as a private school for girls and run successfully by the Pennington family for decades. That was, until the mysterious disappearance and presumed death of a student under questionable circumstances in the early seventies. The case was never solved, which forced the permanent closure of Pennington School and still haunted the family to this day. In the late seventies the property was reopened, after extensive renovations, as a charming New England seaside inn.

During their phone conversation, Nana seemed to think one of the handymen had gone missing. Elizabeth didn't take this news too seriously. Girard was a forgetful old man who was diligent and hard-working, but could easily misplace tools or supplies and be searching for them for days before they showed up in the most unusual places. Perhaps this time he had gone out for an errand and forgot where he was going. All in all, Girard was a pleasant guy and seemed to be an asset to the inn. Conversely, his brother, Renard, who also worked doing odd jobs, was a bit of a nuisance. Clearly infatuated with the sole heir to the family estate, he seemed to go out of his way to be near her during her occasional visits.

Pushing away the uncomfortable memories, Elizabeth switched the portfolio to her other side and pulled her taupe trench coat close to her neckline. Always wanting to be prepared, she'd grabbed drawing supplies before heading out, deliberately neglecting to stop in to see Vera. No telling how long she would have been delayed if she hadn't.

Elizabeth was thrilled to be on her way to Maine, after her grandmother's last minute plea to giver her a hand. She loved the city, but having grown up in the inn, the rugged, rocky coast of Maine with its salty sea air was in her blood.

It wasn't the best of childhoods, but Elizabeth chose to dwell on the positives. She was as close to her grandmother as a daughter to her mother. Amelia had raised little Lizzi after her parents died when she was young. No one ever talked about what happened to them, and Elizabeth had left it that way as a child. As an adult, however, she bore the weight of a nagging urge to find out. And the older Amelia got, there was a real possibility of her taking the story to her grave.

Besides Elizabeth and Amelia, the Pennington family also included Cecilia, Amelia's husband's younger sister, who remained a spinster. Elizabeth remembered her as an angry woman who spent a lot of time in the upper rooms where the family kept house, often erupting in fits of rage toward little Lizzi. A bedroom closet was her refuge when Cecilia was particularly ornery. She felt safe in the small, dark space. When the air had cleared, Elizabeth emerged cautiously and searched out her grandmother. She never spoke of her ill-natured great-aunt to anyone but often wondered why she contributed so little to the day-to-day operations of the inn.

In spite of having to shoulder the responsibility of running a popular lodging establishment while raising her granddaughter, Amelia was a warm, caring individual who ran the inn as efficiently as a ship's captain. Her husband of twenty-nine years *had* captained a large fishing vessel that succumbed to Mother Nature's wrath while trying to outrun an approaching storm, widowing Amelia when she was only forty-nine. The girls' school and subsequent inn had been built by his father with additions and outbuildings added over the years.

Always treating the staff and guests as family, Amelia had a soft voice and a sweet gentleness about her. Elizabeth would do anything for her grandmother, including dropping everything at work to go to her aid. But, at the moment, she was feeling uncomfortable she'd given her boss the slip. She would have to catch up with Vera later by cell.

Engrossed in her thoughts, Elizabeth didn't notice the man who had fallen in behind her, several strides back but maintaining the same pace as her.

She was walking the three blocks to the parking garage on East 45th Street to retrieve her car, a prized silver BMW Z4. It had been a recent splurge she justified as a reward for all the late nights and weekends that had become the norm at Loran Design. Elizabeth was off for what she hoped would be a relaxing couple of days and a reprieve from the grind of her job but wondered what she would find when she got to Pennington Point.

The mist turned into a light rain, but Elizabeth didn't bother with her compact umbrella tucked securely in her purse for those unexpected you-never-know-when-you-might-need-it moments. With only one more block to go, an uneasy feeling crept in that someone was following her. Elizabeth quickened her pace and upon reaching the garage, she headed straight for the elevators. A set of doors opened as soon as she pressed the button. She slipped in and the doors closed behind her. On the roof of the garage, only a few cars remained, owing to the fact it was Friday afternoon before Labor Day weekend.

She beamed as she approached her car, backed neatly into a corner space that allowed ample room on either side. It wasn't easy to protect it in the city the way she wanted to, the way she should, but she did her best. Itching to get out of the city and onto the open road heading northeast, she couldn't wait to get in, start the powerful little engine, and shift into first gear.

Elizabeth skillfully negotiated the downward spiral of the parking garage ramp, pressing the button to lower the driver's side window at the precise moment on the last curve. Reaching the ticket booth, she slipped her monthly parking card into the slot and the gate retreated slowly toward the low ceiling. She pressed the button again to close the window. Slowly releasing the clutch, she gently coaxed the gas pedal. As the car passed through the gate, a man lunged from the left and banged his palm onto the hood of the car, his face pressed up to the driver's side window. Elizabeth shrieked and hit the brake and clutch simultaneously.

It was Lenny from the mail room, towering over her car looking decidedly pitiful, like something the cat dropped on the doorstep after a rainstorm. Certainly wetter than the past few minutes of light rain could possibly have caused. Tufts of chestnut-brown, curly hair poked out from underneath his baseball cap, flipping up and partially obscuring the bottom edge. His bushy eyebrows touched the brim. Water dripped off his hair and glistened on his navy-blue jacket. She felt sorry for him and a bit foolish for over-reacting. Lenny appeared to be a harmless guy, probably the only one who had been working at Loran Design longer than her. No one really knew. He was quiet, kept to himself, seemed to keep his nose clean and avoided Vera as much as possible. Elizabeth wondered how old he was. Hard to tell. She guessed late twenties or perhaps early thirties, she couldn't be sure.

As Elizabeth lowered the window again, she noticed he was tightly clutching a package. Lenny didn't wait until the window was completely down before he poked his head in and began babbling about Sara and the package she thought Miss Pennington needed. Leaning away, Elizabeth couldn't remember ever being so close to him before. His sad, brown, puppy eyes seemed out of place on a face covered in red splotches of acne. Some areas were particularly red and irritated, perhaps infected. Her stomach grew queasy. Elizabeth thanked him and took hold of the damp and dog-eared manila envelope, sure it hadn't looked so tattered when the receptionist sent him on his errand. It appeared to be something one of the courier services delivered. There was no return address. One thing was certain, though, if Sara knew Elizabeth had left the office, Vera would know soon, too. She ran the front desk like a control center and kept their boss informed. Not much got past either of them.

Elizabeth tossed the package on the seat beside her, pressed the button for the window one final time, and set out onto the rain-soaked streets of New York, giving Lenny one final wave. She was on her way. A pit stop at her apartment to pick up the essentials was all that stood between her and a long weekend in Maine.

# CHAPTER THREE

The drive from New York City to Pennington Point could take anywhere from five and a half to six hours, depending upon the traffic, but Elizabeth usually cut the trip down to just under five in her peppy sports car. She spent the time alone with her thoughts, focusing on the radio only when a station started to fade out, compelling her to tune in a new one. With the impending phone call Elizabeth would have to make, her thoughts drifted to what she had left behind.

Bordering on tyrannical, Vera was more than difficult to work for. In all likelihood, her studio led the design industry in staff turnover, due to the unreasonably high standards she held her employees to, as well as herself. Although she was a prime candidate to work with an executive coach to help soften the edges of her caustic personality, Vera undoubtedly had never considered such professional guidance. She probably figured she didn't need anything of the sort, and she would run her business the way she saw fit.

The most seasoned of the design staff, Elizabeth had logged seven years with her so far. Seven *long* years. There had been moments when she wondered how much longer she could endure Vera's wrath. Yet, Elizabeth admired her as a design genius with a head for business, an unusual combination to be sure.

Planning to bide her time, Elizabeth's intentions were to hang on as long as she could and learn as much as possible before launching out on her own. That kind of aspiration, however, was not something she could share with her boss, as Elizabeth was reluctant to test their volatile relationship. On a day-to-day basis, she felt like a lowly staff person Vera enjoyed stepping on and making an example of. Still other times, they seemed, in a twisted, surreal sort of way, like mother and daughter. Of course, that was usually when they went out after work for a couple of drinks and Vera pried into her personal affairs while offering alcohol-induced advice.

The demands of the job, with Vera setting the tone for the office ambience, led to stress-filled, often long, arduous days. Elizabeth had become skillful at escaping this environment by simply hitting the streets for a brisk walk, embracing the city's sights, sounds, and smells: the roar of yellow taxis as they sped by, honking their horns and maneuvering through congestion; the burnt smell of roasted chestnuts or the pungent aroma of sauerkraut on steamed hot dogs wafting from street vendors' carts as she passed; the rumble of the subway below her feet, through the sidewalk grates; and the throngs of people she walked shoulder-to-shoulder with, bumping into one another, jockeying for position on the curb at the red don't-walk light.

Traipsing for blocks, even in inclement weather, she could clear her head before re-entering the quagmire commonly known as Loran Design. This was her survival technique and it served her well.

Central Park was one of her favorite destinations when she had time to linger. Located in the middle of Manhattan and extending nearly three miles long, it was like an oasis in a desert of asphalt, steel, and concrete. In warm weather, rental bikes were available to ride on the paths, as well as remote-control boats to navigate around the ponds. The Central Park Zoo offered an impressive array of wild animals, including an aviary, home to an extensive collection of rain forest birds. The carousel was a perennial favorite for park-goers of all ages, but soaring on a wooden horse in her business suit wasn't her style, so she often made use of one of the benches scattered throughout the park. People-watching made for an interesting pastime which, for Elizabeth, usually turned into dog-watching and made her yearn for a small pup of her own. Perhaps if she had a design studio one day, she could adopt a dog and bring it with her to work. She took comfort in the thought. Someday . . .

With so many art museums to choose from, Elizabeth also enjoyed cultural pursuits. Her favorite was the Metropolitan Museum of Art. Located on the east side of Central Park on 5th Avenue, The Met was surrounded on three sides by the park. The Frick Collection was a stone's throw away, just off 5th on East 70th Street. Elizabeth also enjoyed the Guggenheim, farther north on 5th Avenue, overlooking the park.

Glancing at the green highway signs passing overhead, Elizabeth realized she was just outside of Boston. The jazz station she'd been listening to since Hartford was fading in and out, so she pressed the seek button until she found something with a Latin beat to help keep her awake. Her shoulders responded to the tempo of the new music.

Fellow NYU grad Rashelle Harper had introduced her to Latin music while they were in college. The two became fast friends. While Elizabeth had focused her attention on interior design, Shelle majored in hotel management and hospitality. She now greeted the guests at Pennington Point Inn as their newest hire, ever since Elizabeth convinced her grandmother to delegate part of the day-to-day operations. Rashelle had become a wonderful addition, fitting in with the atmosphere of warm, Down East hospitality, even if her Brooklyn accent revealed her roots. Amelia embraced her like her own granddaughter, visibly relieved to have such qualified help. She didn't hand over the reins outright to Rashelle, but she was gradually entrusting her with more and more responsibility.

One of Shelle's first tasks at the beginning of the summer was to hire a new tennis instructor. The previous one had to be fired because he spent more time trying to improve his relations with the female guests than actually teaching tennis. Complaints of sexual harassment were rampant, not the sort of activity management could tolerate. Apparently, the guy didn't take the news of his firing well, insisting he was an innocent bystander and the complaints were unfounded. His denials escalated into threats, and he had to be physically removed from the property.

Just north of Portland, Elizabeth hopped off Interstate 295 onto Route 1. Years ago, Route 1 was the main road to travel along the coast, meandering through quaint New England towns, twisting and turning along the rugged shoreline, past local lobster shacks and wild blueberry stands. These days, most people stayed on the interstate as far as they could go before getting off, to get to their destination as quickly as possible.

Elizabeth had only a short distance to travel before she reached Route 72, a winding, hilly road that wound its way through seven miles or so of pine trees, punctuated by the occasional dirt or gravel road that led to a residential dwelling. A knitting shop, Dolly's Woolery, sat on the corner of Routes 1 and 72 and had been in the same location for as long as she could remember. Across the street was Ronnie's Clam Shack, a favorite of summer tourists as well as locals.

Slowing down to turn, Elizabeth felt the past several hours of driving taking their toll. She yawned and picked up her empty Dunkin' Donuts cup, hoping for more caffeine, but had already drained the last drop before Kennebunkport. It was getting late, and the lack of street lights and oncoming cars made for a dark back road. Replacing her cup in the holder, she reached for her package of Twizzlers from the passenger seat only to discover it, too, was empty. She pressed on. It wasn't much farther. After the last familiar curve, Elizabeth turned off 72 onto Pennington Road. Nearly there, she cracked the windows for her first sniff of salty sea air, grinning as she felt welcomed home.

Pennington Road was darker than 72 and snaked its way through an expanse of pines, ending in a clearing on a precipice, high above the crashing waves below. Situated on a hundred and twenty-five acres of unspoiled coastline, the main building was an impressive, stately structure set back from the edge of the cliff, similar to many New England inns with its traditional white clapboard siding and multi-paned windows with black shutters. An open porch, where wicker furniture sported worn floral cushions, ran across the front and wrapped around both ends. Double-width steps were set left of center of the porch; ornate carved wooden railings framed either side.

The inn hadn't changed much over the years. It stood strong, proud, and almost defiant against the tumultuous ocean, much like its keeper, Amelia. The property included nearly a mile of an alabaster sandy beach and, in its entirety, was quite a piece of real estate. Any developer would salivate at the possibility of acquiring such a gem. For the Pennington family, it was simply home. Over the years, rumors had surfaced from time to time that the gracious old inn was haunted; but Elizabeth found this notion rather amusing, since she'd grown up there and never experienced anything of the sort. She often wondered if those rumors actually attracted some people to stay there.

At the top of the last hill, the Z4 emerged from the woods into a small clearing where Elizabeth came upon a fork. Slowing the car to a stop, she shifted it into neutral, twisting her mouth into a crooked smirk as a couple clichés came to mind—"the road less traveled" and "the crossroads of life." A weathered wooden sign pointed to the left for Pennington Point Inn and the other pointed to Pennington Point Lighthouse. Entertaining a passing thought, she shivered at the temptation to follow the right fork. Not a good place to be in the dark near the rocks.

Elizabeth put the car back into first gear and started to ease off the clutch when she noticed lights coming down the left fork. Gently, she pressed the brake to hold steady long enough for the oncoming car to pass, as the road to the inn wasn't wide enough to accommodate two cars comfortably. Shortly, a small car appeared from the pines, so she glanced into the driver's side as her headlights shined in. The driver was male, approximately twenty-five to thirty years old, with short, dark hair. Even though he averted his eyes, he looked familiar to her, but she couldn't place him. His name would probably come to her later. He was driving one of those sports car wannabees, probably a Mazda Miata. She couldn't make out the color. Something dark. Maybe blue or green.

After the car passed, Elizabeth steered onto the left fork that meandered through more pine trees for about a hundred yards until she came to another, larger clearing. In front of her sprawled the open sea. Passing the entrance to the guest parking lot on the left, she continued on to the gravel driveway that circled in front of the inn. The placement of the lot behind the main building was deliberate, maximizing the view of the sea from inside. As she rounded the drive, her lights carved a swath in the fog that had rolled in off the water. An outline of boxwood bushes was just visible near the edge of the cliff, planted to keep guests from doing anything foolish.

The sight of her childhood home made her almost giddy. It had been too long. As she pulled the car close to the front door, relief that the trip was complete coursed through her. Shutting down the engine, a myriad of emotions welled up inside. Thrilled to be back, she wondered with uneasiness what was in store.

She gently closed the driver's side door, leaving her bag on the seat and the key fob in the console. Having left the crime-ridden streets of the city far behind, she was in Maine now. No one thought to lock doors or secure their worldly goods in *her* home-town. As she stepped backward to admire her prized possession bathed in the lights of the front porch, she managed a smile in spite of her fatigue. "God, I love that car." She laughed to herself when she realized she'd said it out loud and had sounded like a television commercial. It was just after ten o'clock, but she hoped her grandmother would still be up.

Pausing to gaze out over the water, she listened to the waves out of her line of sight, crashing against the rocks below. The moon was nearly full and directly in front of her, casting its warm glow across the shimmering water from so far away. Turning toward the inn, she caught the familiar sight of a couple Schwinn bikes leaning against the porch railing, a light brown wicker basket hanging from the handle bars of the ladies' version. As she shuffled up the front steps, her feet sounded like sandpaper on the wooden planks dusted with sand from the beach.

She was too far away to hear her cell phone ringing. A disappointed Vera would have to leave a message. Elizabeth hadn't noticed her previous calls that evening, as she'd left her phone on silent.

Elizabeth burst through the front doors into the lobby, stepping onto a natural-fiber sisal rug. Situated halfway between the front door and the reception desk was a substantial turned wood table with a magnificent fresh floral arrangement displaying the waning colors of summer from Amelia's garden.

A travel-weary couple was checking in at the front desk, so Elizabeth slowed her pace and remained behind the urn of flowers to allow them to finish. Thrilled to see they were speaking with Rashelle, Elizabeth guessed her friend must have known she was arriving and gave the front desk clerk the night off.

Rashelle was an energetic young woman with dark brown, almost black hair she sported in a retro-shag. It suited her spunky personality perfectly. Although of average height and build, her outstanding characteristic was her high energy level that rarely could be squelched.

The lobby was centered between a sitting room to the right and the dining room and lounge to the left. Glowing coals in the sitting room fireplace and the lingering smell of smoke were all that remained of an earlier fire, an unexpected, yet welcome treat to ward off the chill of a cool summer evening by the sea. Built-in wooden bookshelves on either side of the fireplace were filled with well-worn hardcover novels, beckoning anyone entering the room to pluck one off the shelf and sink down into one of the oversized chairs arranged in conversation circles around the room.

Situated toward the rear of the building, the dining room was closed for the evening and dark but undoubtedly set up for the hustle and bustle of the morning. Weekend brunches at the inn had become popular, not only for Pennington's guests, but for guests of other hotels and locals as well. A long-standing favorite was Amelia's famous orange-macadamia nut French toast served with warm maple syrup.

At the front of the inn, the lounge was alive with a spirited card game between a foursome of elderly gentlemen. An imposing wooden bar, with dark leather stools pushed up to it, anchored the far end of the room. A large mirror took up nearly the entire length of the wall behind it.

In the sitting room, an old woman occupied one of the wing chairs, her back to the sea. One elbow rested on the arm and long, spindly fingers propped up her head as if she'd fallen asleep reading a book on her lap. A bald spot dominated the back of her head of thin wispy hair. She seemed to be the only occupant of the room.

Rashelle finished with the couple checking in and looked up to see Elizabeth. Her eyes opened wide; she clasped her hands together and squealed in delight. Disappearing to the left of the front desk, she reappeared through a door to the lobby marked "Staff Only." She flung her arms around Elizabeth and they embraced. Emails and texts didn't quite have the same warmth as her hugs in person.

"You made it! So glad you're here. Your grandmother will be pleased. How long are you staying?" Rashelle gushed and didn't give Elizabeth a chance to respond. "We'll twist your arm to stay longer, no matter how long it is. Oh, I'm so glad you're here!" Rashelle clearly couldn't hide her excitement, her Brooklyn accent shining through. "Let's find Amelia. She'll want to know right away you've arrived." Grabbing Elizabeth by the arm, she guided her toward the carpeted stairway that led to the second floor, where the family kept rooms. Stopping mid-step, Rashelle seemed to be rethinking her direction.

"You know, she may still be talking with Tony. She wanted to be sure everything was all set for brunch in the morning."

Anthony had been the chef at the inn for fifteen years, but Amelia still kept her hand in running the kitchen on occasion. Tony, as everyone referred to him, was a man in his forties with a slight build, a French Canadian accent and a fiery temper to compensate for his lack of height. His cooking had been reviewed by some of the most prestigious gastronomic magazines. Having Tony at the helm of the kitchen was a tremendous asset to the inn and the envy of other innkeepers in the area.

The girlfriends linked arms as they sauntered toward the dark dining room. On their way, they bypassed a short hallway that led to the back porch. One flick of Rashelle's finger as they crossed the threshold produced a path of light to the kitchen.

Elizabeth suddenly remembered the woman sitting in the wing chair near the fireplace and wondered why her friend was leaving the front desk unattended. A glance over her shoulder told her the woman was no longer there. Puzzled, she didn't remember seeing her leave and couldn't shake the feeling she should know who she was.

Creaking loudly under their feet, the old wooden plank floor was original to the school's dining room. A wall of windows along the right side of the room offered a beautiful northeastern view in daylight. The wooden bar that stretched out to the left of the door into the kitchen was a smaller version of the one in the lounge. Empty stools lined the counter in silence. Voices emanating from the kitchen assured Elizabeth and Rashelle they'd found her grandmother. Bursting through the spring-hinged, double doors, the girls caught Tony mid-sentence. His and Amelia's serious expressions melted into warm smiles.

"Hey, Nana!"

Standing in the middle of the kitchen was her dear grandmother with a crisp white chef's apron folded in half and tied at her waist. Wire-rimmed half glasses balanced at the end of her nose. Her snow-white, wavy hair was neatly styled to frame her face and accentuated her bright blue eyes. Deep creases punctuated the sides of her mouth and the outside corners of her eyes. At times, Amelia had a way of looking like Mrs. Claus without the extra weight. She certainly had the warm personality to fill the shoes of such an icon.

"Lizzi! It's wonderful to see you." Her face beamed.

They hugged tightly. It had been several months since the last time Elizabeth had made the trip up. Work seemed to get in the way of long weekends or any vacations plans, for that matter. A twinge of guilt pinched her in the gut, but the warmth of Nana's arms washed away the tentative, negative feelings. She wondered if this was what it would have felt like in her mother's arms.

Elizabeth breathed in the familiar scent of Obsession, mixed with whatever hair spray had been on sale. It was great to be in her grandmother's hug. Finally she pulled away and acknowledged the head chef.

"Hi, Tony. How's it going?"

"Great to see you, Elizabeth." He looked like a proud father gazing upon his own daughter.

The squeak of the swinging doors revealed a face Elizabeth had not seen around the inn before. An attractive guy who looked to be about her age with dirty blond hair pushed to one side, his all-white attire suggested he was the new tennis instructor. His eyes surveyed the cramped quarters of the small kitchen, with its two large commercial stoves and cavernous, weathered pots and pans hanging from the ceiling on a rectangular rack, and came to rest on her.

"You must be Elizabeth. I've heard so much about you." He extended his hand and shook hers, grasping onto her forearm with his free hand. She grew tingly and it felt as though an electrical charge passed between them. As their eyes connected, Elizabeth grew uneasy. She pulled back, stepping away clumsily.

Reprimanding herself for letting him pull her in, she couldn't very well fall for a guy based on good looks alone, although she acknowledged her personal life had been lacking.

Rashelle jumped in to smooth things over. "This is Kurt Mitchell, our new tennis pro." Pleasantries and nods were exchanged and then Rashelle moved on. "Hey, Liz, let's grab a glass of Pinot, shall we?" She dismissed Kurt with her shoulder.

A glass of wine sounded divine after her long drive. Then she realized they would have to venture down to the wine cellar and shuddered at the thought. It was located below the kitchen in what used to be part of the tunnel system for the school. Maine winters could be bitterly cold and stormy, particularly close to the ocean, so a system of rudimentary tunnels had been constructed to allow the girls to move from building to building without enduring the elements. Most of the tunnels had been sealed off once the school was converted to an inn. The wine cellar was one exception and occupied a portion of the tunnel that ran under the kitchen.

Elizabeth was relieved to see Rashelle making her way to the small beverage cooler Anthony kept filled with a selection of whites. After pulling out a couple bottles and examining the labels, she selected a magnum of Pinot Grigio, Elizabeth's favorite. Then she crossed the creaky wood floor to the utility closet and pulled out a wine bucket, which she filled with ice from the bin. Using a corkscrew lying on the counter, Rashelle skillfully uncorked the bottle then nestled it into the bucket and retraced her steps across the kitchen, grabbing Elizabeth by the arm. Glancing at Amelia and Tony, she asked, "Anyone care to join us?"

Both declined the offer, citing the late hour and the fact they would be up early for brunch. Kurt shook his head. Amelia added, "I'll catch up with you in the morning, Elizabeth. Oh, and you can sleep in the front room this weekend, or however long you're staying."

Elizabeth nearly tripped over her feet as she turned back. "The front room? Isn't that . . . Cecilia's room?"

"Well, yes," she chuckled. "I don't think she'll mind. And I know how much you like an ocean view."

Elizabeth couldn't shake the feeling she would be stirring up a hornet's nest sleeping there. She didn't want to displace anyone, particularly her ornery great-aunt. Elizabeth straightened her shoulders and stood taller. She was an adult now and should be able to handle the situation. If Nana said she could stay there, she would.

Bidding everyone a good evening, the two plowed through the swinging doors. Rashelle stopped long enough to slip behind the bar and grab a couple of glasses from the overhead rack that clinked together as she pulled them down. She rejoined Elizabeth at the end of the bar, and they linked arms again and started across the room. Before they reached the lobby, Amelia poked her head out of the kitchen.

"You girls are going to stay inside tonight, aren't you? Probably not a good night for a walk, anyway." Her words sounded persuasive, almost pleading.

"Don't worry, Amelia. We're going to find a couple of cozy chairs in front of the fireplace," Rashelle assured her.

Unaware of what they might be referring to, Elizabeth was too tired to pursue it.

"Feel free to put another log on if you're going to be up for a while."

"Okay. Thanks, Amelia."

"Thanks, Nana."

"And I know you girls haven't seen each other for a while, but you don't have to catch up all at once." They all shared a laugh. "I'll stop by on my way upstairs."

As they crossed the lobby and entered the sitting room, Elizabeth surveyed the furnishings and layout, making a mental note to speak to her grandmother about a redecorating project. It was a warm and cozy room—very comfortable for the guests to relax in—but they needed to be careful the shabby chic décor didn't evolve into a worn and dated look over time.

Then Elizabeth remembered the lady sitting in the chair by the window. "So, you're officially off duty, or am I taking you away from something you should be doing?"

"Oh, jeez. I'm done for today. We're not expecting any more arrivals, and all the current guests seemed to have turned in early."

Glancing into the lounge, Elizabeth noticed the gentlemen had finished their card game. The room was dark. "What about the elderly woman who was sitting there when I first arrived?" she asked, gesturing toward the windows.

Rashelle considered her question. "I don't remember anyone there. I thought everyone had cleared out by then."

Elizabeth let it go and sank down into an overstuffed upholstered armchair close to the fireplace, facing a matching chair. Her friend placed the wine bucket and glasses on the oval wooden coffee table in front of them. Glancing at the oversized bottle wedged at an angle in the ice, Elizabeth hoped Rashelle had curtailed her drinking since their college days. She'd been quite the party girl, always ready for a good time, even if it wasn't the weekend. There had been too many occasions when Elizabeth had to drag her back to the dormitory in the wee hours of the morning with Rashelle declaring it was too early to go home. Once she had to rescue her out of the bed of a guy Rashelle had just met at a frat party. The next day Rashelle didn't confront her for embarrassing her, so Elizabeth figured she had no memory of the incident. Somehow she passed her classes and graduated with a degree, but toward the end of their senior year, she seemed to be inebriated more often than she was sober. Elizabeth wrote it off as senioritis and hoped Rashelle would be a little more responsible with her drinking as an adult, especially on the job she'd recommended her for. It concerned Liz that her friend from the big city had wrapped her car around a tree earlier in the summer after a night out at a local bar. She had to rely on others for transportation until she could get a new one.

Approaching the fireplace, Rashelle selected a piece of firewood from the pile next to the hearth and tossed it in. Sparks burst out from under the new log into a gentle explosion and settled back down again. Shelle rejoined Elizabeth, who had begun filling the glasses. As they sipped, they caught up on the small stuff, carefully avoiding anything heavier, happy to be together again. Eventually, Elizabeth couldn't resist pursuing a less comfortable topic.

"So, how's the new tennis pro working out?"

"Kurt? Well, okay. Yeah, I think he's doing a good job. I mean, he arranges round-robin tournaments and does some clinics for the guests. There haven't been any complaints so far, which is an improvement. To tell you the truth, there weren't a lot of candidates to choose from with the paltry salary we were offering. Amelia liked him, so I went along with it." She paused, appearing concerned her salary comment might have offended and then continued. "I think he's bored at times, though, because I do find him poking around, sticking his nose in peculiar places. Says he's interested in the history of the inn, claims to enjoy old buildings. He seems particularly interested in the old tunnels."

Elizabeth shrugged off a shiver at the thought. They were cold, damp, and dark, and gave her the creeps. She couldn't imagine anyone wanting to explore them and did her best to push the thought from her mind.

After finishing their first round, Rashelle reached over and refilled their glasses. The wine was taking effect, and Elizabeth was enjoying its warmth. The friends had been catching up for a while, when the last giggle faded to silence. Only the crackling of the fire was audible. Rashelle sat up, turned serious, and leaned over to place her glass on the table. Scooting ever so slightly forward, she folded her arms and seemed to stare right through Elizabeth. Suddenly Lizzi became uncomfortable. It wasn't as bad as when Kurt held her hand because she knew Rashelle, but obviously something was awry. She began in whispers.

"Elizabeth, I need to tell you what's been going on here. I'm sure your grandmother hasn't told you much, if anything. And this probably shouldn't come from me, but you really need to know."

Sitting up with a jolt, Elizabeth snatched a quick breath. What had her grandmother kept from her? She found her voice. "Girard's disappearance?"

"No. We're not concerned that will turn into anything. Apparently it's happened before. Actually, what's worrying Amelia is some attorney—I think he's from New Jersey—is pressuring her to sell."

"Sell what? . . . The inn?" Startled by her friend's revelation, Elizabeth's voice rose with each word.

Urging her to bring the volume down with a swift hand ges-ture, Rashelle continued. "I don't think she would ever do it. It would break her heart to see this place in the hands of anyone other than a Pennington. But this guy has been relentless. And that's not the worst of it."

"It's not?" Elizabeth bit her lip while relinquishing her glass to the table alongside Rashelle's. She pressed her fingers together and wedged them between her legs near her knees, looking to Shelle to continue.

The creaking wood floor announced the arrival of Amelia and Anthony into the lobby. Amelia bid good night to her head chef as he exited through the front door, and she tottered toward the sitting room, pausing in the doorway.

"Well, girls, it's getting late. I'm going to turn in. You might think about doing the same."

"We will, Nana. We're almost caught up." Elizabeth didn't dare look at Rashelle. They both wished Amelia a good night, and after watching her ascend the carpeted stairs next to the front desk, they turned back to each other.

Elizabeth spoke first. "Okay . . . go on," she pressed.

"Oh, Elizabeth. I don't know if I should—"

"What! You've gone this far. If she asks, just tell my grand-mother I dragged it out of you. Now, spill."

"Okay, okay. The worst of it . . . is the fourteen-year-old daughter of one of our guests is missing. The parents didn't say anything right away, because they thought she'd taken a longer walk around the grounds than expected when she didn't show up for dinner last night. Around noon today, they asked to speak to

Amelia. She called Chief Austin, who was tied up and didn't show up until dinnertime. He left just before you got here. He had his men searching the property, walking through the woods, but couldn't accomplish a lot in the dark. He said he'll return in the morning. Between you and me, I think the parents are afraid she ran away."

*That wasn't the only possibility of what could have happened to her around here.*

There were many other scenarios, including getting swept off the rocks at the lighthouse by a rogue wave. Elizabeth recalled a story that surfaced periodically about a little girl and her father who fell victim to just such a wave. Of course, as a lot of stories went, the details changed along the way. Sometimes it was a little girl and her mother. Either way, it was tragic. Warnings were posted near danger areas, such as the Pennington Point Lighthouse, specifically for the unsuspecting tourist.

Sinking back in the chair, Elizabeth rubbed her temples with the tips of her fingers. Her concern for her grandmother grew. Aware of the stress that came from running the inn on a daily basis, she feared the latest couple of developments could prove to be too much for her nana. And the last thing she needed was bad publicity from a police investigation. It could also feed into the attorney's intentions.

After finishing off the bottle of wine well after midnight, their lively conversation slowed to intermittent spurts between lulls, so the girls called it a night. Elizabeth thought she'd never felt so tired. It took everything she had to hoist herself out of the chair. In spite of the recent events revealed by her friend, she believed things would look better in the morning light. They had to.

Returning to her car to retrieve her belongings, Elizabeth decided not to bother moving her Z4 until morning. All she could think about was getting some much-needed sleep. When she reached in from the driver's side, she noticed her cell phone on the passenger seat next to her overnight bag. "Shit!" She'd forgotten to call Vera. Picking up the phone, she noticed she had a few missed calls. They were probably all from her boss. She would have to deal with her in the morning.

With the strap of the bag slung over her shoulder, Elizabeth eased open the door to her great-aunt's room. Pausing in the doorway and peering into the dark room, fully expecting to see Cecilia fast asleep under the covers, she winced as she flipped the switch on the wall inside the door. A small ceramic lamp lit up on the table next to the bed. Releasing a cathartic exhale, she was relieved to see an empty bed. Her great-aunt must have taken a different room after all. It was uncharacteristically nice of her. Certainly not the Aunt Cecilia she remembered from her childhood.

Crossing the threshold, Elizabeth closed the door behind her and tossed her bag onto a small antique chair with a woven cane seat that let out a faint creak in protest. It was one of a pair placed like bookends on either side of the small round table at a large picture window facing the ocean—the perfect spot to start the day with a strong cup of Earl Grey or to watch dusk creep over the estate with a glass of dry merlot before heading downstairs for a late dinner.

Grabbing her toothbrush from the side pocket of her bag, Elizabeth made her way to the tiny bathroom tucked to the left of the bed. After freshening up, she switched off the lamp and the room took on an eerie glow from the moon. Silence hung in the air with a sense of expectancy. Slipping under the covers, she breathed in the faint lilac scent ironed into the bed linens, an extra-special touch for which the inn was famous, and drifted off. She didn't notice her great-aunt open the door and peek in as if checking on her. It made a soft click when it closed. Elizabeth opened her eyes for a moment, but was too tired to move, so she closed them again until morning.

# CHAPTER FOUR

*fter a restless night*, Elizabeth awoke to a jarring ring. Groggy from the long drive and entirely too much wine the night before, she rolled over and reached for the bedside table where she'd tossed her cell phone in the wee hours of the morning, cringing as she read the caller ID.

"Hey, Vera." She tried to sound upbeat.

*"Elizabeth! Where are you?"* Her boss' voice was loud and grating.

A familiar throb crept behind her eyes.

"We have a lot of work to do! I expected to see you in the office first thing this morning so we could get started."

Elizabeth had the sinking feeling Vera already knew where she was. *Stay calm. Don't get sucked into her wild, irrational emotions.* "Vera, I'm sorry." She spoke slowly and deliberately. "I forgot to call you last night. My grandmother asked me to come up and give her a hand with some—"

"*Elizabeth*! Where's your sense of priority? Drescher is our biggest client and a real power broker in this city. This is not someone you ever want to disappoint. He knows how to make things happen, and he can make things happen for *us*. He's entrusting Loran Design with one of his biggest projects ever. How can you run off at a time like this?"

*Run off? She's heading for the deep end and needs a lifeline before she goes over the edge.* "Vera. I brought supplies with me to get started—"

"Get started? You know how we operate. We brainstorm together. We sit in the same room and think out loud together. That's how we work best. What were you thinking?"

Elizabeth struggled to remain calm. The back of her neck tightened. Springing to her feet, she paced around the room. She could think more creatively while on the move, also defend herself more effectively, if necessary.

"Vera. We can work separately first, and then get together to hash through some ideas. Our time can be better spent if we come up with some original concepts on our own." Elizabeth stopped in her tracks. Had she overstepped an invisible line? Was Vera worried she wouldn't come up with anything fresh working by herself? "I can fax you what I come up with." She was throwing her a bone. Would she grab it or leave it where it had landed?

"All right, but I want you to stay in touch." She seemed to be softening. "Jack is already asking to meet with us again. He particularly wants to talk with you about this. I'll give him your cell number so you can consult with him while you're away. But you take care of whatever it is your grandmother needs taking care of and get *right* back here. Keep in mind you can always hire someone to take care of a lot of things. And let me know when you'll be back. You got that?"

Elizabeth wished her boss could hear how unreasonable she sounded. After promising to stay in touch, she hung up and threw her phone onto the flowered coverlet bunched up on the bed.

Brilliant sunshine spilled in through the windows, which always lifted her spirits. She couldn't wait to get outside. Perhaps she would take her sketch pad on a walk down to the lighthouse. Then she remembered the inn's famous brunch and Amelia's French toast. The light would have to wait.

A knock startled Elizabeth but was followed by a familiar voice. She rushed to let in Rashelle, who was carrying a tray laden with covered dishes and a vase with a long-stemmed yellow rose from Amelia's garden.

"Breakfast, sleepyhead!"

"Oh, Rashelle. Thanks. You didn't have to—"

"Of course I did. Brunch only runs for twenty more minutes, and I knew you wouldn't want to miss the French toast."

"Really? How did it get to be so late?" Elizabeth was disappointed she had slept away part of the morning.

Rashelle carried the tray to the windows and placed it on the small table with a floral tablecloth that didn't match the bedspread.

"Yeah, Amelia has been asking for you. I think she wants to see you as soon as you can get downstairs." She offered no details but scurried out under the guise of returning to work.

Breakfast tasted better than she'd remembered. Savoring every bite while watching the seagulls circling outside the window, Elizabeth was nearly mesmerized. After finishing the last morsel, she pulled herself away from nature's display to get on with her day. She took a brief shower, left her bed as it was when she'd rolled out of it, and went in search of her grandmother.

On her way out the front door, Elizabeth noticed two squad cars parked on the circular driveway. Chief Austin must have returned to continue the search for the girl. She started in the direction of the garden, a half-acre plot located twenty-five yards behind the main building and surrounded by a white picket fence. An oversized gate on the side facing the inn enabled the rototiller to pass through for spring tilling. Elizabeth was pleased to find her grandmother puttering busily. Amelia looked up as she reached the gate and smiled warmly under her wide-brimmed rattan hat. Standing slowly from her kneeling position, she took off her gardening gloves and placed them next to the basket she was using to collect herbs and squash, meeting Elizabeth at the gate.

"Well, hello, Lizzi. You're finally up and about." She turned her frail, narrow wrist to examine a thin, tarnished gold antique watch. "I'm afraid you missed brunch, though."

"Rashelle made sure I didn't. She brought a tray to my room."

Amelia chuckled. "What a good friend. She really looks out for you."

"Yes, she does. It's great to see her—to see everyone."

"It's wonderful for us to see you, too. It's been a long time. We've missed you." Amelia paused, perhaps sensing she might be making Elizabeth feel guilty and changed the subject. "Let's take a walk down to the light," she urged as she closed the gate behind her.

Elizabeth was always up for a walk, but this time she had a feeling the conversation would not be pleasant. As they started across the side yard toward the path down to the breakwater, the breeze off the ocean tugged at the brim of Amelia's hat. Long crooked fingers latched onto a flapping edge and held it tight until they reached the section of the path where the trees protected them from the wind off the water.

"Lizzi, thank you so much for coming up on such short notice like this." She gazed at her granddaughter, beaming.

"Nana, I would do anything for you. You know that."

"I do and I really appreciate it. Things are somehow always better when you're around." They shared a smile between them. Amelia's eyes appeared heavy. "Lizzi, I don't know how much Rashelle told you last evening, but there are some things going on I think you should know about." She searched Elizabeth's eyes, perhaps hoping for a nod of acknowledgment.

"Shelle did tell me about the missing guest and, of course, the real estate attorney."

"Yeah, he's been a bit annoying. Rather persistent, that one. If I didn't know better, I'd wonder if the disappearance has anything to do with him. I have a feeling he won't stop until he gets what he wants."

"Nana!" Elizabeth scolded, stopping abruptly on the path. Her grandmother paused a few feet away, turning back to catch her granddaughter's disapproving scowl.

"Oh, I'm not entirely serious. He's just worn me to a frazzle. I don't know what to do at this point. He calls, writes letters. He won't let up." She threw her hand up in exasperation and then grabbed Elizabeth by the arm, moving again down the path. "That's why I asked you to come. I need a little help with this one. It's getting to be too much. I'm not as young as I used to be."

Elizabeth hated to hear those words but knew they were true. She couldn't imagine the inn without Nana. She couldn't imagine *life* without Nana and endeavored to push that thought out of her mind.

"I'm a little concerned about this girl's disappearance. With these woods and the rocks at the lighthouse . . . well, it doesn't seem like there could be a happy ending in all of this. It's already been since Thursday afternoon that anyone has seen her. What if one of the other guests did something to her? I can't bear the thought."

"What about the police? Have they talked to the other guests to see if anyone saw anything?"

"Oh, I haven't let Chief Austin near the guests yet. I really don't want to involve them . . . upset them until we absolutely have to. Of course, he thinks I'm jeopardizing the entire investigation."

"I hate to say it, Nana, but he may have a point," she countered gently. "If one of the guests did do something, he's not going to stick around long enough to be interrogated the next day." Amelia shot her a look of concern.

Elizabeth suddenly wished she hadn't gone so far. "But in reality, that probably isn't the situation anyway. It may be a matter of the girl wandering off, not knowing the area, and finding herself somewhere she's not familiar. Thank goodness it's summer so the nights aren't terribly cold. It could be a lot worse. The chief and his men will find her this morning. You'll see," she tried to comfort her grandmother. Not having a good feeling about any of it, she only wished she could believe her own words.

The snap of a twig in the woods a few yards in startled the two so they stopped and listened. No discernable movement. The woods got thick a few steps off the path, so whatever made the sound was out of sight. Dismissing it as a couple of scampering squirrels, they resumed their walk down the path.

Anxious to keep the conversation going, Elizabeth continued, even though they were walking single file through a narrow section. "So, what about Girard?" she asked, speaking loudly to send her voice over her grandmother's shoulder.

"Oh, I spoke to Renard this morning and he told me Girard had returned. He said his errand to find the right parts for the riding lawn mower took longer than expected. He had to travel quite a distance and try a few places before he was successful."

*He couldn't pick up the phone and avoid all the running around?* Elizabeth shuddered to herself. The mere mention of Renard's name gave her the creeps. She wished he would leave her alone or, better yet, find someplace else to work besides the inn. She would try to avoid him while she was there. "So you haven't actually seen him? But Renard says he's back."

"Yes. I have no reason not to believe him." She sounded a bit annoyed with the question. "Besides, I think I have more important things to worry about right now."

Elizabeth had to agree.

Amelia stopped at the bluff overlooking the lighthouse, and the two Penningtons leaned against the railing. "You know, I hate to admit it, but this guy has me thinking about what it would be like if I did sell the place."

"Oh, Nana, you don't mean it!"

"Elizabeth, I've been doing this—running the school or the inn—my whole life. Believe it or not, I'm getting tired." She took her granddaughter firmly by the shoulders and looked squarely into her eyes. She spoke softly. "There's no one to take over. It takes an awful lot to run a place like this. I'm not sure I have what it takes anymore. Maybe it's time for a change . . . for all of us. You have your career in the city, and there's nothing wrong with that. No one is asking or expecting you to give up everything you've worked so hard for."

Feeling herself reeling, Elizabeth implored, "Rashelle is working out well. You could give her more responsibility, and I could check in from time to time." She was desperate to change her grandmother's mind. Amelia was giving in far too easily.

"Lizzi, you can't do a good job of running a place this size by checking in once in a while. You would spread yourself too thin and do neither job well. Besides, it's not like I haven't had a long time to think about this. It's not exactly a snap decision."

"But the inn has been in the Pennington family for generations." Elizabeth choked on her words as a tremendous wave of guilt flooded over her. She'd left home and gone off to the big city in search of a place to establish herself as a designer, leaving everyone behind to carry on with the inn. Now her grandmother was considering the wild suggestion of a greedy attorney whose only intentions were personal gain. "I could make it work," Elizabeth continued to plead. Her world seemed to be sliding out from underneath her. She'd grown up there. *How could she possibly say good-bye to her childhood home?* Her heart broke wide open. She fought back the tears.

"Lizzi, if your parents were alive . . . unfortunately, things turned out differently than we all expected. Life works that way sometimes." Amelia's arm around Elizabeth showed concern she was thrusting far too much onto her granddaughter's shoulders.

Although it didn't seem the best time to broach the subject, Elizabeth wanted to know what had happened when she was too young to remember or understand.

"Nana, could you tell me what happened to my parents? I know we never speak of it . . . but I really would like to know."

"Elizabeth, you certainly deserve to know." She spoke slowly, her voice sounding hesitant. "Sadly, no one knows *exactly* what happened. Do you remember them at all?" She was changing the subject slightly.

Elizabeth shrugged her shoulders.

"Your parents loved you so *very* much. Either one would have given their life for you."

Elizabeth stared intently at her grandmother. Voices from below caused them both to turn. The police chief and the inn's tennis pro were making their way up the path from the lighthouse. Chief Austin was a man of insignificant stature yet carried a significant amount of extra weight around his middle. He had a large round head with a receding hairline of stringy, somewhat oily, short, white hair. Carrying a clear plastic bag at his side, he held it close to his leg as if he were trying to be discreet. There was something light purple in it, some sort of fabric. Perhaps an article of clothing. Evidence?

Struck by the oddity of Mitchell traipsing behind the chief, she pressed her abdomen as a nervous flutter crept in. Although there was something about Kurt that Elizabeth found intriguing, she tried to push away the feeling, concerned he could be a suspect. The two men stopped at the bluff to join the Pennington ladies.

"Well, good morning, gentlemen," Amelia offered.

"Good morning, ladies," the chief responded, his breathing labored from the climb up the hill.

"Ladies." Kurt nodded and remained slightly behind the chief, eyes fixed on Elizabeth.

She averted her eyes from his.

"Amelia, I wonder if I might have a moment of your time." The chief got straight to the point.

"Certainly." Amelia turned to Elizabeth and took her hands. "Lizzi, I'm sorry. Why don't we have dinner this evening on the veranda? Anthony's doing a clambake down on the beach, so it should be rather quiet there. We can continue our conversation then."

"Sure, Nana. You go ahead," Elizabeth urged, struggling to hide her disappointment. She watched the trio disappear up the path toward the inn, her eyes stuck on the plastic bag at the chief's side.

Deciding a beautiful day shouldn't be wasted, Elizabeth continued her walk to the light. Anxious to get some design ideas down on paper, she wished she'd brought along drawing supplies. At some point she'd have to get back to Vera with something to show her.

The path brought Elizabeth down the steep hill, out of the woods to a clearing. Just off to the right was a small shed used to store kerosene in the days when a full-time keeper tended to the light. Kerosene was deliberately stored far enough away, so a fire in the shed wouldn't take the lighthouse with it.

Standing stalwart like an old friend was the beacon at the end of the breakwater jutting a hundred yards out into the water. A garrison of sorts. A form of refuge to a young girl escaping a bit of her childhood. A sanctuary to a young woman who needed some time to herself to do some thinking.

While the door to the lighthouse was kept locked, painters and photographers were allowed access and guests were given tours by a member of the staff upon request. Elizabeth knew where the key was kept and proceeded to push open the door to the small shed. Inside was quite dark but her eyes adjusted quickly. She could make out some tools hanging on one wall, boxes of who-knows-what stacked up against the adjacent wall. It wasn't a large space by any stretch of the imagination, approximately fifteen feet by twenty feet with most of it spoken for. Groping in the semi-darkness, hoping the location hadn't changed, Elizabeth's fingers brushed the familiar shape dangling from the nail to the left of the doorway where it had been kept for years.

Grinning broadly at her success, she lifted the key off the nail and stepped back out into the bright sunshine. As her eyes took a moment to readjust, she pulled the shed door closed and then headed out to the breakwater. It was a dicey walk across large boulders with blunt edges lying at precarious angles, like hopscotch with consequences. Many times as a teenager, she'd been in a hurry to get out to the light and caught a foot between two rocks, falling in her haste to escape the inn, scraping knees and hands in the process. She had the scars to prove it.

Elizabeth started out slowly but picked up the pace after settling into a rhythm in her step. Carefully choosing her path across the boulders, keeping her eyes focused on where she placed her feet, she chanced a glance at her target from time to time to check her progress. The closer she got, the more tingly her body became. After several minutes of total concentration, she found herself at the threshold of the lighthouse.

Inserting the key into the lock of the huge wooden door, she willed it to work and turned. Click. Bright sunshine slowly penetrated the entryway as she pulled with all her might. A cool, musty, but familiar smell greeted her. Again, her eyes took a few seconds to adjust to the darkness of the tower. She pulled the door closed behind her, making a loud thud that reverberated in the empty space. Securing it from the inside, she tucked the key in the pocket of her capris. She'd rather not have any company; she wanted to enjoy the solitude—just like years ago when her grandmother came searching for her at dinnertime.

At first, the lighthouse was the last place Amelia checked. Maybe it was because of the rocky hike to get out there. Eventually, she caught on, and the lighthouse became the first place she checked for her granddaughter. Shuddering at the thought of her now-elderly grandmother crossing the treacherous breakwater, Elizabeth headed toward the narrow staircase that spiraled to the top of the light. Her footsteps echoed as she went.

Ascending the worn wooden steps, deliberately aiming for the wider side of the planks, Elizabeth was winded when she reached the top. Pushing open the door, she stepped out onto the balcony, a narrow walkway with a railing sixty feet above the rocks below. The sheer height could make the most sure-footed person feel dizzy. Elizabeth, however, immediately felt right at home; she could see the world from way up there.

Rounding the curve of the wall to the side facing the open ocean, she passed an apparent construction area with yellow tape across a section of missing railing, making a mental note to avoid that area when she was ready to leave. Reaching the far side of the light, she backed up against the outer wall, bent her knees, and eased herself down into a seated position with her legs crossed. She took in the salty sea air. With everything going on at the inn, she had some things to think about, and this was a great place to do it.

Her grandmother needed her help. She was about to throw in the towel and sell the inn, Elizabeth's childhood home. Amelia's age and fatigue aside, she was giving in entirely too easily. There had to be another alternative. Even more serious and certainly more pressing was the matter of the missing guest, a situation Elizabeth feared her grandmother was glossing over and quite possibly hindering the investigation. Imagining Chief Austin didn't have a lot of experience solving a missing person's case, she figured he had even less with a murder case. Murder at Pennington Point Inn? Could it be possible? She prayed it wasn't and moved on to other concerns.

Since her gut was telling her the questions surrounding Girard's disappearance were not actually resolved, she needed to follow through on that. She couldn't simply take her grandmother's word, who took Renard's word. Also, what was the deal with Mitchell? Was he legitimate? He'd been snooping around the inn and seemed overly curious about the tunnels. Was he really a tennis pro? Maybe she should hang around the courts and observe him in action. . . . What about the previous pro? What was his name? Aaron something or other. Where did he end up after he got fired? And who were the parents whose daughter was missing? Who was the daughter? What about the other guests? Who was the attorney harassing her grandmother? These questions all needed answers, too.

Feeling overwhelmed, Elizabeth gazed out to sea with the breeze off the water caressing her face. Completely secluded on the far side of the light in her own little refuge, she stretched out her legs with her back pressed against the wall. It was early afternoon, so the sun was still high in the sky and quite strong, but on its way down to the horizon. The warmth felt good. She embraced it and soon drifted off.

# CHAPTER FIVE

A *loud thud jolted* Elizabeth awake. The lighthouse door. At first, it brought her back in time and she thought it was her grandmother. Then she realized she'd locked the door on the way in, and *the key was in her pocket.* She jumped up and crept across the balcony to the open doorway, venturing onto the first step. Listening intently, she couldn't see anything in the dark and there were no audible footsteps. Was someone waiting at the bottom? Who had another key? Did someone break in? Her mind raced. Wanting to hear a sound, any sound, she could only pray it would come from someone who meant her no harm. There was nowhere for her to go. She was trapped on a walkway with the railing under repair, high above the rocks below.

A gust off the water threatened to push her off balance. Grabbing the door jamb, she leaned in, straining to hear movement. Still nothing. Reaching for her pants pocket, she winced when she realized she didn't have her cell phone. *So much for calling in backup*. She was on her own. Silence rang in her ears. Nearly paralyzed with fear, she couldn't utter a sound. Not that anyone would hear a call for help. Desperate thoughts made her consider if she'd imagined the door slamming. Perhaps she'd been dreaming.

Cursing to herself, Elizabeth started to make her way down, stopping to listen periodically. There seemed to be many more steps than when she ascended earlier. The occasional small windows punctuating the sides of the tower let in just enough sunshine to negotiate the stairs safely, but she couldn't see if anyone waited at the bottom. It was quite dark there, darker than she remembered. Reaching the last step, Elizabeth's body stiffened as she surrendered herself to the shadows. She jammed her fingers down into the pocket of her pants, groping for the key to the door and her freedom. With it clutched in her fist, she dashed toward the exit, fumbling to guide it into the lock, squinting in the dim light. In her haste, it kept missing its mark. Sensing someone lurking behind her, she tried the key again. Suddenly she felt a large hand on her shoulder. Letting out a shriek, she whirled around, slamming her back against the door. The sound of the key hitting the floor took a second to sink in.

"Need help with the key, miss?" It was a low, almost sinister male voice.

A click and Elizabeth was staring into the eyes of Renard, his face illuminated by a flashlight. He was a large man, not very tall but with broad shoulders and proportionate girth. She'd never seen him appear so threatening before. The top of his conical head seemed more sparsely covered than she remembered, and his bushy eyebrows displayed more salt than pepper.

Painfully aware she needed to conceal her fright, she could hear her heart thumping in her ears. Could he hear it? Was she breathing? *Keep breathing!* Her body had an annoying habit of shutting down in extreme situations. But she couldn't afford to pass out at the moment.

Renard bent down to retrieve the key, not taking his eyes off Elizabeth. She feared his intentions. He stood up with the key resting in his palm. She reached for it and he snapped his fingers closed, still staring deeply inside her. She pulled her hand back slowly, returning his gaze, feeling trapped. *What is this guy going to do?*

Elizabeth watched as he tossed the key into the air, a few inches at first, and then higher and higher until it peaked just above his nose. Her nostrils flared as she caught a whiff of his sweaty body odor mixed with the mustiness of the old building. Should she try to grab the key in mid-air? Even if she successfully snagged it, she still would have to get it into the lock, turn it, push the door, and get out. He didn't look like he would allow her to do any of that. Maybe she should try reasoning with him.

Before she could speak, he opened his mouth and barked, "What are you doing here?" His eyes narrowed, demanding an answer.

Who was he to question her about why she was there? She could ask him the same thing but decided to play along and not get him any more riled up than he already was. He literally held the key to her release. And no one knew she was there. With a sickening feeling creeping into her stomach, she wondered if Renard could be connected to the disappearance of the girl.

"Well?" He grew impatient. She needed to choose her words carefully.

"Oh, I used to come here all the time as a kid. My grand-mother, Amelia, would come find me when it was time for dinner." In desperation, she threw that out as a thinly veiled justification.

Deep creases rippled on his forehead. Just as quickly, his eyes brightened, acknowledging his understanding. "Miss Elizabeth, it's you." His voice softened slightly. "I didn't recognize you. You're all grown up now. Look at you." His words were slow and deliberate, stopping short of an apology for scaring her half to death. "I was concerned about someone, ya know, one of the guests, finding their way up here and getting hurt, what with the railing being repaired and all."

"Well, that's certainly understandable . . . and very responsible of you," she added, trying to give him a verbal pat on the back. Lord knew she didn't want to actually touch him. *Please let me out of here.* Panic swelled inside and she fought to repress it. "Thank you for doing that. I'm sure my grandmother would be pleased to hear it. I should go and catch up with her now. Thanks for your help." Did she dare ask a question? "But if the door is kept locked, how would any of the guests be able to get in? That's the key from the shed." Her eyes went to the fist hanging to his side.

He appeared to be carefully considering her question before answering. "Because one of the keys came up missing recently."

*Great! It could be in just about anyone's possession.* Frantic to get out from under his control, she tried again. "Well, I should be going." She looked at him expectantly and stepped to the side so he could open the door for her.

"All right, let me help you with the door. It can be a little stubborn, especially after we had it re-keyed not too long ago.

Gives me trouble now and again, too." Tucking his light into one armpit, he skillfully slipped the metal key into the lock, turned it, but stopped short of actually opening the door. He paused. Elizabeth willed him to push the door. *Please let me out.* Adjusting the aim of his light, he met her eyes. "You need to be careful you don't get hurt while you're here, Miss Elizabeth. I'm sure your grandmother wouldn't like anything bad to happen to you." He leaned against the door, leaving Elizabeth to wonder what he'd meant. Was he simply referring to the railing under repair at the light? Or did he have anything to do with the missing girl? She didn't have long to ponder. He gave the door a solid shove with his shoulder, allowing bright sunshine to flood the small, once-darkened room.

Before he could stop her, Elizabeth pushed past him, brushing against his sturdy body into the warmth of the day and the freedom outside the lighthouse walls. She inhaled deeply. The brisk sea air never smelled so good. Then she considered the key still in his possession. She spun around and boldly put her hand out. Renard kept one foot anchored on the threshold with the door pulled close to him, as if trying to prevent her from seeing what was inside. It made her curious if there was indeed something she wasn't able to see in the dim light, but her desire to flee was much stronger than her curiosity. She would have to return another time. "I should put the key back in the shed," she threw out to see his response.

He didn't move, cemented in place like a sentry at his post. Holding his gaze, he calmly answered, "I'll take care of it when I head up the hill."

Realizing she had no choice, she turned toward the rocky breakwater. Raising her hand above her head in a floppy wave, she offered, "Okay, thanks. See you later." She hoped it sounded as casual as she needed it to be, and then scampered deftly across the boulders, not bothering to look back.

After racing up the hill through the woods, Elizabeth arrived at the clearing feeling unsettled from her encounter with Renard but with a sense of determination to help her grandmother get to the bottom of whatever was going on. Elizabeth also had a nagging feeling about the tunnels. She despised the thought, but her gut was telling her she should see for herself to be sure nothing was amiss below. First, she would find the chief to find out as much as she could.

Just as she reached the front entrance to the inn, Kurt pushed the screen door from the inside and they were face-to-face again, closer than she cared to be. Stepping backward, she bumped into one of the bikes parked near the porch railing. Elizabeth whirled around in time to watch it fall over, knocking over the bike next to it. She cringed. Thankfully it was only the first two and not the entire fleet lined up, waiting for guests to take them for a ride. Kurt rushed to her aid.

"Here, let me give you a hand."

Elizabeth felt her cheeks flush. *Way to make an entrance.* "Thanks, not one of my more coordinated moments," she threw out, trying to make light of her momentary clumsiness.

"So, how about a little tennis?" he offered once the bikes were righted.

"Oh, I don't know. . . . I didn't bring my racquet," she blurted out, as if that was going to make a difference.

"Not a problem. I've got several demos the sales reps have been pressing me to try. Besides, I actually had a cancellation, so I'm free for the next hour."

"Well, I don't know about a lesson."

She was trying hard not to blush any further, uncomfortable with the thought of being one-on-one with him.

"It doesn't have to be a lesson. We could have fun hitting the ball around."

Fun? That wasn't exactly Elizabeth's idea of a good time, but she recognized the opportunity to get to know him a little better and, perhaps, find out what he knew. She wondered what she was afraid of.

"C'mon. What are you afraid of?"

Startled to hear her thoughts, she tried not to react to his question. "All right. Give me a minute to get changed." The chief would have to wait. So would the tunnels.

# CHAPTER SIX

Elizabeth re-emerged from the inn's front door to find Kurt leaning against the porch railing, his wavy hair tossed about by the breeze off the ocean. One hand pressed a cell phone to his ear, the other was poised on a hip. He dismissed the person at the other end and, in one swift motion, slid the phone into the pocket of his white Adidas warm-up pants. One arm slid across the other as a grin spread over his face, a sparkle in his eye. She felt herself being drawn in and fought hard to push away. There was something about him that made her uneasy. She wasn't prepared to trust him yet, if ever, and she hoped she wasn't falling for him.

"All set?" he finally said after gazing upon her for a moment.

"Ready as I'll ever be." She tugged at the hem of a white polo shirt and shorts pulled together with Rashelle's help. When gathering her essentials for the weekend, she hadn't planned on playing tennis while in Maine. Fortunately, she and Shelle were close enough in size to borrow clothes.

Heading down the narrow path to the left of Amelia's garden, they engaged in small talk as they walked through the pines. She was careful what she revealed to him, all the while trying to learn a little something from him. He told her he'd gone to school at Colby, where he played varsity tennis. *Okay, so maybe he could play the sport and might be qualified to teach. Time would tell.*

Arriving at the courts, wrapped by a dark green chain-link fence, Elizabeth was disappointed to see they weren't alone. Standing together on the far court, another couple in tennis whites was sipping water and conversing softly. She couldn't tell if they were finishing up or taking a break. Her time with Kurt might not turn out to be productive after all. She was beginning to wonder why she'd let herself get talked into playing tennis.

Kurt stopped at the small tennis shop located in front of the courts, fondly referred to as "the shack." "I'll just grab a couple racquets for you to try."

Elizabeth nodded and waited outside the door. Kurt popped out again holding three for her to choose from. Feeling completely out of her comfort zone, she couldn't tell one from the other.

"Why don't you hold each one so you can see which feels right."

She took the racquet closest to her.

"Kurt, look. I'm not going to know which is right." *Maybe this wasn't such a good idea.*

"Let me see your grip." He tucked the other two racquets under his arm and took hold of the racquet head. "Here, put your hand on the grip like so." Placing his free hand on top of hers, he rotated it slightly around the grip. She tried to ignore the sensation he was creating and looked to him for an explanation.

He seemed amused. "I'm just checking the distance between your thumb and index finger. Yeah, this one is too large for you." Examining the grip size of the remaining racquets, apparently neither would work as he gathered up all three and disappeared back into the shack for another lot.

"You know, Kurt, this is turning into a lot of trouble for you," she apologized, speaking into the doorway but not setting foot onto its threshold. Kurt reappeared with three more racquets.

"Don't be silly. It's my pleasure." He sounded eager to please. "Besides, it's about time these demos got some use. They're brand-new racquets sitting idle, gathering dust. Sorry it's taking a couple go 'rounds. I didn't realize you had such feminine hands."

Elizabeth took it as a compliment but didn't acknowledge it. Instead she busied herself with comparing the three new racquets. "This one feels okay." She held out her right hand wrapped around a black and green Yonex. He examined the placement of her fingers and adjusted them slightly, making her as uncomfortable as before.

"Looks perfect. Right grip size. Frame is not too heavy, not too light for you. Good choice." He tucked the other two racquets inside the door. "Okay, let's go hit a few." His exuberance was almost contagious. Almost.

Elizabeth's stomach was in knots at the prospect of setting foot onto a tennis court with a guy she'd just met. She couldn't remember when she'd held a racquet and had no desire to make a fool out of herself. To her relief, the other couple was walking off their court. They would at least have the place to themselves.

After exchanging pleasantries with the departing twosome, they turned their focus to their respective tasks, his to give some pointers to a reluctant student and hers, to find out more about him and what he knew about the goings on at the inn. After all, he'd spent some time with the chief. *Was that because he knew something or because he was a person of interest?*

"Uh . . . it actually has been a while since I played tennis—quite a while. I probably could use a lesson," she grudgingly admitted.

"No problem. Why don't we warm up first at the net with some gentle volleys, and then we can back up and work on your ground strokes." He picked up a racquet leaning against the ball basket that resembled a small grocery cart filled with bright yellow, fuzzy balls. Pulling it by the front, he wheeled it to the other side of the net. "Start out a couple of steps in front of the service line. Take it slowly. Nice and easy. Just block the ball. Don't swing." He fed her a slow ball that she managed to return, but was way out of his reach, so he calmly took another and kept the warm-up drill going. "Just squeeze the racquet right before the ball makes contact. You don't have to squeeze hard all the time. In fact, try to relax your hand in between." She took his advice and the volleys improved dramatically, at least they appeared that way to her. *Who knows what he's thinking.* They plowed through two to three dozen balls.

"Okay, let's back it up to the base line and try some ground strokes. Why don't you show me what your forehand looks like without a ball coming at you?"

*Oh, this ought to be good. I was nervous enough* with *a ball, and he wants me to do it without one? Great!* Elizabeth took a feeble attempt at a forehand.

"Pretty good, now try to step forward when the ball's coming toward you and then swing. And follow all the way through so your elbow points toward the net when you're finished with your swing."

Considering his advice, she made two more attempts.

"Very good. Much better, Elizabeth! Now let's try backhand. Show me your swing."

*The infernal backhand. Why did it have to be part of tennis?* Elizabeth felt miserably out of her comfort zone playing tennis and more uncomfortable attempting any kind of backhand. She took the obligatory couple of strokes so he could critique her again, feeling herself blushing. Not having learned tennis as a child, she found taking a lesson rather awkward. The courts weren't built until she was away at college, so she hadn't had the opportunity to pick up the sport as he clearly had. *At least he's trying to be gentle. And he's not laughing. Maybe he* is *a pro.*

"Not bad. Think about what I mentioned for the forehand. Step and then swing, following through so you complete a half circle with your elbow pointing at me. The only difference is you have both hands on the racquet for the backhand. Try a couple more." Elizabeth obliged and he nodded in approval. "Good. Now let's add balls."

The ground stroke drill turned out to be less embarrassing than expected but was not enabling her to speak to Kurt one-on-one. She was learning a lot about tennis but not what she came for. After several minutes of forehands and backhands, she was relieved to see he had stopped feeding balls.

"Well, that wasn't so bad. How about a little help with my serve?" she called across, feeling a bit braver—and it would also get him over onto the same side of the court as her.

"Sure thing." Watching him pull the ball cart around, Elizabeth was surprised at how few were left in the basket. No wonder she felt like she'd already had a workout.

After showing him her version of a tennis serve, he gave her a few pointers to refine it. "Bend your knees. Toss the ball up over your head, but a little in front of you because you want to be moving forward when you make contact with the ball." At first she felt awkward trying to apply his suggestions, but slowly she felt more comfortable as she served her way through the rest of the balls in the basket. Although there was much to be pleased about from a tennis perspective, she needed to get him talking.

"Terrific. You certainly are a quick study. All right, let's get these balls picked up, and we'll play so you can apply everything you've learned."

He retrieved two ball tubes hanging from the fence and handed one to her. As they started for the net to gather the balls collected there, Elizabeth chose to ignore the sheer number of them and the fact they were evidence of her inconsistent effort to clear the net.

"So, Kurt, what do you make of what's been going on around here?" She left the question as open as possible.

He calmly stopped trapping balls and cast a sideways glance. She hoped her question didn't sound as obvious as it felt.

He resumed gathering balls. "Do you mean the situation with the lost girl?"

"Yes, and everything else that might be going on." *Ugh!* She wasn't good at prying discreetly.

"Well, I'm not privy to a lot of what goes on."

*Was he serious? Did he really expect her to believe that?*

"Last time I spoke to Chief Austin, which was this morning when we saw you on the path, he had few leads to go on. He did find a zippered sweatshirt down on the rocks that matched the description of the missing girl's."

"Really?" Elizabeth was thrilled to hear there was progress but then realized it might not mean good news.

"Yeah. Her parents seem convinced she wandered off and was the victim of foul play. Chief's not so sure about that, but he did say the parents admitted their daughter had fought them about going on this trip. It was supposed to be one last weekend away before she started school. But she's fourteen and you remember how it can be at that age. The last place you want to be is with your parents, especially on vacation."

"But he *is* gathering evidence and seriously considering other, more serious possibilities, isn't he?"

"I'm sure he is. He seems to have a handle on it."

Repressing a disapproving scowl, Elizabeth's doubts pervaded her thoughts, but she kept her opinion to herself for the time being.

"So, is there anything else I should know about?" It was worth another shot at prodding him for information.

Kurt chuckled as he emptied his tube of balls into the basket. "What else could be going on? Isn't that enough for this quiet little inn?"

She had to agree it was. Unfortunately, it wasn't all. Was he really oblivious to everything else, or did he know more than he was sharing?

"Of course," she quipped, concealing her disappointment.

"All right then, let's play a little." He grabbed three balls from the cart, handed her two, and jogged over to the other side of the net. "Okay, you serve first," he called.

And so began a set that went on for twenty-five minutes and ended with a score of 6-1. Elizabeth was convinced the single game she won was a token of sportsmanship. He couldn't beat a lady in a shut-out. At least it seemed like the guy was a gentleman.

She approached the net with her arm extended. They shook, but he looked surprised. "You don't want to play another set?"

"No. I think I've had enough of a workout." She wiped the perspiration from her forehead with the back of her hand. "I need to save enough energy to be able to function during the rest of the day."

Kurt chuckled.

"But thank you, though. That was a lot of fun. I learned a lot, too." She handed her racquet to him.

"Elizabeth, you're too modest. You were great. We'll have to play again before you leave." He had that glint in his eyes again.

Turing away to break the connection, she couldn't think of a comeback that wouldn't sound like she was getting sucked in. Suddenly, she felt his hand firmly grasping her upper arm. One foot suspended in mid-step, inches off the surface of the court, slowly she turned back. He leaned in, his face uncomfortably close to hers. Pulling away from him, she winced as his grasp tightened.

"Be careful, Elizabeth. You don't know what you might be sticking your nose into around here. Just—" His eyes narrowed, darting off to the side and back again. "Just be careful. . . . Please." He slowly released his grip, and she resisted the urge to rub her arm to restart the circulation.

Backing away from him, she didn't dare take her eyes off his. "Thanks for the warning," she said in an even, unemotional tone that took everything she had to keep under control. She walked briskly toward the gate, this time unencumbered.

*What had he meant? Was it a warning or a threat?* She would consider it the latter until she could be sure. A chill ran through her body.

On her way back to the inn, hunger pangs gradually replaced the nerves affecting her stomach during tennis. She was anxious to stop into the kitchen to see what Tony had for her to eat. It was already the middle of the afternoon, so he would be working on dinner, but she should be able to grab a quick bite to go.

# CHAPTER SEVEN

After a refreshing shower, Elizabeth emerged from the small bathroom with a fluffy white towel wrapped around her torso, holding it together with one hand at the base of her neck. Reaching for the clothes she'd selected to wear and tossed onto the bed, she froze. Out of the corner of her eye she noticed someone standing by the door. Elizabeth retreated toward the bathroom, her back against the wall.

There stood a woman. The elderly lady from the sitting room the night before. Suddenly, it dawned on her it was Cecilia. *What's she doing here? Elizabeth knew she shouldn't stay in her aunt's room. What was Nana thinking?* Elizabeth tried to speak, but before she could make a sound, her great-aunt was already talking.

"Elizabeth, you have to save the inn." Her voice was barely a whisper.

"I'll . . . I'll do everything I can," she vowed, scarcely believing they were having a civil conversation.

"You must. Amelia has all but given in and walked away. This place has been in the family too long to let it go like that." Her tone was one of desperation, imploring Elizabeth to do everything in her power to rescue the inn from the hands of . . . God only knew. The two women stood facing each other from across the room. No more words were spoken. They seemed to be reconnecting what time had pulled apart.

The moment was shattered by the piercing ring of Elizabeth's cell phone. She could guess who was calling. Lunging toward the bed, she rummaged through the clothes, searching for her phone buried beneath them. Caller ID confirmed her apprehension. A sinking feeling crept into her stomach as she absentmindedly placed a hand on her abdomen. Leaving the phone where she'd uncovered it, she didn't bother to answer. Better to let her leave a message and Elizabeth would call back later when she had something for her. Returning her attention to Cecilia, she was surprised to see her aunt was gone. In her anxiety over Vera's call, she didn't notice her slip out.

Elizabeth threw on a pair of light khaki twill capris and a pink polo with feminine capped sleeves. She put the sneakers she'd used for tennis back on. They were not hers, but they were much more practical for—well, just more practical than what she had packed.

After tossing Rashelle's tennis clothes into the bathroom sink to soak, Elizabeth headed out the door with drawing supplies and a rumbling in her stomach. Thrilled to be setting off for the bluff to immerse herself in a sketching session, she practically skipped down the carpeted hall.

At the bottom of the stairs, one of the inn's regular guests spotted Elizabeth and made a point of connecting with her. Mrs. Leibowitz was a feisty little old lady who had been staying at the inn every summer for many years. What she lacked in stature, she overcompensated with ferocity. The frosty, white hair framing her face was soft and wavy on good days and puffed out and frizzy on the rest. Her nose was large, painfully angular—resembling a hawk's beak. Her dark eyes penetrated through black, oversized rectangular-framed glasses that might have been in style twenty years earlier. Known for enjoying her wine, she preferred a nice dry red but would drink a glass of cognac if someone handed it to her. Curiously, the alcohol didn't seem to take the edge off of her cross disposition. Being a long-standing, regular guest, she tended to throw her weight around, making demands of Amelia and her staff. Elizabeth rued the day Mrs. L. figured out she was Amelia's granddaughter. There was no slipping past her without getting an earful about something. To top it off, she had a grating voice to match her overzealous, in-your-face personality.

Mrs. Leibowitz's lips were pursed and her arms swung alternately at her sides, hands clenched into fists as she strode up to the first Pennington she spotted. *"Elizabeth!"*

Her name sounded more like a squawk.

"What the *hell* is going on around here?"

Elizabeth wondered if she spoke to her grandchildren in the same way. *Was she always this abrasive? Or just when she stayed at the inn?*

"There are cops everywhere! Crawling all over the place, sticking their noses into everybody's business, asking a lot of questions." She stiffened her back, appearing overly indignant. "You know how many years I've been coming here?"

Elizabeth didn't know exactly and also didn't care. She needed to find a way to get past her. Now she understood why her grandmother didn't want to involve the guests unless she had no other choice.

"I didn't come back this summer to be interrogated like some common criminal. This is absolutely ridiculous! Why would I ever come back again?" Her voice grew louder with each word as if heading for a crescendo. "What are you going to do about this?" She wagged her crooked old index finger in Elizabeth's face.

Mrs. L. paused long enough for her to jump in. The situation clearly called for some serious acting, but she had to be careful not to be perceived as patronizing. She did her best to make her voice sound compassionate.

"Mrs. Leibowitz, I realize how much of an inconvenience this is for you, and everyone at Pennington Point Inn empathizes with you. We really do." Elizabeth slowly laced her fingers together, folding her hands piously in front of her. "And we are confident if everyone cooperates with the officers conducting the investigation, they will be able to wrap up quickly and we can all go back to what we'd rather be doing. Please be patient. I'm sure this will all be over very soon. Thank you for being so understanding."

Running out of breath and starting to feel lightheaded, she knew she couldn't ease up until she'd sealed the deal. "Why don't I have someone from our wait staff bring up a nice bottle of Chianti to ease your discomfort? Would that be all right?"

Mrs. L. opened her mouth, but Elizabeth remained in control.

"Let me go take care of it right now." Turning on her heel, she walked briskly to the kitchen, leaving the bewildered guest standing alone in the middle of the lobby with her mouth agape. A quiet "thank you" was all she could muster. Regretting crossing paths with her, Elizabeth hoped she'd put the issue to rest, at least for the moment. Deep down, she knew Mrs. L. would never be happy.

# CHAPTER EIGHT

As expected, *Tony and his* staff were bustling about the kitchen in preparation for the evening's clambake on the beach. Elizabeth watched for a while as Tony skillfully chopped several vegetables faster than she'd ever seen a hand, with a knife in it, operate. The movement was mesmerizing. He looked up to see her watching him, pausing to chuckle.

"Elizabeth, check out my new knife." Tony held it out for her to see more closely. "Believe it or not, the blade is made of ceramic, but it's incredibly sharp. I don't think I've ever worked with anything sharper." Quite a testimonial, considering how long Tony had been a chef. He demonstrated on a nearby tomato, slicing it in half with little effort, using only one hand. Elizabeth was duly impressed. Of course, she wasn't much of a cook, but she had tried to cut tomatoes before and usually struggled to get consistently sized slices, usually ending up with a mushy mess.

Glancing up from Tony's neat line of tomato slices, she was perplexed by his expression. He seemed to be enjoying his new gadget far too much. His eyes took on a glaze as if his thoughts had carried him far from the quaint inn perched on the precipice above the ocean. Tony finally blinked, put down his tool, and cleared his throat.

"If I'm not careful, I could get carried away with such a sharp tool. . . . What can I do for you, Lizzi?" He always had a moment for her. Upon hearing she needed a little something for a late lunch, he quickly pulled together a lobster roll, to Elizabeth's delight, accompanied by a fresh fruit salad, including some of Maine's wild blueberries, and a sparkling water. She was thrilled. Tony's lobster roll was the best she'd ever tasted. Of course, it should not be confused with a lobster *salad* roll that had mayonnaise in it, possibly small pieces of diced celery. A true New England lobster roll was simply generously sized chunks of lobster slathered in butter and nestled in a soft, fresh hot dog roll, slit along the top. Tony probably added a secret ingredient or two. She could travel up and down the rocky coast of Maine and not find a better lobster roll.

With boxed lunch in hand, she passed through the lobby, giving a nod to Rashelle, who was busy with guests at the front desk. They appeared to be husband and wife with two little girls in tow. The man was not very tall, somewhat dumpy with drooping shoulders, and dark, curly hair. The wife seemed like a church mouse, with straight, shoulder-length, brown hair, parted in the middle. The girls appeared to be less than five years old and close in age with curly hair, like their father's, that bounced softly on their shoulders with the slightest movement. The younger one spun around to see who was crossing the lobby. Elizabeth looked back as she reached the door, catching her eye. In a strange way, the young girl reminded her of herself as a child.

Snatching a folding chair from the front porch and tucking it under one arm, Elizabeth descended the broad steps and crossed the circular drive. Her car was still parked at the top of the curve, and she'd have to try to remember to move it later. It was time to get some ideas down on paper and get Vera off her back.

As Elizabeth set off across the side lawn toward the path in the woods, a couple guys from the kitchen staff approached the stairs to the beach. One carried a large garden shovel in each hand; the other was laden with two large bags of charcoal. The beach side of the peninsula was accessed via a set of wooden stairs installed years ago. The steps washed out at the bottom from time to time, usually during the occasional hurricane, and required constant maintenance. They were configured so guests descended about a half dozen or so steps, reached a landing, turned, and descended another half dozen steps in the opposite direction, repeating this pattern several times before reaching the sandy beach below. The key was to refrain from looking down in the process.

On nights of a barbecue or a clambake, Tony and his staff expended the extra effort to transport everything necessary down to the beach. Sometime during the summer, someone had rigged a primitive pulley system to send down as much as possible that would fit in a wooden box measuring three feet by four feet. The rest was carried by hand down the stairs. Since it was so labor intensive, only a couple of beach barbecues were planned per month, but they were hugely popular with the guests. Tony and his crew dug a pit in the sand and roasted corn on the cob still in the husks and steamed native Maine lobsters over coals. He rounded out the meal with coleslaw, rolls, and scrumptious pies made with Maine raspberries or blueberries, depending upon which berry was in season at the time. Tonight's pie would be raspberry. A portion of the berries would be from Nana's garden and the rest from a local farmer who delivered to the inn on a regular basis. Elizabeth loved raspberry pie. It reminded her of when she was little and her grandmother would send her out to the garden to pick berries. Little Lizzi usually ate more than she brought back to the inn, but her grandmother never seemed to mind.

Grown-up Elizabeth needed to get herself focused and find a quiet place to get some work done. On the way through the trees she could hear rustling sounds. Keeping her eyes forward, she tried to ignore the deeper part of the woods, telling herself it was only squirrels playing. Nothing more. She covered the half-mile distance to the bluff in no time. Once there, she plunked down her drawing supplies and her lunch, freeing up her hands to unfold the old-fashioned lawn chair woven with faded yellow and white fraying strips of vinyl, a throwback to the seventies when yellow was the happy color. Situating herself facing the railing with a view to the sea, she was anxious to start sketching, so she let her lunch lie untouched in favor of the drawing pad. Vera often scoffed at her use of paper and pencil, calling it an archaic practice in the modern world of technology. Elizabeth, however, felt a certain sense of control with a pencil in her hand and found her creative juices flowed more easily. So she plodded right along using her old-fashioned equipment, in spite of her boss' objection. It was hard for Vera to criticize too loudly when she saw the design creations Elizabeth produced.

Having already spent time thinking about the possibilities, Elizabeth envisioned the lobby of Drescher's new luxury hotel with magnificent panels of rich fabric draped from the ceiling and from random points high up on the walls. The panels would be loosely woven to allow air flow and be constructed of a heavy-duty faux silk that could be removed periodically to be cleaned. The fabric would look luxurious, but would also help to absorb sound, which was important in a public space like this three-story lobby. She skillfully sketched what she imagined onto the pad of paper on her lap.

Before long, she slid down in her chair, pulling her knees against her body, bracing her heels on the edge of the chair, converting her legs into a makeshift easel on which to rest her paper. After several quick sketches of the fabric panels from different perspectives, she turned her attention to the front desk, the concierge station, and the bellhop's stand, drawing each one with rich Italian marble counters, and then moved on to dark mahogany wood walls with contemporary chrome fixtures and soft lighting. Next she focused on the furniture.

Throughout the lobby, she pictured upholstered chairs and love seats with clean, contemporary lines arranged in conversation clusters. No particular color palette had seemed obvious yet, but she would put that question in the back of her mind to work on while she kept going.

Turning her attention to individual guest rooms, she flipped the pad to a clean page. In a hotel of this stature, they would all be suites, and she thought each floor should have a different design style, perhaps with an international flair. She was in a groove and didn't want to stop sketching before she'd put down on paper everything spilling out of her imagination. Her late lunch would have to wait a little longer, in spite of the noisy protest from her stomach. "Strike while the iron is hot," her grandmother always said. As a youngster it took her a while to figure out what she meant by that, but as an adult, Elizabeth not only understood the cliché, she lived by it.

After about an hour of fluid arm movements, Elizabeth had cranked out a couple dozen sketches. A few discarded pages lay at the base of her chair, scrunched up into balls, but the rest were solid designs she felt confident about. Lifting her head, she let her feet drop off the edge of the seat. It was time for a break. Her body was sending a more desperate signal for food, the beginnings of a headache. Grateful she'd eaten a late breakfast, she never would have lasted as long before having to stop if she hadn't.

While her taste buds delighted in the succulent lobster and sweet crunch of the fruit salad, she closed her eyes and enjoyed the sounds of seagulls playfully floating on the air currents above her. After a few minutes of nature's serenade, she slowly opened her eyes and her gaze fell beyond the railing. A figure stood on the breakwater, near the lighthouse. Chief Austin. His hands were on his hips, and he seemed to be staring out to sea. Perhaps in a reflective mood. He had a lot to ponder. A lot to sort out. She watched him pace as if waiting for something. Or someone. As Elizabeth slowly stood from her lawn chair, a squeak reminded her of its age. Reaching out to grasp the railing, she squinted to see more clearly. What was he up to? She watched a while longer, unable to tear herself away. Suddenly, the chief took tentative steps across the boulders, down toward the water. Elizabeth shifted her focus to where he was heading and noticed a figure emerging. Someone in a wet suit, complete with an oxygen tank, mask, and flippers. In the frigid waters of coastal Maine, such an outfit was necessary in order to spend any time submerged.

Anxious to see if the diver had found anything, she watched with great interest as the black-rubber-skinned person spoke to the chief with gesturing hands. From the distance she was observing from on the bluff, it was hard to tell if the diver was a man or a woman.

She needed a closer look. Shoving the drawing pad and pencils into the portfolio, Elizabeth folded up the decidedly gaudy lawn chair but stopped short of scooping them up. A disapproving click slipped from her lips at the remnants of her lunch scattered at her feet. She couldn't leave a mess behind. That would violate what was, in her mind, the eleventh commandment. Thou shalt not litter the pristine state of Maine. She put down her load and gathered her litter, placing the loose items inside the box. Tucking it under her arm, she picked up the chair and portfolio again and assessed the area to see where she could tuck her stuff out of sight for a while. A large tree on the far side of the clearing, a few feet into the woods, would suffice. She stepped behind the towering conifer and leaned her belongings up against it, freeing her to move unencumbered.

Re-entering the path, she wished she could break into a light jog to get there sooner. Unfortunately, the trail did not lend itself to that. After the bluff, the path became narrower and was riddled with tree roots that could easily catch a toe and send her airborne, landing her face-first in the dirt. Thankfully, branches extended out into the path to grab onto when navigating down the steep slope.

Pausing for a moment to peer through the pines toward the lighthouse, Elizabeth couldn't see the diver talking to the chief. For that matter, the chief wasn't in sight, either. Suddenly, she heard voices below on the path. Elizabeth slipped into the brush on the side of the hill, grabbing onto the trunks of small pine trees as she went. As each step put her farther away from the path, she could hear voices getting closer. Both were male. Hoping to glean something from their conversation as they passed, she squatted to stay out of sight and took hold of the nearest trunk to steady herself on the steep incline. Footsteps grew closer. She slowed her breathing and listened, hoping she was adequately concealed. Then it got quiet, no footsteps and no voices. Even the gulls overhead were quiet. *What was going on?* The idea to hide in the trees started to seem foolish. Then the conversation began again. There was no movement, though. The chief must have had to catch his breath. Only the extremely fit could make it up the hill from the light without getting winded.

"Look, Chief. This is getting us nowhere. Precious time is slipping away. We need to close down the entrance to the inn. No one leaves until we figure this out."

Elizabeth stifled a gasp.

"We have no concrete evidence this is anything other than a teenager who has run away. Amelia will never go for closing down the—"

"It's not her choice!" the other man bellowed. "We have a very serious situation and could be losing vital evidence or allowing key witnesses or even the perpetrators the opportunity to walk away, scot-free."

Elizabeth felt uncomfortable eavesdropping on their conversation. If they could see her, she would look rather guilty crouched behind the tree. Inadvertently shifting her focus from maintaining her balance to what they were saying, her left foot started to slide and the rest of her body followed along down the steep hill. As the trunk slipped from her grasp, she could hear the surf crashing against the rocks below. Panic set in. The edge of the cliff couldn't be far away, but she didn't know exactly how far. She snatched at low branches as she tried to stop herself from sliding. The first branch pulled right off the tree. The second slipped through her hand, but slowed her down a bit. The third branch saved her. Her body jolted to a stop. Grabbing the trunk of the tree with everything she had in upper body strength, her arms ached.

Wondering how much noise she'd made slipping down the side of the hill, she listened. Had they noticed? The air was silent. She couldn't tell if they were pausing in their conversation or listening for her. She prayed it wasn't the latter. It would be difficult to come up with a reasonable explanation if they found her. Glancing down the hill, beyond her left foot, her eyes grew wide. She was mere inches away from an abrupt drop off the edge of the cliff. Stifling even the slightest sound from escaping her lips, she suddenly felt dizzy and her fingers tingled. She was perched precariously where the trail took a turn and zigzagged the rest of the way down the cliff. If she had kept going over the edge, they would have been investigating another mishap at the inn. Elizabeth endeavored to put that out of her head to concentrate on holding on and remaining quiet. Straining to listen to her surroundings, she longed to hear their voices. Hopefully, they'd dismissed the sound as a squirrel or some other small critter. She held still. Eventually the voices picked up again.

"Lieutenant Perkins, we don't know that it's a serious situation. It could just be—"

"Not a serious situation? Check with the girl's parents and see what they think. The evidence we've collected so far certainly indicates it is; and speaking of checking, I'd like to see what Mitchell's been up to. He's been difficult to pin down."

Their voices trailed off, so the chief must have caught his breath while he was getting an earful. The squelch from a two-way radio confirmed they were farther up the path.

*Poor Nana. She will absolutely flip. This will be terrible for business. And Kurt. What did the lieutenant mean by that? Do they suspect him? If he is a suspect, what would his motive be? And are others in danger? And what evidence? What else have they collected?*

Waiting several minutes to make sure the men were far enough away for her to leave the safety of her camouflage, she wondered what her next move was going to be. *Were they investigating a murder or a disappearance? Or two disappearances, the girl and Girard. Were they connected?* As she considered these questions she slowly made her way out of the woods, carefully placing each foot perpendicular to the hill so she wouldn't slip again. She emerged from the pines, relieved the body-sliding was over. Glancing up the hill, she noticed the silhouette of someone coming down the path through the trees. The chief? The lieutenant? It was too late to dive back into the woods, but if she stayed put, they would wonder what she was doing there and why they hadn't seen her on their way up the path. In a rash decision, she decided to continue down the hill. Chances were she could get down to the bottom faster than whoever was behind her and buy herself more time before she came face-to-face with him or them. Being out in the open at the bottom of the trail seemed far safer than cornered on the edge of a cliff.

Grabbing protruding pine boughs as she went, Elizabeth negotiated her way down the steep decline, stepping nimbly around exposed roots. Footsteps thudded behind her. In a panic, she quickened her pace, which made her descent much more challenging. If she remembered correctly, there were two more hairpin turns in the trail before she was safely at the bottom. Curious to see who was behind her but afraid to sneak a peek, she focused on where her feet were landing. Finally, she couldn't resist any longer and took her eyes off to look behind her. As she did, she felt her foot catch on a root or a rock, so she spun around to see the trunk of an evergreen hurtling toward her. Instinctively, she put her hands out to break her fall and landed with a thud on her chest, her forehead making contact with the base of the tree. The impact stunned her for a moment, abruptly displacing air from her lungs. Realizing the person behind her was nearly on top of her, she labored to get her feet beneath her but was a bit dazed. A firm hand grabbed her from behind.

"Lizzi, are you all right?"

Still struggling to breathe, she was relieved to hear a familiar voice.

"What happened? You look terrible. Are you all right? I'm so glad I found you. I should have checked the lighthouse first. That's where your grandmother suggested, but it's such a long walk down—"

"Shelle, I've got my cell phone. Try that next time." Still trying to catch her breath, Elizabeth was sure she looked quite awful, having just cleaned off a five foot section of the path with the front of her clothes. Rashelle helped her sit up. . . . Her cell phone. Had she remembered to put it on silent? Could that have given her away in the woods if it had rung? She decided she needed to get better at being in stealth mode, or she wasn't going to find out much. Worse yet, she could put herself in danger.

"What were you doing?"

"Oh, poking around." Elizabeth brushed off her clothes as Rashelle pulled pine needles out of her hair. "Listen, let's get back up the hill," she urged, pulling herself upright. "I overheard part of a conversation. I need to let Nana know Chief Austin is going to start making things miserable for everyone—"

"Start? The inn's already in lockdown. No one in or out."

"Wow, they move quickly. He must have radioed ahead on his way up the hill." *Great. Vera is never going to believe this!*

"Yeah. Basically everyone is a suspect until proven otherwise."

"What? A suspect for what?" She wondered what the diver could have found.

"Poor Amelia. She's not going to take this well."

Elizabeth grabbed Rashelle firmly at the shoulders. "You and I are going to find out what's going on."

"W-we are?" she stammered.

"We have to!" Elizabeth released her grip and resumed her hike, glancing back to confirm Shelle had fallen in behind her. "My grandmother is on the verge of giving up the inn, which has been in our family for . . . for Lord knows how many years. But generations, anyway. And because some aggressive attorney is harassing her. Do we know anything about this guy?" she asked, turning to see if her friend was getting her point.

Rashelle's lips parted slightly, but Elizabeth continued her rant.

"A young female guest is missing and everyone fears the worst at this point. The inn is in lockdown—not good for business." She gestured with an accusatory finger pointed into the air. "On top of it all, the chief is *way* out of his league here. He's never had any experience with missing persons, extortion, or . . . or worse. He wasn't around when the student disappeared years ago, but that case was never solved and we don't need another scandal." The pace of her words quickened with each sentence. She stopped on a turn to catch her breath.

Silence pervaded as they pondered their quandary. Elizabeth wondered how loudly she'd been speaking and if the woods around them had ears. As she nervously surveyed their surroundings in a 360-degree swath, one thing she knew for sure, they needed to rally behind Amelia.

They continued up the hill in silence until Elizabeth nearly walked past the bluff in her determination to get to the top.

"Oh! I almost forgot. I left my drawing supplies and a chair behind a tree."

"You did *what?*"

"Don't give it another thought. I needed to travel lightly. It'll only take a second," she assured her friend, stepping into the trees. "I put them behind this . . ." Her voice trailed off as she walked into the woods. She darted from tree to tree but didn't find her belongings. "They were right here," she asserted, panic rising in her voice. *Where could they be?* Retracing her steps from the bluff back to the trees, she was certain she knew the area, having played there as a child. Confident she was not mistaken, she kept searching. Even if they had fallen over, she should still be able to find them. The underbrush was not thick. She walked in a circle around the area. Rashelle searched the fringes of what Elizabeth was covering. Crisscrossing the small area above the bluff, Lizzi grew anxious. Her drawings . . . she had nothing to fax to her boss. Vera was definitely not going to be happy. "They're gone." Her words were barely audible. She was devastated.

"Do you think the chief would have picked them up and kept them, thinking they might be evidence?" Rashelle ventured a guess.

"Oh, why would he do that?" she snapped, exasperated with the new wrinkle. "Let's go see."

When the pair reached the top of the trail, Elizabeth looked worse for the wear, but resolute. They walked out into the clearing onto an unsettling scene. Police cars lined the circular drive. Then it dawned on her.

"Shelle, my car is gone!"

# CHAPTER NINE

Reinforcements *had been* called in, causing quite a commotion at the otherwise sleepy seaside inn. State troopers in their crisp blue uniforms milled about in a loosely formed circle. Police radios squawked. Elizabeth searched frantically for her friendly local chief. She found him peering out from behind a couple wide-brimmed state trooper hats. She got as close to the entourage as she could and rose up onto her tiptoes.

"Excuse me, Chief Austin," she shouted, but he couldn't hear her with the din around him. She reached in and grabbed his forearm and repeated more loudly, "Chief Austin!" He spun around to face her, pulling his arm out of her firm grasp.

"What!" he barked, clearly short-tempered and wearing the stress from the situation on his shirtsleeve. "Oh, Miss Pennington." He lightened his tone.

"Do you know where my car is?" She tried to keep her voice from sounding desperate.

"You may want to speak with Lieutenant Perkins of the Maine State Police. From what I understand, they had reasonable suspicion to search the car, and upon inspection, ordered it impounded and towed to the evidence collection center at the Portland barracks."

"What? They impounded my car? In Portland?"

Several officers turned toward her raised voice. She lowered the volume a couple of notches.

"What could they have possibly found that they thought was suspicious?" *What did I leave in it? Did someone put something in it? What the devil is going on?*

"And Elizabeth . . ." He leaned over and put his hand firmly on her shoulder like a father reprimanding his delinquent daughter. "I wouldn't be making any plans to wander too far away. I'm sure the lieutenant will want to have a little chat with you." He glowered with his last words.

The chief removed his hand from her shoulder but held his gaze for effect, then he was swiftly swallowed by the sea of state police as they jockeyed for position to hear instructions from one of the state troopers who was clearly in charge. Lieutenant Perkins perhaps? Elizabeth took a step back to avoid being jostled by the lively group.

Dismayed, she couldn't believe they'd taken her little Z4. How was she going to get back to the city? Then she remembered her portfolio. "Hey, Chief, did they take my portfolio, too?" she shouted across the clamor but doubted he'd heard the complete question. He looked in her direction from inside the crowd as if he thought someone had spoken to him but was brought back to the task at hand by a man in blue. They had a lot of questions for him.

If Elizabeth could have seen through the crowd to the edge of the woods, she might have noticed Kurt lurking just out of sight, keeping his eye on the activity. In particular, he had his eye on her.

Feeling as though she was getting sucked in by the whirlpool of activity, Elizabeth yearned to be in control again. She turned away from the crowd, searching for her good friend Rashelle, who was right where Elizabeth had left her, standing off to the side of the driveway with her arms folded and a look of trepidation. Their little Camelot known as Pennington Point Inn was in a veritable state of turmoil. *Where was a knight in shining armor when you needed him? . . . Or her?*

As Elizabeth approached, Rashelle looked at her expectantly.

"I've *got* to get back that portfolio," she demanded. "I don't know who has it, but my job, my career, depend on it. My boss is going to be on me to get design ideas to her. I already got an earful this morning." Her voice quivered. For now, it was best to keep moving. She would have to deal with the portfolio later.

"One step at a time," Rashelle advised. Extending her arm around her friend's shoulder, she guided her toward the inn. They headed up the front steps and were met by Tony on the porch. He wore an uncharacteristic scowl and stood at the top of the stairs with his hands on his hips, the cool sea breeze tossing his wavy brown hair about.

"Tony, this whole thing is unbelievable," Elizabeth lamented, relieved to have someone else to commiserate with.

"Oui, incroyable!" he agreed with his French Canadian background showing through.

"What's going on?" she pressed, hoping for a fresh perspective on the situation.

"What's going on? *I'll tell you.* I stand here and wait while the police try to decide if it's okay for me to go ahead with the clambake on the beach. The majority of the food is prepared, and the guests are going to start complaining any minute."

"Where's my grandmother?" Elizabeth suddenly realized she wasn't visible.

"Amelia wasn't feeling well, so she went upstairs to lie down for a while."

Concerned for her nana, Elizabeth asked softly, "Is she all right?"

"She's fine, Lizzi. Just overtired. I think this whole ordeal is wearing her out."

Elizabeth feared the mayhem at the inn was causing exorbitant stress on her grandmother, which worried her. *Dear Lord, please help her through this difficult time with her health intact.*

Rashelle grabbed Lizzi's arm and pulled her away.

Bidding Tony adieu, Elizabeth followed her friend through the lobby like a dinghy in tow. Inside, Rashelle confided, "I've got some more info on the missing girl."

Once behind the reception desk, she closed the access door and spoke in hushed tones. "I was here earlier when the chief came into the lobby with a state trooper and the parents of the girl. They didn't notice me because I was seated at the computer down below the counter, updating some reservations that had just come in. They said this girl is fourteen years old, is about five feet, six inches tall, light brown hair, usually pulled into a pony tail. She was last seen about three o'clock on Thursday afternoon when she went out to get some fresh air. She was wearing a pink t-shirt and jeans, with a light purple, zippered GAP sweatshirt—like the one they found at the lighthouse today."

Lizzi considered all the info, and then asked, "Did the parents confirm it was their daughter's?"

"Yes."

"To get some fresh air . . ." Elizabeth repeated. "Is that another way of saying they were having words and she needed her space?"

Rashelle tilted her head, remaining quiet, allowing her friend to continue.

"You know, it's tough to be fourteen. It's even tougher to be fourteen on a weekend away with your parents. What were they thinking?" Elizabeth winced, uncomfortable that she was repeating part of her conversation with Kurt. "This was supposed to be a last fling before she went back to school. For who? Did they really think—what's her name?"

"Uh, Kelsey . . . Kelsey Hutchins."

"Did they think this would be fun for her?"

"Supposedly."

"Did anyone hear them arguing?"

"There was no one in the room next to them. They requested the end room in Acadia House, the one closest to the woods."

"Where are they from and when did they check in?"

"Let's see. I remember I was on duty when they arrived. It was Thursday, around noon. They showed up before check-in time. I wasn't sure their room was ready, so I sent Marion from housekeeping to check."

"What did the Hutchins do while Marion was gone?"

"Mr. Hutchins—Bill—just did a lot of pacing in the lobby and his wife, Lisa, wandered into the sitting room and sat down to wait."

"What about their daughter?"

"Kelsey? I never really saw her. She must have been outside or still in the car."

"So, you wouldn't know what she looks like if you saw her?"

"No."

"Did Bill and Lisa at least have a picture to show the police?"

"I don't believe so. I know they apologized for not being more helpful."

"So, just the three of them registered at the inn."

"Right."

"Doesn't that seem odd to you, in this day and age of having a plethora of photos on a phone, that they didn't have any to share with the police?"

Rashelle shrugged.

"They didn't have any other children?"

"Not that I know of."

"How old would you say the parents are?"

Rashelle appeared surprised by this question. "Well, I would say around mid-thirties."

"That's all?"

"Yeah, they seemed kind of young."

Elizabeth considered the facts and then asked, "How long were they staying?"

"They were to check out on Sunday morning . . . tomorrow. Although, they asked if it would be possible to stay longer, if necessary."

"Really?"

"What does that mean?"

"I don't know. It seems odd. It's Labor Day weekend. Wasn't this the last weekend before their daughter started school? Wouldn't they know how long they could stay when they arrived? Who knows *what* it means, if anything."

Silence occupied the small space behind the front desk for a moment until Elizabeth continued. "Wait a minute. You didn't tell me where they were from."

"Oh! Let me double-check." Rashelle leaned over the ergonomically correct chair parked in front of the computer monitor. Her long slender fingers danced gracefully across the keys until she accessed the screen she needed. "West Hartford, Connecticut."

"And how did he pay for the room? What were the arrangements?"

"Usually we have the guests give us a credit card number at check-in and we settle up when they check out. He insisted on paying in cash up front."

"Cash?"

"Yup."

"Who *does* that?"

Rashelle left the rhetorical question unanswered.

Elizabeth kept going. "Okay, so one theory may be that she went out for a walk and got lost in unfamiliar woods, and darkness fell before she could find her way back."

"But the woods have been searched and they found nothing."

"It doesn't mean there isn't anything yet to find." The friends exchanged looks of understanding. "Another theory could be that she went for a walk on the beach and went too far beyond the breakwater, and the tide came in. It got dark before she could get back. She fell asleep and missed the first low tide so now she's waiting for the next one. Or perhaps she simply left; she'd had enough of the 'rents. She wanted to do something fun for the last few days of her summer freedom. She may show up tomorrow morning in time to go home. . . . Ha! Won't she be surprised to find such a large welcoming party waiting to greet her?"

"Yeah." The friends shared a chuckle.

Rashelle got serious again. "She could also have gone down to the lighthouse and gotten too close to the water. She wasn't with her parents when I passed along the standard warning we give to all our guests about rogue waves."

As images crossed her mind of the chief carrying the purple sweatshirt up from the lighthouse, Elizabeth realized she had to consider that as a possibility as well. And it wasn't just the risk of getting swept off the rocks, the temperature of the ocean in Maine, even in the summer, made it impossible to survive in the water for any length of time.

"I know the diver didn't find anything—"

"You do?"

"Yeah, but like you say, that doesn't mean there wasn't anything to find."

"True . . . I don't know if the current would take a body away from there or wash it back up on shore."

The voice from behind took them by surprise. "It would carry it away, and no one would ever see it again."

The girls whipped around.

"Nana, I didn't know you—what are you doing here?" Elizabeth couldn't help but notice how tired she looked. The dark circles under her eyes told of trials and tribulations that had spanned a lifetime. Lizzi needed to help her get through the current quandary. Returning to Amelia's startling claim when she interrupted their brainstorming session, Elizabeth asked tentatively, "It would wash it away? H-how do you know?"

"Oh, Lizzi, it happened a very long time ago, but unfortunately it did happen." Her grandmother sounded exhausted, spent physically and emotionally. "Different circumstances, but perhaps the same result. Someday I'll tell you about it."

"Amelia, do you think that's what happened this time?" Rashelle chimed in.

"I don't know. Anything is possible. She could have gone too far down the beach and around the stone outcroppings where the tide comes in and cuts off the passage."

Elizabeth's eyes found Rashelle's. They'd already covered that possibility.

"For all we know, she could have found her way into the tunnels and is lost down there somewhere."

"The tunnels!" Elizabeth drew her arms in closer as she attempted to contain her shiver. Her voice was not much more than a whisper. "I thought they'd been sealed off years ago."

"They were, but vandals tampering with the entrances over time have damaged some of the seals and rendered the locks inoperable. Every once in a while one of the staff catches a curious kid nosing around one of the entrances and shoos them away. A couple weeks ago, Kurt mentioned he found two brothers trying to open the hatchway on the back of the tennis shack. That leads to the tunnel that goes between the main inn and Acadia House."

Listening intently, the girls waited for Amelia to continue.

"Acadia was one of two buildings used as dormitories back when Pennington was a school. The other dormitory burned down and was never rebuilt. So the tunnel leads out from the inn and forks partway out; one tine of the fork ends up under the guest rooms in Acadia, and the other eventually arrives at an abrupt dead end. Moosehead Lodge was built after a section of the woods was cleared, near the footprint of the other dorm, not long after we began operating as an inn, but it's not connected to the tunnels."

Elizabeth marveled at how Amelia always had something she could teach her about the old inn yet never seemed to reveal the whole story.

"Well, I came down to find my reading glasses." She glanced at the desk that held the computer. "Oh! There they are. I really should tie them around my neck so I won't lose them all the time." Reaching past the girls, she chuckled to herself. A pleasant fragrance of perfume wafted as she moved. Stepping back to face them, she offered a simple explanation. "I need to lie down and rest for a while. I find if I read first, it relaxes me. I'll see you girls later."

They watched her slip through the door. Elizabeth could tell Rashelle was processing what her grandmother had shared and feared what she was concocting behind her inquisitive look.

"Okay, Lizzi. We've got to check out those tunnels."

"Shelle, you don't know what it's like down there."

"You heard your grandmother. She practically spelled it out for us."

"What?" *Spelled it out? That was a bit of a stretch.* She didn't like where the conversation was going.

"Listen. The police haven't extended their search to beneath the property. They're having a hard enough time covering the grounds. Here, let's grab a couple flashlights." She yanked open the bottom drawer in the desk under the computer. Fumbling around in the back of it, she came out with two old, banged-up metal flashlights she proudly held up like two rainbow trout from a deep-sea fishing trip.

Elizabeth still couldn't wrap her mind around the idea of the two of them descending into the depths below the inn. Having been strictly forbidden from doing so as a child, she had no desire to enter the dark, dank tunnels as an adult.

"How are we going to get down there without being seen? I'm sure they don't want anyone nosing around."

"You heard Tony. He's out on the front porch waiting to get the okay to do the clambake. There's probably no one in the kitchen right now. We'll go through the wine cellar."

Unable to think of a good comeback, Elizabeth had no desire to go, but at least she would have someone to go with her. *What if the girl* was *lost down there? What if the two of them could put the whole matter to rest?*

"All right, let's do it." Rashelle handed Elizabeth one of the two clunky flashlights. As if on cue, they instinctively switched them on in tandem to check the batteries. Both lights sprung to life.

"Wow. They actually work. Who knows the last time these artifacts were used."

Her friend's observation didn't help Elizabeth feel any more at ease about the expedition they were about to set out on.

# CHAPTER TEN

*After slipping through the* empty kitchen, past the wine cooler, down the creaky wooden steps, the girls stood on the other side of the towering racks of wine bottles staring into an unknown black void. A narrow separation between two racks in one corner had allowed enough room for two diminutive young ladies to slip through.

Switching on her flashlight, Rashelle started into the damp, shadowy tunnel, slowly placing one foot awkwardly in front of the other. "Let's meet back here if we get separated," she instructed, taking the lead.

Elizabeth remained behind her, struggling to get her flashlight to stay lit. As she shook it, the large D batteries rattled inside. The dim light brightened and seemed to be staying on. Shuffling toward Rashelle's light, she was surprised by how far her city slicker friend had reached during the time she fumbled with her light.

Constructed of field stones, the tunnels were similar to stone walls found throughout New England that wound their way through open fields in the countryside and, at times, slipped from view as they disappeared into woods. The passageway measured approximately eight feet high by ten feet wide at the largest sections, but there were smaller areas constricted by underground rock ledges. Construction had been long and arduous but critical to the continued success of the school. Rudimentary lighting installed to facilitate the students' passage through the tunnels had long since stopped functioning, however. Without flashlights, the blackness was darker than dark—an abyss completely void of light.

A musty smell hung in the damp air, and the floor was wet from water seeping in through the stones. An occasional drip from the ceiling gave the impression of being in a cave. Over the years, the walls had evolved into a patchwork quilt as sections gave way to frost heave and were replaced with brick and, more recently, with cement. From the initial observation beyond the wine racks, it didn't look like anyone had done much repair work in a while. Errant stones littered the floor for as far as the eye could see with a weak flashlight.

As Elizabeth took a few steps down the tunnel toward Rashelle, something brushed softly against her forehead and she jumped back. Aiming her light to the ceiling, she illuminated an elaborate web, replete with a large black spider scurrying away from the giant human intruder. Shaking off the encounter, she rubbed her face, trying to remove the sensation it was still touching her. Stepping closer, she admired a beautiful pattern of intricately woven fibers, glittering in her beam of light, and wondered how long it must have taken the spider to construct it. It was truly a work of art.

Gazing past the web, Elizabeth noticed Rashelle's light was no longer bobbing in front of her. She didn't seem to be moving. Perhaps her friend was waiting for her to catch up. Elizabeth navigated carefully past the spider and its beautiful home, being careful not to touch the sticky strands again, resuming her trek down the tunnel. She kept the light moving back and forth, up and down, not knowing what she might find. A shaft to the right was partially blocked off with dining room chairs stacked in columns like a wall. It was either a route that led to another building on campus or a dead end. *Only one way to find out.* She couldn't resist the urge.

As Elizabeth approached from behind, Rashelle stood perfectly still. "I can't."

"What?"

"I can't." Rashelle spoke more firmly.

"You can't what?"

"I can't do this."

"What? Why the sudden change of heart?" An otherwise outgoing, gregarious New Yorker had turned into the Cowardly Lion, and they were a long way from Oz.

"I don't know what it is, but I can't do this. It's like the place has a personality, and it doesn't want us intruding. It doesn't feel right."

"None of this feels right. Since when has that stopped us before?" Lizzi was losing her patience. After all, it had been Rashelle's idea to head down to the tunnels in the first place.

"Maybe I just need time to get used to it."

Elizabeth wondered if she would *ever* get used to it. It gave her the creeps. "You stay put. I'll go for a ways and come back. Okay? Will you be all right?"

Rashelle remained anchored to her spot on the dirt floor, staring into the dark tunnel.

"Shelle?"

She flinched. "Y-Yes. You go ahead. I'll be fine. I'll just wait here."

"Okay. Focus on breathing," Elizabeth urged.

"Okay," she muttered, not seeming to hear the words.

Elizabeth made a right to explore the first offshoot from the main tunnel. She wasn't entirely comfortable leaving her friend behind, but she needed to cover some ground, since Rashelle was incapable. Besides, she'd left her near the entrance so she could find her way out if she needed to.

Leaving caution and all sense of reason behind, Elizabeth started off taking small, deliberate steps down the dark side passageway, blazing her way with her light cutting a narrow swath. After several yards she could sense the tunnel was veering to the right. Attempting to shore up her confidence, she tried to reason with herself.

*I can't get lost. All I have to do is turn around and follow the tunnel back the way I came.* After a while she realized her baby steps were becoming more tentative as the flashlight grew dimmer. Banging the bulb end of it on her palm, she coaxed it brighter. It flickered on and off and then went out. The darkness in the tunnel was complete. All encompassing. It felt as though it could suffocate her. Desperate to get the light back on, she banged the lifeless battery holder against the wall. Nothing. Not a flicker.

"Great!" *Time to head back. Nothing accomplished.* Reversing her direction, she ran her hand along the cold, smooth stones as she crept toward the main tunnel, keeping her fingers splayed against the wall. The darkness was overwhelming. She opened her eyes wider, straining to make out a shape or a shadow. Anything. *One foot in front of the other.* With nothing discernible to see, she squinted, fighting the sensation she was going to run into something, reluctant to consider what might be behind her.

Suddenly her feet met the resistance of a slight incline. With the light on earlier, she hadn't noticed she'd been making her way down a slight hill. Now, without the use of her sight, her remaining senses were heightened. Anxious to get out of the dark, she quickened her pace; but in her haste, her left foot slipped on a wet spot, and it shot out from underneath her. As her upper torso snapped backward, she tried to compensate with the rest of her body. Her arms flailing, she managed to throw herself forward again. As her luck was running, she overcompensated and her right foot landed hard on the dirt below. The force of the impact caused her ankle to roll. She yelled out as she went down. Releasing the flashlight in time to break the fall, she landed on the damp dirt floor with a soft thud, sprawled out in the dark with a throbbing ankle.

"Shit!" Groping the ground, she located the useless light and sat up. Forcefully rubbing her ankle, she hobbled to her feet and kept moving, trying to make her way in the dark. It couldn't be much farther, she assured herself. Going off and leaving her friend on her own seemed less like a good idea than when she came up with it. She persevered through the pain and kept walking, more like hobbling, with one hand on the wall, wondering if she should be able to see Rashelle's light by now. Then it hit her. Was she simply taking longer because of her ankle and the lack of light, or did she get up from her tumble facing the wrong direction? Panic welled inside and she endeavored to get her bearings.

She strained to see if she could hear anything. Slow but steady drips of water somewhere in the distance were all that were audible. Bracing herself for what may lay ahead, she made the decision to keep going in the same direction for a while longer. If she didn't reach the main tunnel after a certain number of steps—a hundred steps, she would turn around and go the other way. She couldn't panic, she just had to be methodical about it. "One, two, three." She continued the rest in her head . . . *19, 20, 21 . . .* wondering where Rashelle was and if she would see her light if she got close . . . *34, 35, 36 . . . I never should have left her. I didn't like the idea in the first place. She found the old flashlights, not me . . . 51, 52, 53 . . . This had better be working. I need to reconnect with Rashelle, especially since she has the only working flashlight. Or does she? What if hers died too? Oh, Elizabeth, what have you gotten yourself into? 68, 69, 70. Is this working?*

Then the smell hit her. It was as if someone had whacked her nose with the back of their hand. *What was it?* She obviously had not been that far before and was certainly not walking in the right direction. Her curiosity, though, kept her from stopping. A few more steps. Did she dare? What would she find? Not much in absolute darkness. Without a window in the tunnels or an operating flashlight, there was no chance of seeing anything. Still she held fast, not changing direction. The smell was strong. Sour, like the early stages of something decaying. What was the source? She kept going, completely blind. Two more steps. Then one more and she brought one foot up alongside the other. It was insanity. In a last ditch effort, she switched the flashlight on, only to see the bulb flicker in a soft glow and then die out again. She whacked it against her palm but to no avail. *No choice but to turn around.*

Very carefully she pivoted in place, one hand on the wall to stabilize herself. In a somewhat irrational moment, she decided to count her steps again, this time backward. She was fairly sure this was the right direction, but she wasn't going to take any chances. Where had she left off before? Somewhere around 70 or 80? She decided to go with 73 . . . 72, 71, 70 . . . She wanted out of the tunnel . . . 66, 65, 64 . . . Hopefully Rashelle was okay . . . and was not getting lost . . . smart enough to stay put . . . 53, 52, 51 . . . Counting her steps had turned into a nonsensical exercise, but it gave her something to do besides panic. Reaching the decline in the floor, she slowed to prevent herself from slipping. Where had she left off counting? She couldn't remember. *Just keep walking. This has to be the right way.* With her hand running along the wall, she pressed on. *Not too fast. But keep moving.* She fought to hold panic at bay.

As she felt the wall veering slightly to the left, a wave of relief poured over her. Remembering the wall turning to the right not long after she started down the side tunnel, she believed she was close to where she was then. She kept moving but held herself back from going too fast. Just a few more steps. It had to be only twenty more? Thirty? *Keep going. Don't let go of the wall.* It seemed as though it was getting brighter. Was it her imagination? *A few more steps.* The suffocating darkness was lifting. She could make out the outline of her hand holding the dead flashlight. She grinned when she noticed it was pointing backward. *Just a few more steps.*

What she saw next made her stop with a jolt. A figure was walking on the other side of the stacks of chairs where the side tunnel met up with the main shaft. It was Kurt, inching along toward where she had left Rashelle, but he didn't notice Elizabeth approaching. Terrified of what his intentions were, Elizabeth quickened her pace, risking slipping again, not wanting to let him out of her line of sight.

As she crept closer she could see Rashelle directly in front of him, farther down the shaft than where she'd left her. A mere dozen yards separated them. Elizabeth had the element of surprise on her side and was going to do everything in her power to prevent him from hurting her friend. Clutching the clunky flashlight with both hands, she raised it above her head as she snuck up close behind him. She drove it down onto his skull with all her weight behind it and watched him fall as his legs buckled beneath him. Rashelle spun around and looked into Elizabeth's eyes, a look of terror in hers.

# CHAPTER ELEVEN

"*I'm sorry.*" *Elizabeth didn't* know what else to say. She felt helpless looking at Kurt holding an ice pack to the back of his head.

He appeared crumpled and disheveled, slouched at the far end of the faded plaid couch tucked under the front windows of the sitting room. Chief Austin hovered nearby like a doting nanny.

"I'm really sorry. How was I supposed to know you're on our side? I'm sorry I hurt you. I thought you were about to hurt Rashelle."

Her friend shot her a troubled look.

Kurt perked up. "What were you doing down there in the tunnels, anyway?" His voice was half whining, half demanding.

"Oh, they're my old stomping ground," she fibbed with a flourish of her hand. "I did grow up here, ya know." Trying hard to convince him of her confidence, she had a nagging feeling he wasn't buying any of it. He certainly wouldn't have if he'd caught

Rashelle's raised eyebrows. "I could ask you the same thing," she tossed back his way with a tone of indignation. The air between them suddenly turned adversarial. The chief mumbled something and headed outside. Now that he'd straightened out the mess from the tunnel mishap, he had other, more important, matters to attend to.

Mitchell, in his rumpled and soiled tennis whites, removed the ice pack and cradled it in his palm, hovering over his lap. He sat forward on the couch with a look of sheer annoyance. "Listen, we need to work together here."

"We do?" Elizabeth wasn't sure she liked the idea. Still harboring a measure of anger toward him, still unsure she trusted him. What exactly had his intentions been in the tunnel? What would have happened if she hadn't stopped him? Just because Chief Austin said Kurt was one of the good guys didn't make it so in her book. Did the chief have a clue what was going on?

"Yeah, I've been doing some digging around on my own and I could use your help—both of you." He glanced from Lizzi to Rashelle and back again. "You in particular, Elizabeth. As you mentioned, you grew up here. You know the place inside and out."

Regretting she'd led him to believe she was comfortable in the tunnels, Elizabeth wondered what he had in mind. More importantly, she needed to find out what his agenda was.

The sound of the screen door banging shut caused everyone to turn their attention to the state trooper who had stepped inside. He stopped on the threshold of the sitting room. Elizabeth recognized his voice when he spoke. "Miss Elizabeth Pennington?" It was the same voice she heard talking with Chief Austin while she was clinging to the side of the cliff earlier. His name tag read, "Lt. Perkins." He was a tall slender man with short-cropped blond hair and dark, piercing eyes that exuded maturity and experience beyond his years. Perhaps he'd been in the military before he wore the proud, blue uniform of the Maine State Police. She imagined he didn't have much of a sense of humor.

"Yes?" She blushed, wondering if he knew she'd been hiding in the woods when he walked by earlier.

"Ma'am, I need to have a word with you . . . in private. Would you mind stepping outside with me, please?" His voice was calm, but firm. He was someone in authority, to be sure.

Once again she was going to fall short of her objective to extract more information out of Mitchell. That would have to wait. "Sure," she agreed, trying to sound more cooperative than she felt. "Carry on without me, guys. I'll be back," she threw out. Hoping their little chat wouldn't take long, she conceded that maybe she could find out about her car while she was at it. Reluctantly she traipsed to the front door with the trooper on her heels.

Once outside, Lieutenant Perkins took the lead and seemed to be walking to a police cruiser with an impressive rack of lights on top. He approached the passenger side and opened the front door.

"Are . . . are we going somewhere?" She could feel herself putting on the brakes. *What was going on?*

He appeared to be stifling a grin. "No, ma'am. We just need a quiet place to talk. I figured this was as good as any." His voice was low and rough. With a bit of levity, which could only be described as police humor, he added, "Step into my office," while motioning toward the open door.

Never having sat in a squad car before, she didn't feel completely comfortable. Hesitantly, she slipped into the front seat without a sound. Once her legs were clear, the officer closed the door firmly behind her, making her jump at the sound as nerves crept in. A deafening silence followed. She began to feel guilty without having done anything, as if she was sitting in the principal's office waiting to be scolded. Catching a glimpse into the empty back seat, she imagined what it must feel like to be confined there in cuffs. She shuddered as the lieutenant reached for the handle of the driver's side door, opened it with a quick jerking motion, and dropped down into his seat. A strange aroma she couldn't place entered the car with him. Stale cigarettes? Cheap aftershave? Fighting the urge to run, her eyes locked on the door handle.

"Miss Pennington, during our initial sweep of the premises, we entered and searched any and all vehicles parked at the inn. One such vehicle was parked out front on the circular drive."

*My car!* Elizabeth didn't like where the conversation was going.

"It turned out to be your vehicle. Upon searching it, we located an item that placed you on our list of persons we are interested in."

"What? I can't imagine what you could have found. What is it? What does it have to do with? I'm sure I can explain." She didn't like the sound of panic in her voice. Were they going to take her somewhere for questioning, lock her up? She wouldn't be able to help her grandmother if she was behind bars. Feeling trapped, her breathing quickened. Her hand slid onto the handle.

"All I can tell you is it's related to the missing girl."

"It is?" His words weren't making any sense. She was stunned. *How can that be?*

"So you need to stay put at the inn until we can figure this all out."

It took her a moment to realize they weren't detaining her or transporting her anywhere. Clearly they'd be keeping an eye on her, though.

Lieutenant Perkins let his last words sink in for a moment before reaching for the door handle and exiting the cruiser. The door closed with a loud thud. Elizabeth jumped again. He left her sitting in the vacuum of the squad car. As the seconds ticked silently away, she felt anger rise up inside. *Why was this happening?* He practically accused her of being involved with the girl's disappearance. She grew furious. Grabbing the handle, she forced the heavy door open, slamming it behind her. As she stepped onto the uneven lawn, her ankle, which was already weakened by her earlier spill, turned awkwardly so her knee gave way. Landing on her hands and knees, she rolled over and rubbed the throbbing ankle. Determined to shake it off and get back on track, she picked herself up and strode straight for the front steps, deliberate in her stride, arms swinging alternately with each wobbly step.

Bursting into the foyer to rejoin Rashelle and Kurt, she stopped short of entering the sitting room. It was empty. *Where had they gone? Why did they leave without her?* She told them she'd be right back. Her anger found a new target.

# CHAPTER TWELVE

*Dabbing the edges of* her face with a towel after splashing on cold water, Elizabeth headed for the seating area by the windows. Dropping into one of the creaky antique chairs, she fought off exhaustion. Somehow she'd become inexplicably involved in the police investigation. A person of interest. *How could that be? Had someone planted something in her car? If so, who? And why?*

Deciding it would be best to stay out of sight from the police while she nosed around, she realized she would need to buy herself some time.

Her grandmother was expecting to have dinner with her that evening. She would leave a note to beg off that commitment. Looking around the room to locate something to write on, she remembered she was sitting at an old desk that had been transformed to a table with a circle of plywood, a tablecloth, and a piece of glass, the same size as the wood. Scooting out her chair, she lifted the floral fabric and peeked underneath. Fortunately the drawers were situated facing her, so she crawled under and pulled the old wooden knobs one by one. Wood dragging across wood, the drawers groaned in protest. They all seemed to be empty, having been cleaned out when the desk was repurposed. She extended her arm down into each one to be sure. As her fingers explored the depths of the drawer on the bottom right side, she felt some sort of paper wedged way down in the back. Whatever it was, it would have to do. She would have had plenty of paper to use if someone hadn't taken her portfolio with all her supplies in it. Kicking herself for not remembering to ask Lieutenant Perkins about it during their chat in the squad car earlier, she hoped it was in good hands. As her thoughts slipped toward her tyrannical boss, she pushed them away and retrieved what turned out to be yellowed newspaper clippings from the drawer. Gently unfolding them, her eyes grew wide as she read the headlines.

August 5, 1984 Portland Herald

## THREE SWEPT OFF ROCKS AT PENNINGTON POINT—
## Search Continues

August 7, 1984 Lewiston Sentinel

## ROGUE WAVE CLAIMS TWO LIVES

There were half a dozen articles, all with similar headlines. Elizabeth wondered briefly why there seemed to be a discrepancy in the number of victims and then let it go. This must be the event she'd only heard people mention from time to time. It made sense she didn't remember it because she was only four years old at the time. Re-folding the articles, she put them back where she found them for safekeeping. She would sneak another peak at them later.

Giving the drawer on the old desk a final shove, she adjusted the tablecloth to its original position. Returning the chair to its place, she headed for the door but stopped abruptly. The sound of running water coming from the bathroom gave her a chill. She thought she'd turned off the faucet. Wouldn't she have heard it before now if she hadn't? Creeping slowly toward the sound, she reached the doorway and peeked in. Water spilled freely from the tap. No one else was there. Keeping most of her body safely on the threshold, she leaned in and reached for the handle, carefully shutting off the water. She stood for a moment, half expecting it to turn on again.

Backing out of the small bathroom, she tried to rationalize the phenomenon, but there was no time to dwell on it. She needed to catch up with Rashelle and Kurt, grabbing paper from the guest reception desk to write a note to her grandmother on the way by. Retracing her steps to the door, she reached for the knob, only to freeze again. Something was sticking out from under it. Elizabeth's eyes locked on a piece of white paper folded in half with no visible markings. Bending down to retrieve it, her unsteady slender fingers opened it to reveal a handwritten note. Bold, fairly neat letters with random capitalization announced:

### I knoW wHere the Girl Is

It appeared to be scrawled in grease pencil. Elizabeth gathered a shallow breath. *Who had slipped it under the door?* Refolding the note, she tucked it into her pants pocket. It was time to get back in the game. Things were about to get interesting, it seemed.

Elizabeth hurried down the carpeted stairway, turning at the bottom toward the dining room. She nearly ran into Rashelle as she burst through the doorway with a tray in her hands.

"Shelle! Whatcha doin'?" She was relieved to find her.

The tray contained two covered dishes, two glasses filled with ice, and a couple cans of ice tea. A basket of rolls, pats of butter on a plate, napkins, and silverware rounded out the presentation. A single rose from Amelia's garden teetered in a slender, cut-glass vase, looking out of place, considering the circumstances.

"Tony asked me to drop this off at the Hutchins' room. They didn't request it, but Amelia figured they would need it. Wanna come?"

"Would I!" Elizabeth was thrilled with her fortuitous timing.

"Oh, thank you. I really didn't want to go alone," Rashelle gushed, sounding relieved.

Elizabeth reached over and snatched the vase from the tray and took hold of Rashelle's upper arm as if to escort her.

"I'll carry this so you don't have to worry about it falling off." They went out through the porch to make their delivery.

The narrow path from the inn was part brick, part stone, with a patch of dirt here and there, and it meandered through the shady pine trees on its way to the rear buildings. Elizabeth followed behind Rashelle and before long, they arrived at Acadia House, which was much more modest than the grand, main building of the inn. The one-story structure was sided with simple white, clapboard siding; large windows marched across the front in a neat row. A narrow wooden porch, painted white to match the rest of the building, ran the length of the front. The Hutchins' room was an end unit, farthest from the ocean, but closest to the woods. Steps on either end of the porch led up to the building. Rashelle headed for the nearest set with Elizabeth right behind her, vase in hand. When they got to the top of the steps, the door to the Hutchins' room lay in front of them. Curtains were drawn on the windows to the left side of the door.

Pausing on the welcome mat, Rashelle straightened up and knocked firmly. As an afterthought, Elizabeth returned the vase to the tray. Several seconds lapsed. The girls listened for movement inside the room. Elizabeth raised her fist to knock again when she heard someone fumbling with the knob. A stocky man with a tousled mop of medium brown hair opened the door a few inches and peered with little emotion through the narrow opening at the duo standing outside. Elizabeth presumed this was Mr. Hutchins. Dark circles under his eyes suggested a couple of sleepless nights. He looked numb. The girls couldn't see far past him into the dark room. Rashelle was the first to speak.

"Mr. Hutchins, we thought you and Mrs. Hutchins might be hungry . . . that you could use some food. . . . You really should eat." She was struggling to find the right words. "Anthony, our chef, prepared a couple of dishes for you. Let us know if there is something else you would like instead."

His face lit up slightly, and then he seemed to think better of himself and became more subdued. He reached out to take the tray.

"Thank you for thinking of us. I'm sure this will be fine." His voice was soft and his head was bowed toward the tray, not making eye contact with the girls. "We appreciate this—everything you're doing. Thank you." He withdrew into the room and closed the door, leaving the friends to exchange glances without uttering a word. On their way back to the inn, Rashelle found her voice first once they were out of earshot of the Hutchins' room.

"He looked so sad."

"Yeah."

"Hope they find her."

"Me, too . . . alive." Elizabeth thought of the note scrunched up in her pocket but decided to keep it to herself for the time being and share it with the police instead.

Katydids chirped in the long grasses along the edge of the woods. Elizabeth drew in a long cleansing breath of briny sea air.

In the waning daylight, their surroundings were becoming bathed in shadows. Elizabeth much preferred the inn and the extensive grounds around it in bright sunshine when everything was sharp and clear. Yet, even in the limited light, something caught her eye as the two walked along.

"Shelle!" she half-whispered, half-yelled. Rashelle stopped abruptly and spun around in one swift movement. "Look at this!" Elizabeth was already off the path and moving toward the dense trees a few feet away. She pointed to a couple of branches of a low bush that were broken but still dangling. "And look at this!" She examined the ground next to the bush. It appeared to be soft and sandy with a couple of small, narrow footprints embedded in it.

"What do you think it means?"

"Well, I'm not sure it means anything. But this is directly across from the stairs up to the Hutchins' room. What if Kelsey ran out their door after an argument and headed straight into the woods? This could be the lead the troopers need to find the girl."

"Maybe we should go in. See if we see anything." At the moment, Rashelle seemed far bolder than Elizabeth.

"We'll just let them know what we found." She grabbed Rashelle's arm and pulled her toward the inn. She was not about to start into the woods at dusk. That was not her idea of fun.

# CHAPTER THIRTEEN

Unusually *adept at* slipping into the kitchen to gather food even at the height of activity, Rashelle had scavenged enough to make a full sit-down dinner for the two of them, including a lobster and several clams for them to share. Dining with minimal conversation, the girls were wrapped up in their thoughts, Elizabeth regretting she'd forgotten to cancel dinner plans with her grandmother. With the jalousie windows cranked out as far as they would go, the cool evening breeze filtered through the screened-in porch, but the picturesque setting was lost on both of them.

The sudden ringing in Elizabeth's pocket startled her. Cringing as she pulled it out, she fully expected it to be Vera. To her surprise it was an unfamiliar number with an area code of 917. Elizabeth was fairly certain it was one of the codes for Brooklyn, and then it dawned on her. Drescher. Her eyes went to her friend.

"I'm sorry. I really should answer this."

Rashelle shrugged as if assuring her it wasn't a problem.

Elizabeth stood up, turning away from the table, and did her best to summon her professional tone. "Hello, this is Elizabeth." Her back stiffened in anticipation as she began to pace.

"Elizabeth, how are you?" His voice was smooth and lilting.

"Fine, Mr. Drescher. And you?" With a nervous tilt of her head, she pushed a section of hair behind one ear.

"Elizabeth, please . . . Jack. Please call me Jack. We've known each other too long to keep up such formalities."

A shiver coursed through her body. "All right, J-Jack. If you insist." She reached the end of the porch and pivoted to retrace her steps.

"Of course I do. That's much better. Thank you. So what are you up to? You mentioned you were going away for the weekend. Anyplace exciting?" Silence occupied the other end as he waited for her to respond.

Her mind raced. Her boss thought she should be in New York City working on a project for him, and if she wasn't careful, it could appear she'd cast her responsibilities and priorities aside for a mini-vacation. "I'm actually visiting my grandmother in Maine."

"Maine. That's quite a hike from the city, isn't it?" His voice was calm and soothing, one that could talk anyone into almost anything.

"Yes, well, I came up to give her a hand with some things. It was kind of last minute, but I have also been working on your new project," she assured him.

"Well, I hope you fit in some relaxation while you're there. You work so hard. You need to reward yourself once in a while."

Although disconcerted by his suggestion, she was relieved he didn't seem angry she'd taken time off. Cautiously, she started to let down her guard.

"And I hear the lobster there is like no other. Make sure you get one of those red crustaceans before you leave."

She raised her brows. "As a matter of fact, I'm having one for dinner right now."

"Nice! Where are you dining? A favorite restaurant of yours?"

"Not exactly. My grandmother runs an inn up here, and a friend of mine and I are having a quiet dinner on the back porch." Then she thought she should clarify. "A girlfriend and I. There is a clambake down on the beach for the guests so the veranda was available for us to enjoy." Suddenly she felt silly, sharing her trivial details with such an important man.

He feigned interest, however. "Sounds absolutely wonderful."

There was an awkward pause while Elizabeth scrambled to think about how to turn the conversation around so it was no longer about her.

He came to her rescue. "Well, I didn't intend to interrupt your dinner. We'll talk again, Elizabeth. I would like to go into more detail about my project."

"Absolutely, Mr. Drescher—Jack. I would be happy to go over the concept of my designs with you, if you'd like." She hoped that was sufficient to keep him happy for a while.

"That sounds great, Elizabeth. I'll call again." His voice was unusually gentle. It crossed her mind he probably didn't speak to everyone in that tone.

"Good-bye." She spoke softly. As she returned to the table, it sank in she'd had a conversation with Jack Drescher, outside of work, that had nothing to do with work. "Wow, that was lame."

Rashelle looked up.

"I just talked to one of the most powerful businessmen in the city, perhaps on the East Coast, and all I could talk about was eating dinner on the back porch. Clearly I don't have much of a life. And I hate it that I get so nervous when I talk to him. He's such a huge client of Loran Design. Extremely successful with his real estate empire. Very powerful. If his name is associated with a project, it seems as though it's an instant success, or at least a guaranteed success in time. He has a way of making things happen."

Elizabeth recalled part of a phone conversation she had inadvertently overheard, not long after she'd first met him, during which Drescher yelled at the person on the other end of the line. Not intending to eavesdrop, Elizabeth happened to be walking past the office he had taken over at Loran Design, and the volume of his voice made her jolt to a stop. Clearly, not someone to cross.

"Probably travels to exotic places and has vacation homes in every corner of the world. He lives a life you and I can't imagine. Nothing I say could sound very interesting to him. All I do is work. I don't have much of a life outside of it," she confessed, feeling sorry for herself.

"Maybe you should do something about that." Rashelle made no attempt to suppress a smirk.

Lizzi considered her friend's flippant suggestion.

"Interesting he wants to speak to you about his project, not Vera."

Elizabeth scowled at her implication.

"I just mean that speaks well for you. Obviously, you're a very talented designer and he recognizes that."

Lizzi dismissed the compliment with a swish of her hand.

"You are, Lizzi. Think about it. You have seven years of incredible experience at one of the top design firms in the city. This power broker wants to discuss his project directly with you. I wouldn't be surprised if Vera feels a little inadequate around you. At this point in her career, she probably finds it more difficult to come up with fresh, new design ideas and to stay on top of the latest trends in the industry than she did when she was your age. Her energy is waning, and she has to try to keep up with the likes of *you*."

"Oh, Shelle. You exaggerate so!"

"Don't believe that for a minute," she asserted with a firmness she rarely exhibited. "I'm serious. Don't sell yourself short. And if this guy is so influential, he could be a big help to you when you decide to break out on your own . . . leave Vera behind and start your own design firm. I bet he would jump ship and give his business to you."

"Vera would have my head if that happened. Good God." Frightened at the thought, she wrapped her arms around herself in a protective hug. "Besides, he scares me a little bit. I'm not sure I want to be alone with him when the day comes he doesn't get his way."

"Doesn't sound like that should be a problem for you." Rashelle had a twinkle in her eye.

Elizabeth cringed. Her friend had no idea what the man was like, and she wanted to put him out of her thoughts. She would deal with him when she returned to the city. That would have to be soon enough.

"Well, at the moment, we've got more important issues to worry—"

From behind Elizabeth, the screen door squeaked on its hinges. A young man in his twenties, who appeared to have a Latino background, entered the porch and passed next to their table.

"Excuse me, ladies." Reaching down and picking up Elizabeth's napkin off the floor, he placed it onto the table, to the right of her dish. He looked directly at Elizabeth. "You dropped this." His interruption startled her, having been completely engrossed in their discussion.

"Oh, thank you," she stammered. Once he had cleared the porch, she leaned over to Rashelle. "Who's that?"

"That must be the new guy—" Rashelle paused as though she was trying to recall the details.

"Another new guy? I thought Kurt was the only one."

"I think his name is Jimmy. He's kind of an all-around guy. Goes where he's needed. He is a friend of Slater's. Tony must have needed his help with the clambake tonight."

Slater was a local fisherman who took guests out on his lobster boat, teaching them about lobstering while pulling up traps on an abbreviated version of his regular route. Although only in his thirties, he was a seasoned fisherman and the son of a retired fisherman who now captained a successful tour boat company farther north in Boothbay Harbor. Slater kept to the lobstering. It wasn't as seasonal as the tour boat business and he was comfortable with it, having grown up in a family of lobster fishermen. Around the bend from Pennington Point to the east was a quiet little cove that boasted a small dock where Slater kept his boat.

Elizabeth picked up the ivory cotton napkin next to her plate. Sliding it across her lap, something fell to the floor that caught Rashelle's eye.

"Liz, you dropped something." Leaning over, she picked up a folded piece of paper and handed it to her friend.

Elizabeth slowly opened it, holding it so Rashelle could see, too. Another brief note scrawled in grease pencil, the handwriting identical to the first note. It wasn't directed to anyone in particular, but it was blunt.

*wHerE's tHe gIrl?    do yoU wANt tO knOW?*

Elizabeth feared what it meant. "Who could have written this?" she whispered. "This is the second one I've seen today." Was it in her napkin when she dropped it? Or did Jimmy leave it for her to find? Completely absorbed by the note, they didn't notice Amelia approaching from behind Rashelle.

"Hey, girls. I see you found something to eat." Amelia's voice sounded upbeat, even though her eyes reflected exhaustion.

They jumped at the sound of her voice. Elizabeth scrunched the note into her fist.

"Nana, I . . . uh . . . I'm sorry. We were supposed to have dinner tonight—"

"Don't give it another thought, hon. I'm the one who should apologize. I forgot, what with all that's going on around here. I'm glad you were resourceful and got some food for yourselves."

"What about you, Nana? Have you eaten?" A twinge of guilt pinched her stomach for not checking up on her grandmother earlier.

"Oh, I grabbed a bite already. I was with the police officers when Tony brought them dinner."

Elizabeth wanted to believe her grandmother, but something told her she was covering up so her little Lizzi wouldn't feel guilty about standing her up for dinner.

"Girls, I'm afraid I have more bad news." She wasted no time with small talk. "Lieutenant Perkins has informed me there's a hurricane they've been watching down the coast, and it's now heading right for us. At first, they forecasted it to go out to sea, but it hasn't taken the path they expected it to take. It's barreling up the Eastern Seaboard . . . on its way here."

Amelia's stunning revelation silenced the girls for a moment. With an eyebrow raised, Elizabeth was the first to regain her voice. "That's awful, Nana. What do we do?"

"Well, at the moment there's not much we *can* do." She looked like she was struggling to maintain her composure. "They'll keep monitoring the storm while they continue their investigation, which they hope to complete by the time the hurricane arrives. All the guests will have to evacuate by then."

"When do they expect it to hit?" Rashelle chimed in.

"It's hard to say exactly, seems to change by the hour. It's a rather volatile storm. Could be sometime Labor Day or Tuesday morning. Hopefully not as early as tomorrow evening. In the meantime, we need to assist in any way we can with the search and investigation. Hopefully we'll find the girl safe and sound somewhere. Maybe she's playing a teenage prank on her parents, and it will all be over soon."

"Wouldn't that be nice?" Elizabeth joined in on her grandmother's daydream, despite its unlikelihood.

Appearing to play devil's advocate, Rashelle offered, "Of course, if she's caught wind of the commotion she's caused here, she may not surface for quite some time."

Amelia gazed toward Rashelle's general direction and seemed to be considering her point. "Well, I hope it all turns out all right. We have to keep believing it will . . . praying it will. It's so unproductive to think otherwise." Her tone seemed to reprimand Rashelle for not being more optimistic.

Although Elizabeth knew her grandmother believed in the power of positive thinking, this situation was going to take a lot more than that to have a happy ending. And she didn't dare tell Amelia about the note she held crumpled up in her palm or the one shoved deep into her pocket. Her grandmother had more than enough to handle already. Those would be shared with a different set of eyes.

"Nana, do you happen to know where Kurt is? We haven't seen him around in a while."

"Oh, I don't know." She sounded uncharacteristically impatient. "He may be helping Chief Austin with something. I know the chief has his hands full, and Slater didn't return from his lobstering trip this afternoon when he was supposed to. Chief needed to follow up on that. Maybe he sent Kurt."

"Slater didn't come back yet?" Rashelle glanced at her watch and slid to the edge of her chair, sounding anxious to hear more.

"I'm afraid not. Hope everything's all right and they just got delayed. Do you know if any of our guests were aboard?"

"Not exactly, but I can go check." As Rashelle rose, Lieutenant Perkins appeared in the doorway.

"Ladies." His voice was firm. He was the man in command. "I need to have a word with you."

"All of us?" Amelia queried.

"That would be fine." *Steady as he goes.* He paused for effect or to gather his thoughts and then continued. "Miss Pennington, first of all, we analyzed the contents of your car. We found a necklace we've determined to belong to the missing girl."

"*What?*" There was a collective gasp among the three women.

"Yes, ma'am." His penetrating steely eyes focused on her.

*What is he talking about?* Elizabeth shifted in her seat, scarcely able to take in air. Nana jumped to her rescue.

"Officer, there must be some mistake. That can't be possible."

"Well, ma'am, I'm afraid it is." His voice was deep and firm.

"She didn't know the girl. None of us met her," Amelia implored him to listen.

"Is that so?" He was as calm and firmly in control as at the start of the conversation.

"As a matter of fact, it is. And Elizabeth didn't arrive here until late Friday evening because I called and asked her to come.

She wouldn't have had the opportunity to meet the guest who is missing. She couldn't possibly have any connection."

"Well, ma'am, I understand what you're saying, but it does appear there is a connection." There was no swaying him.

Speaking directly to Elizabeth, he pressed her. "So you have no idea how the necklace made it into your car?'

Elizabeth swallowed hard. "No, sir."

He turned to leave the porch and stopped just short of the doorway. With a pudgy finger pointed at Elizabeth, he warned, "I don't think I need to remind you what that means. . . . Stay put." With that, he left the three ladies alone with their mouths agape.

Rashelle leaned over to Elizabeth. "What was *that* supposed to mean? He can't be serious, Lizzi!" Her voice was loud and demanding.

Amelia jumped in. "All right, Rashelle. Calm down. This whole mess will get sorted out and everything will be all right." She seemed to be trying to convince herself as she spoke. "I'm sure this is simply one big misunderstanding." Without another word, she exited the porch, leaving the two friends with the remains of their cold dinners.

They ate in silence. The food didn't taste quite as good as it had when they first sat down. After a long day, Elizabeth ached with uncertainty and trepidation of what lay ahead. Lieutenant Perkins' comments didn't make any sense. Feeling anger rising up inside of her, she felt compelled to engage in the search. The trained professionals had to be missing a key piece of information. She knew the grounds of the inn and the people that worked there better than they did.

"C'mon, Shelle. Let's get rid of these dishes." As an afterthought, she added, "Want to grab a glass of wine? I think better with one."

Sharing a nervous giggle, they gathered their dirty plates and headed to the kitchen. A hinged door without a window, it tended to be more stubborn than the swinging door from the main dining room into the kitchen. Turning sideways to use her shoulder for better leverage, Elizabeth gave it a firm shove with her entire body behind it. When it flew open, she lurched into the kitchen, struggling to hold onto her plate and keep herself upright. As the door thudded against something behind it, Elizabeth glanced down and let out a bloodcurdling scream.

# CHAPTER FOURTEEN

Rachelle stumbled through the doorway. "What, Lizzi? *What!*" With her dirty dishes in one hand, she grabbed onto the swinging door with the other to stabilize it. Panic flashed in her eyes as she slipped into the kitchen and joined her friend in the narrow space at the end of the prep station. "What happened?" Rashelle's mouth twisted as it gaped open.

Elizabeth stared in disbelief.

There, in a heap on the floor, was the body of a middle-aged man wearing a crisp white chef's jacket with black and white houndstooth checked pants. His jacket was soaked with blood oozing from the wound caused by a chef's knife sticking out of his chest.

Rashelle tried again. "What the *hell* happened?"

"I just opened the door!" she shrieked, pleading her innocence.

"Was he standing behind it?" Her voice quieted to a whisper as she took hold of Elizabeth's upper arm, pulling her closer.

"I have no idea! I pushed the door open and it hit something."
Rashelle let an anguished moan slip through fingers splayed across her mouth.

"I don't think I did anything, but this looks terrible!" Fear gripped Elizabeth as her eyes traveled the length of the lifeless body to the bloody wound and the handle of the knife. Her first instinct was to run. The lieutenant had accused her of having a connection with the missing girl, and now she was standing over the body of a dead cook. But she didn't recognize him. Was he new? Could he be a guest? If so, why was he dressed like a chef? She took a closer look at the black handle protruding from his torso and reluctantly conceded it appeared to be Tony's new knife.

"Liz, let's get out of here!" Shelle hissed. "We're lucky everyone's down at the clambake, but at any moment someone could come bursting into the kitchen and find us in this very incriminating situation."

"We can't just walk out of here. We need to let someone know—"

"No, we don't! The next person through the door will have to handle it. It doesn't have to be you. He's obviously dead; he can wait. You can't do anything for him." She swatted toward the lifeless body. "If Perkins sees us here, he won't waste any more time. He'll cuff you and take you away. They'll probably charge you with the disappearance of the Hutchins' girl, too. You've got to get outta here!" Still holding her plate and silverware, she grabbed Elizabeth with her free hand and led her back out onto the porch. Returning their plates to the table where they'd sat for dinner, they arranged them exactly as they'd been earlier to look as if they had just walked out after eating, never entering the kitchen.

Squirming from an awful twisting sensation in her stomach, Lizzi knew what they were doing wasn't right but couldn't come up with a better idea. Stepping into the hallway, they watched in horror as Lieutenant Perkins slipped into the dining room from the foyer. They hurried to the doorway to see him striding toward the kitchen with a determined gait. They both gasped. What they did next was a split-second decision, but one they made simultaneously.

"Lieutenant!" they shrieked in unison as he lifted his hand to push open the swinging door. He stopped in mid-stride and turned to respond to the girls. Clearly they'd startled him.

Not trusting what Rashelle was going to blurt out next, Elizabeth did the talking. "If you're looking for Tony, he's down at the beach." Her voice sounded calmer than she felt, and she prayed her expression didn't reveal the terror within.

Apparently Rashelle couldn't resist chiming in as well. "And if you'd like coffee, Tony set up a beverage station in the sitting room." She motioned across the foyer.

Perkins examined the girls' faces, perhaps detecting a hint of an ulterior motive, still poised near the door. Seeming to consider their suggestions, he lowered his hand. "Thank you, ladies." His voice was low and steady. Striding back across, the click-thud of his firm footsteps on the old wooden floor echoed in the unoccupied room.

The girls stepped aside to allow him to pass, and then followed behind, making their exit to the left up the carpeted stairs.

Out of their line of sight, the kitchen staff were returning to the inn through the back porch, each one loaded down with the essentials from the clambake on the beach. The first guy in the door dropped the heavy box he was carrying when he stumbled onto the body. The loud crash reverberated throughout the first floor.

Once the girls reached the landing, out of Perkins' earshot, Elizabeth stopped long enough to strategize and grabbed onto Rashelle's forearms, her voice barely a whisper. "Now what!"

"Let's go to my room. I've got a stash there," Shelle suggested.

"A what? A stash? What do you—"

"Wine . . . I've got a little fridge with a few bottles of wine." Rashelle set her straight.

"I don't care about the wine." Lizzi was losing her patience. "If you haven't noticed, the situation has deteriorated dramatically over the last half hour and just took a bloody turn for the worse."

Rashelle extended a flat palm, motioning for her to lower the volume. "I realize that, but I also know you could use a glass of wine, too." Tilting her head, the corners of her mouth slipped into a crooked smile.

Lizzi almost responded in kind. Probably would have under different circumstances. She thought about Rashelle's offer for a moment but decided against it. "No, not now. I'm going to go down to the beach and take a look around."

"The beach? A look around? It's dark out!"

"I know. The moon is out, though. I want to see what's down there. Satisfy my curiosity."

"Satisfy your curiosity," Rashelle repeated, clearly not liking the idea. "And I suppose you want me to go with you."

"That would be great, but you don't have to." Elizabeth sounded braver than she felt.

"All right, let's go." Rashelle reluctantly took her friend's arm. Just as they landed on the second step, she stopped abruptly. "Hold it!"

Elizabeth had to grab onto the railing to keep from falling forward with her momentum.

Rashelle reached into her pants pocket and retrieved her vibrating cell phone. "Hello?"

Elizabeth listened to the one-sided conversation.

"Uh-huh . . . Yes, of course . . . Yes, I'll take care of it right away." Shoving her phone back into her pocket, she turned to Elizabeth. "I'm sorry. There are some things I need to take care of. I . . . I can't go with you."

"What kind of things? They can't wait?"

Shelle shook her head but remained tight-lipped about the specifics.

Elizabeth was curious but decided she wouldn't pursue it. Instead of sticking her nose into Rashelle's business when it pertained to her job, she would just trust her. Of course, that was the tough part, knowing who to trust, including her friend. Suddenly she was not as forthcoming with information as Elizabeth would have expected. "Okay. I understand. You do what you need to do. I'll go alone."

"Are you serious? I'm so sorry. I would go with you if I could—"

"Don't sweat it. I'll meet you back here, in your room. We'll have that glass of wine."

"Sounds good." Appearing uncomfortable with Elizabeth going alone, Rashelle added, "Ya know, Liz, I'll try to finish up quickly and meet you down there on the beach. Okay?"

"Great." Trying to sound as noncommittal as possible, she didn't expect to see her friend on the beach. Not at night.

Reaching the bottom of the stairs, they parted ways, leaving Rashelle to tend to business behind the reception desk.

Skipping down the stairs of the porch, Lizzi set off across the front lawn at a steady clip, resolved in her purpose. The long grass that tickled her ankles and the scraggly, misshapen hedges along the edge of the cliff gave the impression Renard and Girard had been slacking off a bit.

An invigorating salty sea breeze off the water caressed her face. Fog hung in the night air illuminated by the moon as she descended the wooden stairs. Grasping the railing, she tried not to look down. She moved at a steady pace, not too fast to risk tripping or slipping, but fast enough so she could cover ground in a reasonable amount of time. The sound of waves crashing against the beach drew her focus, and she could just make out the movement. The impending storm had stirred up the ocean ahead of it.

The whir of a car engine approaching caught her ear. Elizabeth dashed back up the stairs far enough to peek around the bushes. She watched a small car round the circular drive and come to a stop in the glare of the porch lights near the front door. Who had been allowed in? Wasn't the inn in lockdown? She watched to see who got out. Instead, the car remained idling at the base of the stairs. The front door opened and a female scampered down the steps—Rashelle—opened the passenger side and slipped in. What was she doing? The car sped off, leaving a cloud of dust from the gravel it had stirred up in its wake. Elizabeth was left to wonder if it was the same sports car that had passed her on the way in on Friday evening. Then it dawned on her. The man driving the car was Aaron, the tennis pro who had been fired the prior spring. She wondered how Rashelle knew him. Elizabeth's mind raced. She needed more answers from her friend. In the meantime, she was going to return to her task of surveying the beach.

Reaching the bottom of the stairs, she took her first step onto the sand but hesitated before setting off, feeling regrettably alone. The evening had turned chilly, so the guests must have cleared out right after dinner. Suddenly, her idea of walking the beach by herself didn't seem so smart. She shored up her shoulders and started off anyway. With the thickening fog limiting visibility, her eyes strained to see in the dim light. She could only hear the waves crashing on the beach. A few more steps and Elizabeth's foot landed on something hard embedded in the sand. She reached down and picked up a cylindrical object. "Corn cob," she announced, disgusted, though her words fell only on her own ears. A leftover from the clambake. "No one knows how to pick up after themselves." She tossed the cob to the side and kept walking, feeling vulnerable in the darkness.

After a while, she could just discern the outline of the rocky outcroppings on the east end of the beach. Elizabeth stopped. Was there something ahead, partially obscured by the fog? Catching a glimpse of what appeared to be a person standing several yards away, Elizabeth squinted to see more clearly. The figure seemed to be looking her way. A young girl? Was the fog playing tricks on her? Slowly she moved closer. Heavier fog enveloped her, making it more difficult to see. "Who's there?" Elizabeth called over the roar of the surf. Would the girl be able to hear her? No response. In a blink, she could no longer make out the outline of a person. The fog had completely obliterated her view. Pressing forward in the direction she'd seen the girl, it seemed like she should have caught up to her already. "Hello!" Where could she have gone? Elizabeth stood still. As the fog swirled around her, she wondered if anyone had been there at all. Listening to the waves crashing against the shore, her thoughts turned to Slater and his boat, *The Seaward Lady*.

It wasn't a large boat by any stretch of the imagination, probably forty feet in length with a main deck and a lower level only Slater and his crew frequented. Bench seating along the stern had been installed so passengers could observe them pulling in lobster traps. About a third of the way from the bow was a primitive captain's deck with a windshield and small roof with three sides that offered modest protection from inclement weather. On the starboard side was a rig with a pulley system Slater used to pull up lobster traps. A buoy bobbing on top of the water had a rope attached to the bottom of it, the other end of which was secured to a trap sitting on the ocean floor. Each lobster fisherman had a specific color pattern he or she had the exclusive right to use on their buoys so there would be no mistaking who laid claim to them. Most could rattle off who owned each pattern. Using a long-handled tool with a hook on the end, Slater would snag the buoy and pull it up onto the side of the boat, threading the rope onto the pulley, and then use the crank to pull the trap to the surface. Fingers were crossed that, after all the cranking, there would be a lobster in the trap and it was large enough to keep.

Strict guidelines dictated the minimum size, and each lobster-man had a measuring tool handy to verify his catch. In addition, any female lobsters carrying eggs had to be returned to the sea, even if they were otherwise large enough, so the eggs would have the chance to hatch. These rules were in place so the lobsters were not overfished and the industry could sustain itself. Since the work required long, back-breaking days, those who lasted usually had lobstering in their blood, often hailing from a long line of lobstermen.

With a sad heart, she worried what had become of Slater and his passengers. The situation sounded dire, particularly with the approaching storm.

Shrouded in fog, feeling uneasy out on the beach alone, Elizabeth had seen enough. It was time to return to the inn.

Had she taken a few more steps, she would have kicked something solid lying in the sand. A life preserver with a name emblazoned on it: *The Seaward Lady*.

Turning back toward the stairs, Elizabeth froze. Since she'd first touched her toes in the sand, the fog had rolled in and completely swallowed the beach. There was nothing discernable in the murkiness. Fighting panic, she struggled to remain calm.

Waves crashing onto the shore to the left assured her she was facing the right direction. She needed to keep that sound metaphorically anchored there as she crossed the sand. Without any visible reference points, she reluctantly set off across the beach. Had the young guest found herself in a similar predicament and gotten too close to the powerful waves?

In an attempt at a positive distraction, she reminisced about walking the beach with her grandmother after a storm, the best time to find spectacular shells and sand dollars, veritable treasures left by the sea. The roar of the waves was much like what she was listening to now. Larger conch-like shells faintly mimicked the sound if you held them to your ear.

Elizabeth had traipsed a few yards when she realized the texture had changed beneath her feet. What had been soft and transient was now flat and firm. She was on wet sand, veering toward the ocean. Redirecting herself a little farther to the right, soon her feet were sinking into the soft sand again, albeit at a snail's pace. Walking with her arms out in front of her, she kept hoping to feel the railing of the stairs. But what if she'd passed them? She decided to try sidestepping. If she was facing the right direction and she stepped to the right, eventually she would run into the side of the cliff. Then she could run her hand along it until she found the stairway. Slowly she stepped, over and over, shuffling along. Was it working? Or was she too far to the right and heading back toward the rocky outcroppings? She listened for the waves. It sounded like they were still directly to her left, so she resumed her sidestepping with her right arm extended, longing to feel the cliff. Was she staying on course? As her palm pushed against a cold, rugged surface, relief flooded through her.

Picking up her pace, she moved through the loose sand while her outstretched fingers brushed across occasional tufts of grasses and caught on a cliff rose along the way. She stretched her other hand out in front, anticipating the railing. *One foot in front of the other. Keep going.* Finally she could just make out the stairway and lunged at it, landing on the bottom step with both feet. She scampered up the stairs, firmly grasping the railing.

When she reached the top, the fog was not as thick as it had been down on the beach, but it was rolling in off the water rapidly and obscuring the inn and its outbuildings. The roar of an engine caught her attention again. All she could catch was the rear lights of a car disappearing down the access road. If anyone had gotten out of it, they were safely inside. Retracing her steps across the front lawn, she hoped to hook up with Rashelle again—if she was back yet.

To Elizabeth's surprise, her friend met her at the front door. Though dying to ask where she'd been and whom she'd been with, Elizabeth decided to keep her questions to herself for now. "All right, let's go get that wine now."

Rashelle nodded and they crossed the lobby to the stairs.

The swarm of police occupying the dining room told them the dead cook had been found.

# CHAPTER FIFTEEN

Third door on the right, Rashelle's room was directly across from and a mirror image of Elizabeth's. As promised, she pulled a chilled bottle of Chardonnay out of a mini fridge doing double duty as a table on the side of the bed closest to the door. Apologizing for not having Lizzi's favorite, Rashelle had the bottle opened in no time and poured two large glasses.

"Oh, at this point, I'll take anything." Elizabeth eagerly put the glass to her lips and took a sip. Without a word spoken, the bloody kitchen encounter became the third party occupying the room. Stunned to be in territory neither had visited before, they stood silently and sipped the dry white wine, unable or unwilling to put their thoughts into words.

Finally Elizabeth spoke. "Rashelle, what is going on? And how did I get so involved?" It seemed surreal. "Things only got worse after I got here—like *I've* made it all worse."

"Lizzi, don't be ridiculous. This nightmare has nothing to do with you. Unfortunately, you've gotten all wrapped up in it by showing up. Your intentions were good. You came to help."

"And I didn't help matters by leaving the scene of a crime earlier. What was I thinking?" She navigated around a laundry basket to the other side of the bed.

"Liz, you had to." Her Brooklyn accent burst through. Clearly recognizing their voices were escalating, she spoke more softly. "You know how that would have looked if someone had seen us." With the heel of her hand she jammed the cork back down into the neck of the bottle, returned it to the small refrigerator, and flopped down on the bed, fluffing the pillows behind her.

Elizabeth's face flushed with anger. "Thank God no one did! I thought for sure someone was going to walk in on us. That was a close call with the lieutenant." She sank into the overstuffed floral armchair near the window.

"That's for sure."

"I wonder how long it took them to find the body after we did." She kicked off her shoes and propped her feet up on Rashelle's bed.

"I don't want to think about it."

"Obviously they've found it, though." Elizabeth took a moment to picture who might have been unfortunate enough to be the next one to open the kitchen door. Hopefully it wasn't Amelia. "Tony's crew would have come back at some point after the clambake."

Their conversation trailed off.

After polishing off the bottle, they considered opening a second, but soon drifted off to sleep, Lizzi in the chair and Shelle on her bed.

What seemed like seconds later the two friends were awakened by a hard knock. Clumsily they got to their feet, still half asleep. Rashelle, chilled from lying on top of the covers most of the night, wrapped her arms around herself. Groaning, Elizabeth rubbed the side of her neck, aching from sleeping in an awkward position in the chair. The firm knocking escalated into pounding. Rashelle rubbed both eyes with her fists as she headed for the door. Glancing back to Elizabeth, she nervously grabbed the knob, her lips pursed into a thin line of concern. Slowly she pulled the door open.

There stood Lieutenant Perkins holding a computer disc tightly between two pudgy fingers, a laptop computer tucked under one arm. "Ladies . . ." Perkins spoke sharply. "You have a little explaining to do." With that, he pushed his way into the room.

Rashelle took a step back but made it clear she was in no mood for his intrusion. "What are you doing?" she demanded, her voice reverberating in the small room. "What time is it? How dare you barge in here," she bellowed.

Elizabeth grew concerned her friend was overstepping her bounds, taking on someone she had no business grappling with.

"Silence! Miss Harper, Miss Pennington, you both need to take a look at this." The lieutenant wasn't taking questions.

The girls ventured a glance at each other while the lieutenant strode toward the table by the window where he set up the computer. Elizabeth's eyes wandered beyond him to the thin band of light on the horizon, but the sun was nowhere in sight. It was still the wee hours of the morning. Wondering what kind of a day it was going to be, she knew it wasn't promising if it began with the state police barging in, interested in a chat.

Once the lieutenant was ready to share his discovery with them, he demanded, "All right, ladies, see if you can explain this." Moving aside, he pressed a key to set the screen in motion.

Tentatively, the two friends stepped closer, fearful of what they were going to see. As the video advanced, the setting became all too familiar. The kitchen at the inn with Elizabeth straddling the bloody body, one hand on the swinging door, the other holding her dinner plate. A collective gasp escaped their lips. *How could it be?* Rashelle then entered the picture and suddenly they were reliving the nightmare from which they had fled hours earlier. *How could they possibly be watching what they'd been replaying in their minds? Who could have recorded it?* Elizabeth looked into Lieutenant Perkins' expectant gaze. Panic swelled within her. He wanted an explanation, and she wondered if she needed a lawyer before she opened her mouth. To her surprise and horror, Rashelle spoke first.

"It was all my fault. I told her to run."

"I can see that." His tone was firm, almost scolding. "What we would like to know is what happened before the video starts."

It was Elizabeth's turn. "I know this looks bad—"

"Yeah, it looks bad." The lieutenant's voice boomed. "Like you guys have been caught red-handed."

"Red-handed? We didn't do anything. We walked in on this."

"So why did you run? It makes you look guilty as hell when you take off like that."

"I know. It wasn't the smartest idea." Elizabeth cast Rashelle a fiery glare. "We were scared with everything going on at the inn. You had just accused me of having some sort of connection with the missing girl. But you have to believe me that we stumbled into the kitchen and found this body. I don't even know who it is." Her voice trembled on her last few words. She hoped it went unnoticed.

"Well, lucky for you we're more interested with who shot the video than in how you ended up in the middle of the crime scene. Most likely, the person recording the event set it all up."

"Where did you get the CD?" Elizabeth couldn't resist asking.

Perkins grunted. "It mysteriously showed up on the front seat of my cruiser."

"I see." His answer didn't explain much.

"What can you tell me about the events leading up to it? Was there anything unusual that caught your eye?"

Elizabeth regretted she didn't have any information to help him. They hadn't lingered long enough to notice anything out of sorts besides the deceased. "I wish I knew . . ."

Slamming the laptop shut, Perkins grunted in disgust. He snatched it up and stormed to the door where he paused, creating a deafening silence. Thankfully, he threw out a suggestion that broke the tension.

"Why don't we get some coffee? It's going to be another long day."

"Yeah, great idea. We'll catch up with you," Rashelle added.

"We, uh . . ." Lizzi realized they were still fully clothed in the previous day's outfits, never having taken the time to change into pajamas. "We need to freshen up a bit." It certainly sounded plausible to her.

The lieutenant acknowledged her with a nod. "Okay. See you downstairs," he grumbled.

Once he'd cleared the doorway, Lizzi watched as he padded down the hall. Gently, she closed the door and turned to Shelle. Their eyes locked.

"We need to find out who tried to set us up." Elizabeth restrained herself from scolding Rashelle with a version of "I told you we shouldn't have run." They needed to focus on being more productive than that. "Let's go grab some caffeine and get in the game."

Rashelle mumbled something unintelligible but followed along behind.

# CHAPTER SIXTEEN

*A*fter the unsettling awakening*, Elizabeth and Rashelle trudged to the sitting room, finding a small round table still set up from the night before. They emptied the carafe into two Styrofoam cups. Rashelle sipped hers black while Elizabeth stirred in some milk and a little sugar and then pressed the cup to her lips. The liquid morning was barely lukewarm but nonetheless welcome. They busied themselves at the table, trying to shake off their drowsiness.

Nearby, Kurt sipped his early morning java, standing by the windows gazing out to the tempestuous sea, seemingly lost in thought. Elizabeth wondered why he was there.

The lieutenant burst through the front door with two people in tow. Elizabeth looked up to see Mr. Hutchins along with a woman she presumed to be his wife. They were escorted into the dining room where a sleepy Chief Austin and other police officers milled about and were no doubt dealing with the body discovered in the kitchen. Perkins was obviously interested in what connection the Hutchins might have with the victim.

Glancing at Rashelle, Elizabeth did her best to look disinterested. Mitchell appeared from behind them and exited the sitting room as if he had been beckoned by a silent pager. His curiosity seemed to be getting the best of him. Once he was lost in the crowd Elizabeth felt comfortable to speak.

"Shelle, we need to get out of here."

"What are you talking about?"

"Trust me." She grabbed her friend and headed toward the back porch, treading quietly as they passed through. As they neared the door to the kitchen, Lizzi tried to put out of her head the grisly scene they'd witnessed and become part of earlier. Slipping out into early morning darkness, Lizzi let go of Shelle's arm long enough to catch the screen so it wouldn't slam shut. She re-established her grip and led her down the path to Acadia House. Rashelle seemed to be catching on.

Before long they were standing in front of the Hutchins' door. Rashelle stood back as Elizabeth reached for the knob. It turned slightly, but soon met with resistance.

"Who locks their door?" She threw her hands up. Rashelle seemed to understand it was a rhetorical question.

They tried the windows on the left side of the door, grunting with each attempt. Neither would budge.

Heading down the steps with Rashelle behind her, Elizabeth wasted no time going around to the side of the building. She was grateful it was an end unit, but the lawn sloped downward, dropping to an elevation several feet below the double-hung windows that ran along the side of the Hutchins' room. Reaching up to the nearest one, she grabbed onto the sill but couldn't get enough leverage to push it open.

Rashelle laced her fingers together with her palms facing upward and formed a stirrup.

"Here, I can give you a boost."

Without hesitation, Elizabeth stepped into her friend's makeshift stepstool and slid up the clapboards, clawing until she was waist high with the sill. Working on borrowed time, she gave the bottom half of the window a good shove. To her surprise, it slid easily. They'd forgotten to lock their side windows, at least that one.

"Shelle, we did it!"

In their excitement, they both jiggled a little too far in opposite directions and Elizabeth toppled out of Rashelle's hands. Head first, she plummeted to the ground. She reached out to break her fall, landing hard on the grass, stunned by the jolt to her body. For anyone observing them, this would have been hilarious, but neither was laughing.

"Liz, I'm so sorry!" Rashelle rushed to her side.

"Shhhhhh." Having no time for apologies, Elizabeth scrambled to her feet and brushed off her pants. Speaking in hushed tones, she motioned frantically for Rashelle to re-engage. "Don't worry about it. Just get me up there again."

They repeated the steps leading up to her fall, being careful not to get too exuberant in their success. Elizabeth pushed the window again, and it slowly moved a little farther. Fighting to keep her foot from slipping in Rashelle's grip, she gave the window one more push, praying it would be enough to squeeze through. She grabbed onto the sill and hoisted herself up with a grunt. For one crazy moment she balanced on her stomach, half-in and half-out, with the ends of her hair mopping the floor and her legs dangling outside. It was almost comical.

There was no turning back. She was practically in. Dangling her arms, her fingertips touched the floor, but clearly there was nothing soft for her to land on. With no comfy couch below the window, she would have to try to land as gracefully as possible. A couple more wiggles and her rear end cleared the bottom of the open window. Pulling her legs in, she spilled into the Hutchins' room with a quiet thud and a groan.

Gathering herself, Elizabeth made a beeline for the front door, which she unlocked and yanked open. No Rashelle.

"Where the—?" Darting onto the front porch, she lunged for the railing at the end. On the lawn below stood Rashelle in the quiet before dawn, her arms folded across her torso as the cool air off the ocean gently played with her hair. Her eyes were fixed on the dark woods that loomed a few yards away.

"Pssst!" Elizabeth motioned for Rashelle to move. "Come on!" she beckoned.

Rashelle sprinted to the porch and followed her friend inside. They closed and locked the door behind them to leave it exactly the way they'd found it.

"What are we doing here?" Shelle sounded uneasy.

"We just need a closer peek. It could be nothing, but something about these guys . . . well, I don't know. We've got to grab the opportunity while Perkins has them occupied."

"Hopefully it's long enough."

The room was set up in an open floor plan divided into three areas, each with its own purpose. Just inside was a sitting area with a solid blue, denim loveseat positioned under the front window and facing two tulip chairs, upholstered in a complementary floral. A floor lamp in the corner to the left was the only light on and was set on low, providing a soft glow in the room. The focal point of the seating arrangement was a distressed pine armoire positioned on the outside wall. The doors were closed but, presumably, they concealed a television. The window Elizabeth had shimmied through was to the right of the armoire. Magazines, empty snack food wrappers, as well as a couple soda cans, were scattered haphazardly across the top of the coffee table in the center of the seating area. She picked up the closest magazine, folded it in half and slipped it into her back pocket.

Moving away from the front door, they pushed farther into the room, away from the only light source, but they didn't dare switch on any other lights. Elizabeth led the way with Rashelle close at her heels. Catching movement out of the corner of her eye, Lizzi stopped suddenly and Rashelle nearly ran into her. Glancing back at the front windows, she could just make out the face of a young girl before the ephemeral image faded away.

"What?" Rashelle whispered, sounding anxious to know what her friend was looking at.

"The window . . ." There was nothing left to see.

"What?" She obviously hadn't seen anything.

"Don't worry about it. Let's keep going," she urged, trying to shake off the unsettled feeling she was left with.

Forging ahead into the middle section of the room, Lizzi bumped into one of the chairs pushed up to a small dining table cluttered with papers. A fax machine, printer, and laptop occupied the center of the table, making the Hutchins' room look more like an office than a vacation destination. Other items took up space on a credenza against the outside wall, but it was hard to tell exactly what they were in the limited light. Elizabeth dismissed them and kept walking. Not knowing when the Hutchins would come strolling through the front door, they needed to find their way out the back. Getting caught in a guest room without authorization would not look good for either of them.

Beyond the dining area they came upon a small kitchenette to the right with a microwave, mini fridge, sink, and a few cupboards with limited storage. To the left they passed through a doorway into the bedroom, which was pitch black, too dark to see what might be lurking in the corners. On the far wall was a small bathroom and the outline of the bed next to it. Groping alongside the bed and wading through what felt like clothes strewn about the floor, they made their way to the rear door.

As the girls passed a stand-up dresser, they heard the distinct sound of breaking glass behind them, near the front of the unit. Counting on the shadows to conceal them, Elizabeth whispered, "Let's go!" She grabbed Rashelle and they slipped out, closing the door softly behind them, praying their presence would not be detected. Once clear of the stairs, they ran along the back of Acadia. When they got to the end they rounded the corner to return to the main building.

"Good morning, ladies." Elizabeth and Rashelle looked like two Stooges, trying to stop without bumping into Mitchell. "Funny time of the day for a stroll. What brings you out here?"

Elizabeth hesitated and didn't dare make eye contact with Rashelle. Had he seen them entering the Hutchins' room? She knew they didn't have a good answer but was annoyed by Kurt's questions.

"Oh, for God's sake, would you get out of our way. I could ask you the same thing." She moved toward him intending to push her way through, but he reached out and grabbed her arm so firmly it exploded in pain. What had she been thinking, that she could muscle her way past him? Reality check.

"You listen to me." His tone was threatening as he pulled her closer, his face inches from hers. "This is not the time for being a smart ass. There is a murder investigation in progress and we all need to cooperate." He loosened his grip and let her pull away slightly but still had her in his control.

"Okay, okay. We needed a little fresh air and thought it wouldn't hurt to take a walk." Elizabeth hoped her off-the-cuff explanation would fly. He held his scowl as if considering her excuse and then released his grip. Falling backward, she caught herself after taking a couple steps, indignant he'd treated her so brusquely.

"Kurt!" Rashelle came to her defense.

He shot her a glare.

"So, how is it you're so involved in all of this?" Elizabeth couldn't resist pushing back a bit.

"Involved?"

"Yeah, with the investigation. The police." She gestured with a nervous flourish.

Frowning slightly, he looked put off by her question. "I'm just trying to help. Besides, there's not much tennis going on this week, so I've got time on my hands."

Returning to a more serious tone, Mitchell continued, "We're all under a lot of pressure. We don't need anyone fooling around, sticking their noses where they don't belong." His glare underscored his words. "Follow me," he snapped.

With eyes rolling, Lizzi motioned for Rashelle to follow Kurt. It looked like they'd been able to slip out of the Hutchins' room without being detected. They formed a single file behind the tennis pro like they were back in elementary school on their way to gym class. The horizon had grown brighter. Although the day was breaking, it was an overcast Sunday morning with an ominous gray sky, portending worse weather to come. Dark clouds enrobed the inn in a blanket of sadness.

# CHAPTER SEVENTEEN

The comforting aroma of fresh-brewed coffee greeted the threesome as they re-entered the inn through the back porch. In the time they were gone, Anthony had put out food for everyone. Instead of the elaborate weekend brunch he and his staff usually prepared, it was a simple breakfast buffet spread out on a narrow table along the wall of windows in the dining room. It was less a celebration of food and more a sustaining meal to keep everyone going, nothing fancy, just the basics. Scrambled eggs, blueberry pancakes, fruit salad, bacon, and sausage. There were urns with coffee and hot water. A toaster stood by, plugged in, ready to make toast or crisp a bagel. The plates and cups were sturdy disposables.

Bypassing the food, the two friends grabbed coffee and headed into the sitting area as directed by Mitchell, who entered the room behind them and took his place in a worn leather chair near the doorway. Elizabeth sat next to Rashelle on the edge of a flowery sofa with the disconcerting feeling that bad news was imminent.

With few words exchanged, they sat in silence and watched as a couple of state troopers entered the lobby, disappeared into the dining room, reappeared with coffee and food to go, and exited through the front door. They were certainly well fed.

Before long, Amelia appeared at the guest reception counter, seemingly consumed with matters behind the desk. She looked up and noticed the quiet occupants of the sitting room. "Well, good morning, everyone." Bless her heart, she could be so chipper at such a God-awful early hour and under such circumstances. Her eyes didn't seem to have their usual sparkle but, instead, held a hollowness that sent a chill through her granddaughter. *Lord, help her to hang on and get through this ordeal.*

"Morning, Nana."

"Morning."

"Morning, Amelia."

"Did you help yourself to breakfast?"

"No, not yet. We'll get it in a minute. We thought we'd start with coffee."

Voices at the dining room doorway announced the re-emergence into the lobby of Lieutenant Perkins with Chief Austin at his heels like an obedient child.

"Good morning, Lieutenant. Morning, Chief," Amelia called from behind the counter and then slipped through the staff door into the lobby. The men paused long enough to offer a proper greeting and then followed her as she joined the threesome in the sitting room. The two officers lingered just inside the entryway, filling up most of it. Elizabeth felt confined, boxed in, as if they were going to be in for a briefing or an interrogation, so she shifted farther onto the edge of the sofa in an attempt to ready herself for anything.

Renard slunk into the lobby behind the uniforms, his shoulders slumped, arms down at his sides. Appearing disheveled, his clothes were wrinkled and dirty. His greasy silvery gray, shoulder-length hair was plastered to his head. There was a foul, somewhat sour, odor emanating from him. When he spoke, the officers spun around in sync with a semblance of precision as in a military maneuver. The rest of the occupants of the room sat up and took notice when they saw who was speaking. Perkins and Austin tentatively backed farther away, granting him some space. All eyes went to the small pistol in his right hand.

"I've held the secret in for too long. It's time I confessed."

A muffled gasp. A soft moan. He had everyone's undivided attention. Speaking as though he was talking to himself, gesturing with the gun from time to time, he looked anxious.

"It was an accident. I was only trying to help. I didn't mean for her to get hurt." His voice cracking, he seemed to be struggling to keep his emotions in check. The lieutenant, who was positioned to Renard's right, kept a close eye on him, on his gun. Renard became visibly distraught as he unfolded the story for his captive audience. Suddenly, he looked directly at Elizabeth and appeared uncomfortable, scuffing his shoe nervously on the floor like a schoolboy admitting he'd pulled the braids of the little girl sitting in front of him.

"I'm so sorry, Miss Pennington . . . to you too, Mrs. Pennington." He glanced awkwardly toward the family matriarch. "I wish I could change it all. But I can't. I've ruined everything." He burst into sobs, which the trooper apparently took as a sign to act. Renard detected movement and recoiled, pointing his gun at him. "No, don't move. Don't come near me." he lashed out, his eyes possessed with terror.

The situation was deteriorating. Appearing to have nothing to lose, Renard was a desperate man. They had to proceed cautiously. Elizabeth scanned the room discretely, keeping an eye out for anyone else who thought they could take him. Renard was a live grenade, but there had to be a way to calm him down. The trooper had only made matters worse. Now, he was undoubtedly gun shy. She decided to take action.

"Renard," she spoke as softly and gently as she could, like a mother speaking to a small child, hoping to quell a tantrum and soothe his spirit. "Renard, no one's going to hurt you. Just talk to us. Go on with your story. What happened?"

"Miss Pennington, I'm so sorry."

"I know you are. You didn't mean for things to happen the way they did. It was an accident." Her voice seemed to be calming him.

"Yes!" He looked at her, spoke directly to her.

As far as he was concerned, no one else was in the room. He was talking with Elizabeth. She understood.

Sweet, adorable, little Lizzi who had grown into a beautiful woman. She'd always been so kind to him. He'd had a wonderful fantasy that someday she would care deeply for him. She would see what a good job he did taking care of her Pennington Point Inn and realize how much he cared for it, how much he cared for her.

"So go on, Renard. Tell us how it went."

The room got quiet. Renard averted his eyes from hers, as if trying to recall the details, perhaps embarrassed to be confessing to her. He raised his left arm, with what looked like a great deal of effort, and wiped sweat from his brow. His other arm was limp at his side, the gun dangling from his pudgy fingers. Regaining his composure, he picked up his head and stared at the far wall across the room, avoiding all eye contact and continued.

"I was walking by the building. The door to her room was open and I saw she needed help. I don't remember exactly what she was doing . . . hanging something above a window or something like that. She was up on a chair. The window was open. I didn't mean for anything to happen. I know I'm not supposed to go in girls' rooms. Girard always told me that. I *knew* that. He knew I knew, but I was just trying to help. . . . Well, lately he kept saying he was going to tell if I didn't." He broke down, sobbing again.

"Renard, it's okay." Elizabeth confirmed Perkins and Mitchell were holding steady. She—they—needed to hear his story. "What happened?" she implored.

"I must have scared her—I didn't mean to. I guess she didn't know I was there. When I asked her if she needed help she spun around on the chair and lost her balance." His eyes glossed over as if he were reliving the horror. "She fell backward through the open window. It was awful. I tried to grab her before she fell but it happened so quickly. I couldn't get to her in time. I ran outside and she was lying there on the ground all contorted, not moving. I knew she was dead. I'm just so sorry. . . ."

The weight of his confession was too much for him. He dropped to one knee and his head drooped. As if on cue, Mitchell and Perkins dove for him from either side and tackled him to the ground. The tennis pro skillfully kicked Renard's gun well out of his reach while the trooper cuffed him. A well-orchestrated team maneuver. The rest of the room let out a collective breath as the two musclemen hoisted Renard to his feet. His shoulders slumped, his hands shackled behind him.

Elizabeth's anger exploded within. *How could Renard have let it happen?* She wasn't finished with him yet. Jumping up, she lunged toward the trio, grabbing Kurt's forearm to impede his progress to the door. "So, Renard, where is she now?" She spoke directly to him, but the sweet tone of her voice was a loosely veiled attempt to hide her anger. She needed the rest of the story. They all deserved to hear it. Not wanting to miss a word, she inched as close to him as she dared.

"I buried her in the woods," he mumbled, as if to himself. Elizabeth was close enough to smell his rancid breath. Wrinkling her nose, she turned away and released her grip on Kurt's arm. The duo escorted the beast out the front door—one he'd walked through many times over the years—and it would undoubtedly be his last time over the threshold. Everything had changed in a horrible twist of fate.

His final comment hit everyone hard. There had been such hope the situation would end positively, that the girl would be found alive, just in a lot of trouble with her parents for wandering off. One thing was certain. If he had misinterpreted her unconsciousness as absence of life, she was dead now. Elizabeth struggled to get her head around Renard's bombshell. What a terrible, senseless tragedy. For the girl's parents. For her grandmother and Pennington Point. It could spell the end for a wonderful seaside inn that had been in the family for generations. No one was going to want to stay there anytime soon once the media caught wind of recent events. It looked like the real estate attorney was going to get his way after all. Elizabeth was livid but not yet ready to give up the fight.

"Nana, I'm so sorry. This couldn't have turned out worse." For a passing moment, she wondered who was going to have to tell the girl's parents.

"Oh, Lizzi, it *is* awful. These poor parents. That poor little girl . . . at least it's over. I hate to say it. I know it sounds terrible. But I don't know how much more of this I . . ." Her voice was barely audible. "It was so agonizing not knowing. And I never had a chance to meet her. I usually meet all of my guests, at least before they leave." Her eyes brimmed with tears.

Elizabeth reached out for her grandmother and held her tight, not wanting to let go, wishing she could take away the heartache.

# CHAPTER EIGHTEEN

The ceiling fan on the porch rotated lazily above Elizabeth, its reflection in the bowl of her spoon nearly hypnotizing her. The two friends shared a few minutes together over breakfast to sort through the startling confession they'd witnessed. Neither particularly interested in the food, they pushed fluffy scrambled eggs that had grown cold around their plates. Elizabeth broke the silence.

"It just doesn't make sense." She tried to gather the pieces. "Something Renard told us in his confession doesn't jive." She rubbed the deepening crevices in her forehead with outstretched fingers, still gazing at the flickering fan blades in the spoon. Scooting to the edge of her seat, she sat forward. "Rashelle, think about it. He said she fell out the window backward and when he went back outside, she was lying on the ground, all contorted. The front of the Hutchins' room looks out onto the porch. Not onto the bare ground."

Rashelle bantered back, "Maybe he meant the porch floor."

"But how could she die falling from the first floor?"

"What if she hit her head the wrong way or snapped her neck?"

"I suppose that's possible, but from the first floor?"

"He did say she was standing on a chair."

"That's true." Elizabeth considered Rashelle's retort. "But he also said he knows he's not supposed to go in girls' rooms. Did he mean girl apostrophe 's' or girls apostrophe?"

Rashelle looked to her for clarification.

"In other words, did he mean one girl, like the guest Kelsey Hutchins, or several girls—like the girls who were students at the school many years ago?"

Rashelle sat up straight. "Do you think he was talking about the death of that student?"

"I don't know. He was certainly around back then. Besides, it was a student's disappearance and *presumed death*," she corrected Rashelle's misstatement. "The body was never found. And going back to what he said about her lying on the ground, the porch didn't exist on that building until renovations were done to convert the school into an inn."

"Lizzi! What if you're right?"

"Well, it would mean the mystery of the student's disappearance has finally been solved, but we still have a present-day mystery on our hands. We may not be finished yet." With a renewed sense of urgency, she continued. "We need to find the chief. The Hutchins' girl may still be alive."

Leaving the remains of their breakfast behind, they dashed into the lobby but didn't have to go far before they found the chief on the phone at the front desk. Standing off to the side to wait patiently for him to finish, they could overhear part of his conversation, even though he was obviously trying to be discreet. "And you're sure it was from his boat . . . no survivors? . . . Okay . . . all right, thanks . . . yeah, okay, thanks."

"Sounds like they found the boat," Rashelle whispered. "But no survivors."

Elizabeth's shoulders fell. "How awful."

As she watched the portly constable rub his pale sweaty forehead with thick fingers, Elizabeth felt sorry for him. He was clearly out of his league in what must have been a humiliating predicament with the state police swarming in and taking over his jurisdiction. As he wrapped up his conversation, the girls crept across the lobby toward the reception area and staked out their positions like bookends, each resting an elbow on the counter.

Appearing anxious to move on from his phone conversation, the chief spoke first. "Rashelle . . . just the person I need to speak with." He made his way out from behind the counter and into the lobby to confront the girls.

Elizabeth watched for any body language to see if he meant for her to excuse herself, but the chief kept going, directing his questions to Rashelle. "Were you the staff person who was on duty when the Hutchins checked in?"

"Yes . . ." she answered cautiously, looking uncertain where the conversation was headed.

"Did they show you any ID when they registered?" he pushed further.

Elizabeth knew her friend needed to tread carefully and choose her answer wisely. If Chief Austin was getting desperate and needed someone to pin something on, he could be turning the tables on her.

"No, they paid in cash. I only need to verify ID if they are paying with a credit card or personal check."

Pausing for a moment, the chief cleared his throat. "So you don't know if they really were Mr. and Mrs. Hutchins or anyone else, for that matter." His tone bordered on condescending.

Taking one step closer to him, Rashelle held her ground. "Until now, we have never had a reason to question the identity of the guests who walk through our doors. We welcome them with open arms and treat them like family. That's the way we do business here. Amelia wouldn't have it any other way. And until I have been instructed otherwise, I will continue with this procedure." She held her gaze for effect.

Elizabeth had goose bumps. She was proud of her friend. Although a relatively new employee, Rashelle had demonstrated incredible loyalty to Amelia and the entire Pennington Point Inn family and staff.

Seemingly pushed off his stance, Austin stammered, "Uh . . . well, it certainly seems it might have helped in this situation." He was struggling to regain his composure.

"What do you mean? They aren't who they said they were? They're not the Hutchins?" Elizabeth felt compelled to ask.

"I didn't say that. We're still trying to confirm their identity in West Hartford, Connecticut, which is where they said they were from. The address they gave when they checked in is coming up as invalid. Of course, it could be a new address. I can't very well accuse the distressed parents of giving us a fake address. Unfortunately, we also haven't been able to search for their daughter, Kelsey, in any schools in the area since it's the holiday weekend. Seems the superintendent of public schools is away, and there are quite a few private high schools in the area, so it will take some time to contact the administrators of each one. We don't know where she was enrolled. Of course, if we don't have a valid last name . . . we'll have to keep working on that piece."

Curious, Lizzi and Shelle couldn't keep themselves from asking, alternately, "What does this mean? Why would they give a fake name?"

He screwed up his face and grumbled, "Who knows, and we don't know that they did yet." His patience seemed to be wearing thin. "We don't really have any answers." His voice turned gruff. Mumbling something about being back to square one with a hurricane barreling down on them, he pushed between the two, brushing both with his shoulders, and disappeared through the front door.

Remembering her back porch revelation over breakfast, Elizabeth darted after him, calling out, "Chief, I need to talk to you!" As she reached out to keep the screen door from slamming shut, he turned at the bottom of the stairs with an impatient glare. Ignoring his unprofessionalism, she continued, "Renard's story . . . some of the pieces don't make sense. He—"

"We know, Elizabeth. That seemed rather obvious."

Confounded by his patronizing tone, she watched him strut off across the driveway in a determined gait. Not one to be pushed around, she continued, "And there are notes. I've found two so f—"

Without looking back or missing a step, he swatted the air at an imperceptible pest. "Yeah, yeah, I know."

Frustrated he'd dismissed her before hearing her out, Elizabeth at least took solace in the fact he seemed aware of what she had wanted to share with him. She would catch up with him later to pin him down. Very little was making sense.

The matter of the missing guest was far from resolved.

# CHAPTER NINETEEN

*A*fter Chief Austin's abrupt departure, Elizabeth and Rashelle were left standing in the lobby with mouths agape, but not for long. Footsteps shuffled up the same porch steps the chief had just descended. An unseen hand held the screen door while Amelia stepped inside and was soon followed by Mitchell.

"Girls! There you are. Kurt has some information for us. I thought you'd want to hear, too."

As he started to explain, Amelia slipped away in the direction of the dining room. Elizabeth casually wondered why he was the messenger but surmised the chief could use some help.

"Ladies, I was telling Amelia about the man found dead in the kitchen."

Unsure she wanted to know any more about him, Lizzi figured the less she knew, the better, but allowed Kurt to continue anyway.

"He'd registered as Joseph Stevens with his wife, Suzanne, from New Canaan, Connecticut. Apparently this checks out. He's an accountant, a CPA, with clients in the Tri-state area—Greater New York City, New Jersey, and Fairfield County, Connecticut. One of the partners in his firm knew he was heading up to Maine for a long weekend but was, of course, shocked when he was told of Stevens' demise."

Elizabeth interrupted. "So, how do you know all this?"

He answered with a quip, "I just happened to be standing next to the chief when he got word."

Elizabeth figured it was more like eavesdropping and wondered where else he'd been lurking.

"Besides, he's pretty overwhelmed with the situation and sent me to ask Rashelle if any of the guests of the inn had made a reservation to go out on Slater's boat."

"Oops, I got sidetracked. I was supposed to look that up. Let me get on it." Throwing up her hands, she took a step but hesitated. "First I'd like to hear the rest of what you were saying about Mr. Stevens. And if he was a guest, why was he dressed like a chef?"

"Maybe someone's twisted sense of humor, who knows."

"And where is his wife now?" Elizabeth wondered.

"I don't know the answer to that. Maybe she's off-property under police protection? I don't know."

"All right. Go on with the rest of what you do know."

"Well, the state police ran the prints found on the knife and only Tony's were identified. Unfortunately, he can't be eliminated as a suspect yet. Before Mr. Stevens passed out he was able to type a few numbers into his cell phone. They're still trying to decipher what the numbers could mean."

Following along closely, Elizabeth felt she could help solve it as much as the next guy. *Bring it on.* "What were they?"

A dimple formed in Mitchell's cheek. He looked pleased she'd asked. "Let's see." He appeared to be straining to remember.

With her arms folded, she shifted her stance to optimize her height, becoming irked by how much time he was taking to answer the question. *Can we get on with it already?*

"8, 7, 0, 7 . . . 8707."

"Well, it's not seven digits like a regular phone number."

"No, it's not," Mitchell agreed.

"Maybe it's only part of a phone number because that was as far as he could get before he died."

"Could be."

"What about the letters on a phone that represent each number pad? Maybe he was trying to spell out something," Rashelle joined in, thinking out loud.

Elizabeth frowned. "That would have taken a tremendous amount of concentration to spell something out while he was busy dying."

Rashelle shrugged her shoulders as if that was all she had to contribute.

"It had to be related to something he was familiar with, something he's done many times before. You know, second nature to him." Elizabeth stayed focused on her train of thought.

Silence took over while everyone tossed around the last couple of ideas. Then, Lizzi's face lit up. "Rashelle, you have an adding machine in the office, don't you?"

"Yeah, it's on the desk." Leading the way, Rashelle burst through the door into the reception area with Elizabeth following closely behind. When she reached the desk, Lizzi pulled her cell phone out of her pants pocket. She looked from the phone to the adding machine and back again several times. The other two waited in silence while she sorted through her thoughts.

"That's odd. . . ."

"What's odd?" Rashelle took the bait.

"Did you ever notice that the keypad on the adding machine is upside down from the keypad on a phone?"

Mitchell and Rashelle seemed intrigued.

"See? The top row on the phone is 1, 2, 3. But the top row on the adding machine is 7, 8, 9. Think about it. This was an accountant. He was undoubtedly innately familiar with the adding machine. It's a tool of his trade. But he probably also used his cell phone a lot, too. What if he was trying to leave a clue to his killer's identity but did it as if he was using an adding machine instead of a cell phone? After all, we should cut him some slack. He was dying and probably knew it."

"Okay." Kurt was willing to play along. "So what are the equivalent numbers on the adding machine?"

"Let's look." Elizabeth compared the two. "2 . . . 1 . . . 0 . . . 1." The three thought on this for a moment. No one came up with anything obvious.

"Maybe it's a date. February 1st, 2001. That could be a significant date to this man," Rashelle offered. Elizabeth and Kurt nodded as they politely considered the idea.

"Or could it be 1901?" Kurt added.

Ignoring his suggestion, Lizzi threw in her two cents. "What if the first two numbers are the day and the last two digits are the month? In European order. That would make it January."

"Or it could be that it's not a date at all." Kurt turned the discussion upside down. "Could it be part of a license plate or a room—?"

"Miss Pennington!" The lieutenant's voice boomed behind them from the center of the lobby. "You need to come with me."

"Wh-what?"

Rashelle sprung to her friend's defense. "Lieutenant, what are you talking about?"

"I need you to come out from behind there." His eyes focused on Elizabeth.

With Rashelle close at her heels, Elizabeth shuffled into the lobby where Perkins yanked handcuffs off his belt and reached for her arm.

"Oh my gawd!" Her Brooklyn accent intensified in her excitement. "What are you doing? You don't need to do this!"

Amelia came running from the dining room. "What's going on?" Her pale face appeared drawn as her eyes landed on Elizabeth standing helplessly with her arms behind her, Perkins clamping on cuffs.

"Lieutenant, what are you doing? This is not necessary!" her grandmother shrieked. "Take those off of her! What do you think she's done? Take them off." The panic in her voice mirrored the terror in her eyes.

"I'm sorry, ma'am. There's too much evidence against her to let her stay here."

Elizabeth figured Perkins must be getting pressure from a superior to get someone in custody and get the situation under control. He was only making matters worse.

"Evidence? Your evidence is wrong. She hasn't done anything. You're taking the wrong person. For God's sake, take off the handcuffs. She's not a criminal."

Wincing, it pained Elizabeth to hear her Nana's voice quivering as she pleaded on her behalf.

Perkins clearly had heard his fill. He turned away from Amelia and manhandled Elizabeth to the door.

"No, Lieutenant, you listen to me," Amelia implored.

Lizzi felt a tug in her gut. If only her grandmother didn't have to see her being led unceremoniously away like a common thug.

"There's no need for this. If you're going to take her, at least take off the cuffs. Who's the bigger person here? Look at her. Do you really think she could overpower you? Please, I beg of you!" Her voice wobbled on her last few words.

Elizabeth knew she hadn't done anything wrong, but all eyes were on her. It felt like she'd let everyone down, in particular, her grandmother. Movement at the end of the porch turned out to be Mrs. Leibowitz standing with hands on her hips, her lips pursed in disapproval. Clearly she'd drawn her own conclusion, and she'd never let Elizabeth forget about it.

Amelia must have hit a nerve. The lieutenant's shoulders drooped and he reluctantly shoved his hand into his uniform pants to retrieve the key. Deftly slipping it into the narrow slot, he popped the handcuffs off. Elizabeth took a moment to massage her wrists while he returned the cuffs to his belt. Then he guided her down the porch steps to a waiting squad car. Opening the back door, he motioned for her to get in. It looked like she would get to see the rear seat close-up after all.

Amelia dashed down the steps with Rashelle behind her. "Where are you taking her? For God's sake, *please* don't take her. She hasn't done anything. I need her here," Amelia continued to beg.

The lieutenant slammed the door and then pivoted to address Amelia's hysteria, leaving Elizabeth in the quiet of the car. Leaning against the seat, the binding of the magazine she'd shoved into her pocket earlier dug into her back. She reached behind and pulled out her random snatch from the Hutchins' coffee table. Unrolling it, she flipped it over to the front cover and gasped. The last name on the address label did not read "Hutchins." Were they related to the girl? Were they behind her disappearance and did they know the accountant? She intended to find out. The safety of the rest of the guests and staff, including her grandmother, could depend on it. Shoving the magazine back into her pocket, she set her sights on escaping police custody. She had the makings of a plan, which started with slipping under police radar.

While Perkins remained distracted by her grandmother, she slid across the seat, away from the heated discussion. Thankful that Amelia had convinced him to let her out of the cuffs, Elizabeth scanned the vehicle for a flashlight. Peering through the cage separating the back seat from the front, she noticed a sturdy metal one tucked neatly in the pocket on the driver's door. That would do nicely. Reaching for the door handle, she pulled up short of her mark. The doors of a squad car were designed not to open from the inside where prisoners were confined.

Trapped with no way out, her throat tightened with a dull click. It couldn't end like that. Scanning the tight confines of the back seat, something caught her eye, and she leaned closer to the door. Scratches encircled the opening for the handle as if a screw driver or pocket knife had been used to jimmy the lock mechanism. It sagged just below horizontal. Perhaps the last guy to get nabbed had done the work for her.

Tugging the handle, her body jolted when she felt the door give. Someone hadn't inspected his cruiser thoroughly before his shift started. Pressing her shoulder into it, she slipped out, crouching to stay out of sight. She didn't close the door tightly, so as not to draw attention. Grabbing the handle on the driver's door, she listened for conversation on the other side.

"We'll bring her back as soon as we can." As he rounded the rear of the cruiser his voice grew louder. In a desperate move, she hit the ground and rolled under the vehicle, listened as he opened his door but didn't enter the car.

"What the hell!"

*Not much gets past him.*

"Where is she? Damn it!" Footsteps led away from the car.

Elizabeth lay still, listening for voices. After what seemed like an eternity, she scooted out from under the car, surveying the immediate area. It seemed clear. Pleased to see Perkins had left the driver's door ajar, she pulled it open just enough to reach the flashlight, trying not to set off the cruiser's overhead light on such a gray, overcast day. Leaning in farther, she jiggled the end of the flashlight out of the pocket. One more inch and she would have it. With the tips of her fingers around it she yanked it out just as the dome light popped on. Staying low, she sprinted for the woods, anxious for the trees to swallow her up and hide her from the police, who were undoubtedly scattering to search for her. Elizabeth knew she'd lost precious time retrieving the trooper's light, but she'd need it later.

Once in the thick of it, she pushed through the trees with both arms out in front of her. She kept her eyes focused on the ground to keep from tripping over an errant root, glancing up periodically to avoid running headlong into a tree. Twigs snapped beneath her soles. The farther in she went, the darker it grew. She stopped and listened for a moment, growing uncomfortably aware she was the only creature making a sound. The shadowy woods were eerily quiet. A silvery gray mist nearly choked the air. She couldn't shake the feeling something evil had happened or lurked nearby. The thought of going deeper made her stomach turn. But she had no choice. Unable to return to the inn, she had to put as much distance as possible between her and what she'd left behind. She set off again, glancing around to check for movement.

Escape while in custody. Elizabeth tried that on for size. More than just a sticky situation, but she couldn't dwell on it. *One foot in front of the other.* She had to keep—thud! Her arm hit a tree, knocking the flashlight loose and landing it in the brush below. "Shit!" Dropping to the ground, she frantically groped for the light. It had to be close by. Did it bounce? Widening the circle, she patted the ground, ignoring jabs from the prickly dried pine needles, sticks, and pinecones. Where was it? Panic crept in. Stretching to reach under the wide boughs of a big, old pine, she hit metal. "Yes!" Grabbing it tightly, she crawled out from under the conifer and stood up, backing into someone's arms. A hand clasped firmly onto her mouth, allowing her only a muffled scream. She surmised it was a man who had her in a tight hold. His strong arms held her firmly in place. Struggling to pull free, she heard the thud of her flashlight making contact with the ground for a second time. *So much for using that as a weapon.* As she fought to scream and wriggle out of his grasp, her muffled shrieks drowned out her captor's words.

"Elizabeth!" His voice was barely above a whisper. It was Mitchell. She stopped squirming. "Shut up already. Hold still and I'll let go of you."

Releasing some of the tension in her body, she stood still. Kurt held his arms around her and kept one hand over her mouth.

"Okay? Have you calmed down? Remember, I'm on your side."

Elizabeth wasn't so sure, but she was willing to pretend if it meant he would let go of her. She nodded. He slid his hand from her mouth, paused, then eased his vice grip from around her upper body, hanging onto her arm as insurance she wouldn't run.

"All right, already. I'm not going anywhere." Her voice was hushed but firm. She jerked her arm out of his grasp. If it wasn't so dark in the woods, she imagined she could have seen a red spot on her arm where his overzealous hands had gripped her. She rubbed it to relieve the pain. "And where has that hand been, for God's sake? Wash them once in a while." She pretended to spit off to the side.

"What are you doing? You were in custody. Perkins will be having a canary about now."

"A canary? Kurt, no one says that anymore."

"This is serious, Elizabeth."

She didn't give a damn about Perkins. And she needed to ditch Mitchell. Not only did she not trust him, but he would be dead weight to slow her down. "Look, I need to get back into the tunnels to check things out." More like they'd have to be her hideout for the time being. "I can't help my grandmother if I'm in custody. And I don't care how mad Perkins is. I'll just have to steer clear of him."

"Well, the tunnels would be a good place for that. Let's go." He tugged on her arm again.

"Wait! I need the flashlight."

Mitchell pulled a miniature light that dangled from a key chain out of his pocket and snapped it on, painting the ground in wide swaths. Together they scanned in a circle until the concentrated beam landed on the lieutenant's light. She reached down and snatched it up.

"Good, that'll come in handy." He started off deeper into the woods.

Following behind, she wondered what he was up to. Was he actually going to help her, or was he leading her back into Perkins' custody?

# CHAPTER TWENTY

Reaching the perimeter, Elizabeth and Kurt stopped short of emerging from the woods. She searched his face to discern his intentions. He spoke first.

"We need to get you to the entrance . . . behind Acadia."

Elizabeth wondered how he knew it was there.

He surveyed the grounds in front of them, and then stepped out of the safety of the woods. "C'mon," he gestured with a nod of his head.

They stayed low and dashed across the grass toward the end of the building. Elizabeth followed behind as he passed the first set of steps on the rear of the building, going directly to the bushes beyond them. She watched as he reached into the greenery and yanked on a hatchway door. It opened fairly easily as if it was used regularly. There was a sliding latch to secure it from being blown open in the wind but no padlock dangling from it. Vandals must have taken care of that.

"Ladies first." He motioned for her to enter.

Oh, how she hated the tunnels. At least she had a decent flashlight this time. Curious about what she would find starting from this end, she cautiously descended the steps. As she reached to switch on the lieutenant's light, footsteps approached. Her body stiffened.

"Mitchell!" a gruff voice called out.

Perkins. Had he seen her enter the tunnel?

"What are you doing?" the lieutenant barked.

She squeezed her eyes shut and prayed she hadn't been detected.

Kurt slammed the door behind her with a loud bang. "Just checking the tunnels, making sure the access points are secure." The sound of the latch sliding into place confirmed Mitchell's agenda.

"That bastard!" she hissed. She *knew* she couldn't trust him. "Damn it!" The black of the tunnel enveloped her. She waited for her eyes to adjust, but the absolute darkness remained.

Straining to hear if they were still lingering outside the door, she didn't dare turn on her light yet, terrified of being caught by Perkins. As their voices trailed off, she could make out a dripping sound somewhere off in the distance. Damp, musty air permeated her nose. She waited until she couldn't stand the dark any longer and pushed the switch so the flashlight sprung to life, piercing the pitch black. Glancing around her, she saw it was not unlike the other end of the tunnel. Taking what comfort she could from that, it didn't change the fact she was locked in.

Mitchell had her right where he wanted her, and she had a burning desire to get out. Her cell phone! She could call Rashelle to come to her rescue. All her friend would have to do is slide the latch on the hatchway. . . . Of course, calling her would be risky. As with any fugitive, they were probably monitoring her cell phone. One call and more than Rashelle would know where she was.

"All right, Elizabeth. Think." Her voice was rough and echoed within the damp stone walls, sounding odd to her. With the tunnel feeling colder and more desolate than before, she did her best to shake off a shiver. Shining the flashlight down the shaft, she listened. No detectible sounds. Shifting her hand to her hip, she thought for a moment. It looked like she had no other options than to find her way to the main building. Could she garner enough courage to veer off into side tunnels to try to find the girl? No one else seemed to be venturing down to search for her. And what would she do once she got to the other end—if she found her way out? Who would be waiting for her? She'd have to devise a plan as she went. Then she realized the hand on her hip should have brushed the magazine she'd swiped. Had she dropped it in her haste to get away from the police? Did Mitchell slip it out of her pocket? It wasn't productive to think about either possibility. She needed to start moving. If she was going to be a target, it would be better to be moving.

Hesitantly she stepped off. Since the trooper's light was of much better quality than the two rusty castoffs Rashelle had rescued from the desk drawer, she was fairly confident this one might actually stay on. Working her way through, she took small steps and stopped periodically to listen. It was no wonder she was forbidden from exploring the tunnels as a child. God, how she hated them as an adult.

Barely a few feet from the hatchway, she jumped as her cell phone sprang to life. "Shit!" She plunged her hand deep into her pocket to retrieve the noisy offender. Area code 917. Drescher again. He was certainly persistent. She had to give him that. After two rings, she pushed the "decline" button and abruptly ended the call, preventing it from ringing any longer. Was it enough for the police to pinpoint where she was? She shut off the phone and shoved it back into her pocket.

Pressing on, she ambled a few dozen yards until she noticed the reflection of a dim light bobbing along the wall. Freezing in her steps, she snapped off her light, watching as the approaching flicker grew brighter. She had company, and there was nowhere to hide. Nowhere to go. All she could do was wait to confront the person. A police officer? The missing girl? Her breathing quickened. Her palms began to tingle, forcing her to focus on not dropping her only means of navigating the otherwise dark abyss. The sound of footfalls got closer. Almost on top of her. A bright light flashed in her eyes. Switching on her light, she countered the intruder's beam, aiming for the general location of a face. In disbelief, Elizabeth strained her eyes to focus.

"M-Mrs. Leibowitz? What the—what are you doing here?"

Standing in Elizabeth's beam, she struck a pose like they were casually meeting in the lobby of the inn. Of course, no encounter with Mrs. L. was ever casual. Noticing she was holding something down at her side, Elizabeth shifted her light.

"A bottle of wine? Mrs. Leibowitz, you're sneaking a bottle from the inn's wine cellar?" Dismayed at the audacity of a loyal guest using the old tunnels to steal wine, she moved her light back up to Mrs. L.'s face, waiting for a response.

"Bah!" She gestured as if to say, "It's no big deal." "The wine you'd sent up earlier was of questionable quality, so I thought I would make my own selection."

Clenching her teeth, Elizabeth refrained from pursuing the discussion further. It wasn't the time or the place, yet it was disturbing to realize the old woman had obviously traversed the tunnels previously and knew exactly where to go to find the wine cellar. What was more, she clearly thought her indiscretion should be overlooked. Without so much as an explanation, the defiant guest pushed past her and headed for the end of the tunnel Elizabeth had come from. As the darkness swallowed her up, Mrs. L. called back, "I'll leave the unopened bottle in my room to be picked up." Her light bobbed for a few seconds and then disappeared.

"Oh my God, what a bitch," Elizabeth whispered to herself and stood alone with her narrow swath of light in disbelief. She wasn't about to do the crotchety old woman any favors and tell her the hatchway was locked. Figuring she would see the wine-pilfering guest on the rebound, she resumed her hike to the main tunnel entrance.

Shaking off her run-in with Mrs. L., she turned her focus to more pressing matters. Would she find the missing girl? If only it could be over—for the girl, for everyone. She prayed she was still alive. It would certainly make it worth walking into the hands of the police on the other end.

Her feet had settled into a steady rhythm when she smelled it. The odor was so strong, it almost made her eyes water. She wasn't sure she wanted to see where it came from but reluctantly crept closer. The smell was strong. It couldn't be too much farther. Then her light shined on something dark lying in the middle of the floor. Taking a few more steps closer, she squinted to make out the lifeless form just in front of her. Then she noticed the fur. An unfortunate animal had met its untimely demise in the bowels of the inn. Not very large. A raccoon? Opossum? Hard to tell what it was and what did it in, as it had obviously been decomposing for a while. Relieved the carcass was not human, she gingerly stepped over it and moved on. The more space she could put between herself and the smelly mess, the better.

Elizabeth picked up her pace as much as she dared but kept her feet close to the ground to avoid slipping and falling on the damp, packed dirt floor. Her thoughts returned to Mitchell. Did he have the Hutchins' magazine? If so, what was he going to do with it? Had he seen her entering their room? Her fingerprints had to be on it. She feared Mitchell would turn it over to Perkins so he could use it to charge her with breaking and entering. Had the police figured out who the Hutchins really were? If only she could call Rashelle to ensure someone was going to be on her side when she reached the other end of the tunnel.

Becoming aware of how fast she was moving, it seemed as though she'd sped up while her mind wandered. Eager to stabilize herself, she reached out with her free hand to run it along the rough surface of the damp wall. Feeling alone down below the ground, a chill ran through her as the tunnel grew icy cold. The urgency to see daylight was stronger than ever, but she stopped for a moment to listen. It was too quiet.

*"Get out!"*

The voice startled her. It was a whisper in her ear. Jolting in place, she swiveled her head trying to determine where the sound came from. It was a woman's voice but not one she recognized. It certainly wasn't Mrs. L.'s. She couldn't tell where it had originated. It seemed as though it was all around her.

With her instincts urging her to heed the warning, Elizabeth frantically resumed her trek toward daylight. She moved at a pace flirting with the danger of slipping on the wet ground, but her desire to escape took charge.

The hand running along the wall absorbed a subtle vibration, which made her stop. *What was that?* She took a few tentative steps, keeping her hand on the cold damp stones, stopping to listen again. Somewhere nearby came a creaking sound, almost a groan, like a heavy weight causing something to give under pressure. Elizabeth blacked out before she hit the ground.

# CHAPTER TWENTY-ONE

*Struggling to open her eyes*, Elizabeth became acutely aware of searing pain shooting up the back of her head. Moaning, she stirred from her prone position on the damp floor.

"Liz! Are you all right?" A familiar voice. "Lizzi! Oh my gawd. Tawk to me."

As Elizabeth slowly regained consciousness, her eyes darted to locate her friend. The bright light made it difficult to see past.

A gruff voice barked directions. "Get the light out of her eyes, for God's sake. Give her some room to breathe!"

Perkins had found her. *Was he responsible for the throbbing in her head?* Her stomach turned over and she suddenly felt nauseous. Straining to remember what had happened, she was frustrated she couldn't recall. That couldn't be good.

"Liz. What happened? Are you all right, girlfriend? Tawk to me. Can you sit up?" In her haste to help, Rashelle grabbed onto one of her arms to encourage her to move.

"Whoa, Miss Harper. Give her a minute to gather herself. She'll be fine. Give her some time."

*What was Perkins up to? He was sounding entirely too compassionate.* Elizabeth wondered who else was hovering over her. There were several people, like a morbidly curious crowd gathering at a car accident. Blinking while squinting to see past multiple flashlights, Elizabeth reached to the back of her head to perform a tactile examination. She located a large, excruciatingly painful lump, and her fingers felt wet when she pulled them away. Throbbing rocked her skull. Damn, she could use some ice and several hundred milligrams of ibuprofen.

"Take it easy, Miss Pennington. You've suffered quite a blow. Take your time. If need be, we can carry you out of the tunnel."

The urge to get out of the limelight took over. Trying to sit up, everything around her began to spin. A wave of nausea rolled through her stomach again. She leaned to one side and let loose, wiping her mouth with the back of her hand. Not very ladylike but necessary, nonetheless.

Someone latched onto her left upper arm to steady her. There was a new voice.

"Elizabeth, you heard the lieutenant. There's no rush. Take your time."

It was Mitchell. She shouldn't be surprised he was with Perkins. *But Rashelle?*

"I know, I know. I'd like to get out of here. For God's sake, what happened?"

"We can fill in the details in time. Let's first get you to safety."

*What was Mitchell up to?*

"Do you think you can stand up?"

"Let's give it a try. I really want out." The sense of urgency in her voice seemed lost on the others.

Another unidentified voice broke in. "Actually, sir, we need to vacate the tunnel now. It's not very stable. We don't know how long we have." Perkins and Mitchell reached down and grabbed onto her upper arms.

"Ready, Elizabeth?"

She nodded. "Let's do it."

The two men lifted her into a standing position. Her knees buckled, so they tightened their grip and held onto her until she was steadier. Her world swirled and a stabbing pain sliced through her skull, but she was glad to be upright. Having her fill of the tunnels, she wanted out. As they progressed toward the exit, Elizabeth willed herself to keep going. Plodding along, forcing her legs to move, she was acutely aware of her adversaries; Mitchell was on one side with Perkins on the other. Wondering if they were taking her into custody, she almost didn't care. She hoped she never saw the tunnel walls again.

After several yards of shuffling her feet across the uneven surface, she felt drained and slowed down. Her head throbbed harder. The pain was unbearable. Dizziness crept in. Everything around her began to spin. Blacking out again, her body crumpled into a heap on the cold hard floor.

# CHAPTER TWENTY-TWO

Coming *to for a second time* in the familiar territory of the sitting room, Elizabeth cautiously groped through her hair, discovering someone had applied a bandage while she was unconscious. Pain pulsed though her head, threatening to split it in half, but she was, nonetheless, thrilled to be above ground again. Sensing a commotion out in the dining room, she tried to sit up to see what was going on. With the movement, a stabbing pain shot between her eyes. Dizziness returned. Flopping back down on the worn-out floral couch, she noticed it didn't seem to be near the fireplace where she and Rashelle had talked late into the evening on the night of her arrival. The room had been rearranged. Though she was curious about the reconfiguration, she was more anxious to find out what had happened down in the tunnels. Struggling to sit up, but only making it as far as resting on the arm, Elizabeth listened closely to the din nearby.

"Lizzi." The sound of her grandmother's voice felt soothing.

Oh, how she yearned to reach out and hug her, feel her warmth. "Nana, what's going on? What happened?"

"Are you all right? You look dreadful, you poor thing. The tunnel you were in had a cave-in. Young lady, you're lucky to be alive." Amelia was clearly grateful to see her granddaughter had survived a potentially deadly situation, relatively unscathed.

"Nana, I'm okay. I'll be fine." Blinking her eyes to fight back the pain, she endeavored to put her grandmother's mind at ease. "Don't worry about me. What's going on?"

"Liz, the hurricane has taken a turn. It's heading inland . . . right for us." Bending toward Elizabeth with deep concern in her eyes, she took hold of her hands. "We're evacuating the inn."

"What about the missing girl?"

"Oh, the officers—"

"Excuse me, ma'am." Perkins spoke directly to Amelia. She turned abruptly. "We really need to continue the evacuation."

"Yes, of course. I'll be right there." She leaned closer to her granddaughter.

Looking mildly disinterested in Elizabeth's direction, Perkins hovered behind Amelia with his hands on his hips, working hard to maintain a position of authority.

"I have to help the officers. You need to rest, dear. You stay put and I'll be back as soon as I can."

The lieutenant couldn't resist interjecting and spoke in a stern voice. "Elizabeth, if I didn't have more pressing issues to address, you'd be back in custody for running off like that. As it stands now, the investigation took a turn which may get you off the hook . . . but I still want to talk with you later."

He and Amelia disappeared into the dining room before Elizabeth could offer a retort. It seemed as though a lot had happened while she was down in the tunnels.

Eager to find a few ibuprofen, she sat up again. This time, thankfully, the room didn't spin quite so fast. Resting on the couch, she surveyed the room while gathering the energy to stand up. The furniture had not only been rearranged, it had been pushed to one side to make space for outdoor chairs and bikes from the front porch.

She eased herself off the couch but hung onto the arm for a while to make sure she wasn't going to take a nosedive. Taking little steps toward the registration desk, she counted on Rashelle to have something strong stashed in one of the drawers. She got as far as the old, round, wooden table when her head felt fuzzy again. Lunging for the edge, she grabbed hold of it, pushing the table off balance enough to tip the container of flowers. It wobbled precariously close to toppling and crashing to the floor, but she reached out and snatched it in time. Elizabeth cringed, imagining Amelia would have been sorely disappointed.

When she felt strong enough, Elizabeth dashed for the front desk. She let go and fast-walked, in a wobbly zigzag, and grabbed on for dear life when she reached the counter. Pulling herself across to see if there was anything obvious on the desktop below, she hung on for a moment while her head throbbed, straining to see more clearly. It looked like there was something resembling a medicine bottle next to the phone, but the label was facing the opposite direction. She'd have to make her way around to the inside of the office to check it out.

Realizing that would take a great deal of effort, she waited to gather her strength, and then skirted around the corner, running both hands along the walls for support. Reaching the office door, she hit it with a thud, jarring her body and reawakening the throbbing. She fumbled for the knob and managed to turn it enough to release the catch and allow her weight to push open the door. Momentum carried her into the tiny space where she aimed for and landed in the desk chair, which spun around to the desk. With pain pulsing in her head, she scanned the tiny office. The bottle she'd noticed from the other side of the counter turned out to be an antacid. The drawers. There had to be something in one of them. She scooted the chair toward the antique Chippendale-style handles and pulled them one by one. Looking deep into the back, she hit pay dirt with the second drawer. A well-worn bottle of pain reliever rattled around inside when Elizabeth gave it a good tug. She poured half a dozen gel caps into her palm. Wondering what she was going to wash them down with, she spotted a half-full water bottle sitting on the far side of the desk. Ordinarily, she would have been repulsed by the idea of drinking out of someone else's bottle. She had no idea whose it was, but she was desperate. The ibuprofen slid down easily. Longing for them to take effect, she closed her eyes and tried to will away the pain still throbbing. Easing the chair into a semi-reclining position, her body shut down for a third time.

While she lay in the relative quiet of the tiny office, the rest of the inn was in chaos as the staff and troopers labored to reach every guest and instruct them in the evacuation procedures. A couple local schools had opened up to take in evacuees of the impending storm. Meteorologists were particularly concerned about a string of towns along the coast, and Pennington Point was one of them. There was talk of the hurricane sustaining its Category 4 rating. Such a strong storm had not hit Maine for as long as even the old-timers could remember.

# CHAPTER TWENTY-THREE

Waking to the ringing of her cell phone, Elizabeth lurched forward in her chair and grabbed it from her pocket out of habit before she was fully conscious. "Hel—hello!" Elizabeth tried to clear her thoughts while listening to the voice on the other end. Suddenly she realized it was Vera. *Oh my God, why did I answer the phone?* "Yes . . . yes. Vera, is that you?"

"Of course it's me! I've been trying to get ahold of you for quite a while. Drescher has too. What is going on with you, Miss Pennington?" Vera's loud, grating voice awakened a stabbing pain through the center of her head, more intense than before.

Elizabeth regretted answering the phone. It was bound to happen, though. She'd been dodging her boss since she'd arrived at the inn. This was not the responsible Elizabeth Pennington, the professional interior designer Vera knew and loved—well, knew. She'd have to talk to her at some point. Just not now.

"Vera, I'm sorry. Things are a little crazy here right now."

"That's not my problem! I've got Drescher on my back looking for design ideas for his new building. He wants to meet tomorrow afternoon. What am I supposed to tell him, Elizabeth? Sorry, my top designer was busy over the weekend and couldn't be bothered to work on our most important client?" she demanded, emphasizing the last few words.

"What?" Vera was being completely unreasonable, and she certainly didn't have time to deal with it.

"Elizabeth, I need your designs!" Desperation was evident in her tone.

"Vera, there's a hurricane headed our way. At the moment we're evacuating the—"

"Fax me what you have. Damn it, Elizabeth, do you want a job when you get back?" Vera shrieked in her ear.

"I can't right now. I have to go." Lizzi pushed the button to end the call. Throwing herself against the back of the chair, she couldn't believe Vera was being such a bitch. *Is New York City that far away that she and Drescher had no idea what was happening in Maine?* Sitting for a moment to reflect on the brief, but ridiculous conversation, she conceded her response was probably grounds for dismissal.

Having her fill of her tyrannical boss, Elizabeth switched her focus to the inn and the impending hurricane. Anxious to help with the evacuation, she stumbled for the door, nearly tripping on the edge of the circular braided rug she'd inadvertently flipped over on her way into the office. Dizziness pervaded, so she grabbed onto the door frame for support and took a moment to gather herself. Then it hit her. She thought she'd shut off her phone when she was down in the tunnel.

# CHAPTER TWENTY-FOUR

*aving been transformed* into central dispatch, the dining room was bustling. Staff and law enforcement officials loudly bantered, discussing the procedures necessary to make sure everyone got out safely and no one was left behind. Peeking in from a safe distance, she listened to the buzz.

"We tried that door. No one answered. How are we supposed to know if they have already left?"

"Amelia has the master list of guests checked in for the weekend. She's also maintaining a tally of who has left, when they left, and who has yet to check out. Let's ask her to give us an update so we can divide and conquer. We need to accomplish this as quickly as possible."

It sounded like things were under control, even under the circumstances. Elizabeth felt compelled to lend a hand, though, and she ambled toward the front door. Besides, the fresh air would do her good.

Once at the bottom of the porch steps, she could hear the roar of the waves crashing on the beach below. A light rain was falling. Heading around to the side, she figured she would aim for Moosehead to start knocking on doors. She would have to keep track who she was able to reach and which doors were unanswered.

As she approached Acadia House, she realized she wasn't thinking clearly. She didn't know what the evacuation instructions were. Figuring the painful bump was to blame, she slowed her steps to think for a moment. She could at least direct the guests to central dispatch in the dining room. Resuming her pace, she rounded the back of Acadia and up the sidewalk between the building and a long narrow strip of pines that ran parallel. Before she got to the end of the building her legs became weak, and she grabbed onto the nearest stair railing, breathing in a deliberate, even cadence.

As the rain grew heavier, large drops pelted her face, helping to clear her head, but served as a harbinger of the tremendous storm barreling toward them. Tempted to sit on the steps for a moment, she didn't dare, knowing it might be difficult to get up again.

Near her was the sound of a door latch. Glancing up to see who it was, she noticed where she was standing—at the bottom of the back steps leading to the Hutchins' room. "Oh, you must be Mrs. Hutchins, I didn't mean to disturb you. Surely you're aware that the hurricane is—"

Strong hands grabbed her from behind, yanking her arms so tightly she yelled. Something sharp at her throat forced a soft gasp to escape her lips. Mrs. Hutchins stood at the top of the stairs looking impassively then turned away, retreating inside her room.

Puzzled by the woman's aloofness, Elizabeth then realized Mrs. Hutchins must know the person who had her arms pinned behind her, rendering her completely defenseless.

Judging from the strength the person exerted, Elizabeth was convinced it was a man. She was guessing it was Perkins . . . or Mitchell. She didn't have the energy to put up a fight this time. "Okay, already. You don't have to be so rough. Ease—"

"Oh, yes I do. All the other tactics don't seem to be working."

Elizabeth's eyes got wide. The man's voice wasn't familiar.

"For God's sake, Elizabeth, why did you come up here? Everything was going swimmingly into turmoil, and then you arrived to save the day."

It was difficult to draw in air and she swallowed hard. The man's hand, with what she imagined must be a knife, pressed against her neck. Elizabeth struggled to speak. "Wh-what are you doing? Who are you?"

Perkins appeared from around the corner at the end of the building with his gun drawn, facing Elizabeth and her unknown captor. "Hold it right there."

The man tightened his grasp and pulled her closer to him. The knife cut into her neck. Cold trickled down.

"Don't come any closer! I'll slit her throat with your next step."

"Hey, take it easy." Perkins' voice was assertive yet deliberately calm. "You don't have to involve Eliz—"

"*I* don't have to involve Elizabeth. She already involved herself."

Elizabeth didn't like the sound of desperation in his voice.

"She should have left well enough alone and stayed in New York City. After all, she does have enough work to keep her busy for a while. But she chose to throw that aside and run to her grandmother's rescue."

Elizabeth searched her memory to figure out who had her by the neck.

"So . . . you may have underestimated how close she and Amelia really are. Obviously the bond of love shared by these two is very strong. But evidence was planted on her just in case she decided to head up to Maine and stick her nose into things, screw up the plan." Perkins seemed to be fishing.

"Evidence?" Lizzi could barely utter enough sound to make the word heard. The man's grip tightened.

"Yes, Miss Pennington," Perkins continued. "There was a package planted on you before you left the city."

Elizabeth racked her brain. Then it dawned on her. She had all but forgotten Lenny from the mail room had brought a manila envelope to her as she was pulling out of the parking garage.

"It was still on the front passenger seat when we impounded your car. So we took the liberty of opening it for you. In the process, we were able to lift prints from the packing tape used to seal the package. It was a long shot, but we decided to give it a try and run them through the FBI's database. Inside was a box with a necklace, the description of which the Hutchins' had given to us when they described what their missing daughter was last seen wearing. We were disappointed not to find any DNA on the necklace, but our disappointment turned to suspicion when the jacket found on the breakwater didn't have any DNA on it, either. But we did determine that the couple who had checked in as Mr.

and Mrs. Hutchins are actually James and Ann Rizzo. Isn't that right, Rizzo?"

*Rizzo was the addressee on the magazine she'd picked up in the Hutchins' room.* Elizabeth grew more terrified as the man's grip tightened. She snatched shallow breaths to keep from passing out. As the wind picked up, the rain got heavier, stinging her face.

Perkins continued. "All right, Rizzo, it's over. Give it up." He shouted to be heard over the wind in the tall pines behind him.

"Oh, no." Rizzo's voice was still remarkably calm, but firm. He spoke as if he was the one in control. "This is certainly not over, is it, Elizabeth?" *How did he know her?* He pressed his warm sweaty cheek up next to hers, which made her cringe. Cheap aftershave accosted her nose. Her stomach responded with nausea. Desperate to get out of his grip, she squirmed. His knife cut deeper into her neck. God help her.

Suddenly, the man's arm pulled away and she was knocked to the ground. Feeling dazed, she blinked her eyes, struggling to stay conscious. Two guys scuffled on the ground next to her. Mitchell had arrived on the scene. He swung his leg over and straddled Rizzo, easily overpowering him long enough for Perkins to slip on a pair of cuffs, and then pull him to a standing position. A couple of beat cops rounded the corner on a dead run and came to an abrupt halt as they stumbled onto the scene.

Two more cops exited the Hutchins' back door onto the landing with Mrs. Hutchins/Rizzo in cuffs.

Elizabeth scrambled to get to her hands and knees as the two suspects were swiftly escorted around the corner, presumably to waiting squad cars.

Kurt kneeled next to Elizabeth. "Are you okay, Liz?" He took hold of her shoulders and lifted her. His eyes went to her neck. "You need to get that checked out."

Gusts of wind tossed her hair wildly about. Bits of sleet stung her exposed skin. Grateful that Kurt had rescued her from an uncertain fate, she was beginning to like him after all, but at the moment they needed to get to safety. "I'm okay . . . or at least I will be. Just help me up, please."

Standing on two wobbly legs, she ran her hand across the front of her neck. A smear of blood covered her palm, but, otherwise, there didn't seem to be too much damage. Dismissing it with a swipe down her pants leg, it felt good to have the Hutchins, or whoever they were, out of her sight. Shouting over the wind, she demanded, "What the *hell* just happened? What's going on?"

Amelia and Rashelle appeared around the same corner from which the officers disappeared with their perps in tow. They were a sight for sore eyes. Elizabeth yearned to run to her grandmother and hug her tightly. Unfortunately, there were more pressing matters, like vacating the premises before the storm grew worse.

"All right, Lieutenant, we have checked and double-checked every room," Amelia shouted in a quivering voice. "All guests have been evacuated. The only staff left are the ones standing in front of you. Everyone else is safely at the shelter or on the way."

Perkins looked relieved, the stress of the past few days etched in the lines of his face. "Right, then. Let's get out of here. Mitchell, you see that Amelia and Rashelle get to the shelter. Elizabeth, your car has been returned to you. It's parked out front where you left it. Are you up to driving, or do you need someone to take care of that for you? I'm assuming you wouldn't want to leave it here with the hurricane coming."

Elizabeth had never let *anyone* drive her car and she wasn't about to let it happen now, no matter how dire the situation. It was bad enough the police had snatched it out from under her nose without her consent in the first place, and there had better not be a scratch on it or there would be hell to pay.

"No, I'm good. I'll drive. Thanks." Eager for an explanation, she tried again, "But could someone explain what just happened?"

"Miss Pennington, I'm sorry. That's going to have to wait. We'll rendezvous at the shelter and debrief you then. All right, let's move out!" The lieutenant barked the order and everyone turned in response.

Fighting back her building frustration, Elizabeth was going to have to wait to hear the details, although everyone else seemed to be clued in. She could hardly stand it. Anxious to know if the girl had been found and if she was alive, she couldn't bear the thought of leaving her behind. As the last five people at the inn rounded the side of Acadia House, the force of the wind hit them, pushing them onto their heels. Mitchell and Rashelle led the group. The two Pennington ladies were in the middle. Perkins brought up the rear.

Amelia put her arm around Elizabeth and yelled to be heard above the roar of the wind, "Are you sure you're all right, honey?"

Elizabeth nodded in response.

"Are you okay to drive?" Amelia pressed further.

She nodded again.

"Well, I'm going to go with Kurt and Rashelle. I'll meet you at the shelter. Okay?"

Grinning, Elizabeth recalled Amelia had never felt comfortable riding in her little sports car.

"Okay, Nana," she yelled. "No problem. I'll see you there."

Lunging forward, she grabbed onto Mitchell's arm, pulling him back. Rashelle stopped, too. "You take care of her. Do you hear me? Take care of my grandmother," Elizabeth shouted.

"Got it, Liz. She's in good hands. Now let's get out of here before it's too late to leave."

They all picked up the pace, nearly jogging by the time they reached the front of the inn. Near hurricane-force winds off the ocean forced them to lean forward to walk against it. In the semicircle were three cars. Mitchell's modest import of some sort was located farthest down the drive nearest the ocean, with Lieutenant Perkins' squad car in front of it and Elizabeth's Z4 closest, parked alongside the front porch. Lizzi was thrilled to see her pride and joy again, anxious to get in it. Amelia hung onto Kurt and Rashelle as they pushed their way through the storm toward his car, their ticket out of there.

Suddenly Elizabeth whipped around to Perkins. "Lieutenant! There's one more guest left at the inn!" Was it possible Nana could have missed someone in her haste to complete the evacuation? Elizabeth felt compelled to check just in case.

"What?" He scowled in disbelief.

"Yes, I'm absolutely certain," she shouted. "Come with me, I'll need your help."

Setting out on a dead run with the lieutenant on her heels, Elizabeth led him back around the corner of Acadia House to the spot they'd just fled. She knew they were running out of time and Perkins was anxious to vacate. She'd better be right.

Elizabeth ran up to the hatchway Mitchell had secured behind her earlier.

"Mrs. Leibowitz is still in there. I passed her in the tunnel when I was heading toward the main building. She was walking in the opposite direction. The hatchway was locked so she couldn't have gotten out, and she couldn't have made her way back to the inn because of the cave-in." As she paused to take a breath, she was relieved to see Perkins considering everything she'd blurted out.

For a moment, Elizabeth considered the possibility Mrs. Leibowitz had perished in the cave-in. She doubted anyone knew the extent of the damage to the tunnel or had investigated beyond rescuing her. Then again, the tough old lady could have been spared any injuries and was down there trying to figure out how to get out. Hopefully it wouldn't take long to find her. They were already working on borrowed time.

As Perkins brushed the branches away from the hatchway door, Elizabeth's eyes went to a padlock that wasn't there earlier. He wasted no time pulling out his revolver, and she cowered behind him as he took three shots to knock off the lock. Perkins coaxed the latch to the side and gave the door a tug. Sitting halfway up the steps was Mrs. L. holding a wine bottle. The neck had a jagged edge where she'd broken it to access the wine. Her red-stained shirt evidenced she'd missed her mouth a few times. Lieutenant Perkins reached down, grabbed her firmly by the arm, and yanked her up the steps. Obviously feeling no pain, the old woman stepped like she couldn't feel her feet. When she reached the top, he snatched the bottle out of her hand and threw it aside. Slamming the hatchway, he shouted that they needed to clear out. Elizabeth grabbed onto Mrs. Leibowitz's other arm to speed up the process of getting to the last two cars at the inn. The old woman was wobbly but they dragged her through the wind and sleet, loading her into the back seat of the cruiser. Perkins slammed the door, turning to address Elizabeth.

"You have to get out *now*. No one stands a chance in this storm. You have no reason to stay any longer. Get out *now*, Miss Pennington." Rounding the front of his cruiser, the state trooper had done his duty.

Elizabeth took a look around while Perkins entered the driver's side of his squad car. The storm had intensified since they began the evacuation a few hours earlier. Windswept rain and sleet whipped her hair, forcing her to wipe wet strands from her eyes and pull them out of her mouth. It was becoming difficult to stand in place without getting pushed to the side.

Although she felt the urgency to evacuate, Elizabeth found it hard to leave her beloved childhood home. She hated to think about what it might look like after a Category 4 hurricane plowed through it. Watching Lieutenant Perkins disappear down the access road, it was her turn to leave. With her eyes brimming with tears, she reached for the door handle and gave it a pull, but it didn't budge. She tugged again and screamed into the roar of the storm.

# CHAPTER TWENTY-FIVE

The state police had returned her car to her but had neglected to give her back the key fob. Was it inside? Powerful winds pelted the rain and sleet so hard against the window she couldn't see in. In frustration she banged on the glass with her fist, but it didn't give. Even if she was able to break it, she was still stranded unless the fob was inside. Panic gripped her. A strong gust of wind pushed her to the side, forcing her to shuffle her feet to keep them under her. Scanning her surroundings, she searched for somewhere to wait out the storm. *But where was it safe?* She shuddered at the idea of the tunnels. Before the cave-in she might have considered them, but no longer. Then she remembered her cell phone.

Dashing for the porch, she hoped for some refuge from the storm to make a call. If she could reach Rashelle, they could come back to get her. She wiped the rain off the screen. No service. The storm had probably already taken out cell towers along the entire East Coast. No way to call for help. Then she thought of the landline in the inn. She grabbed the knob on the front door. Through the windows she could see the porch furniture stacked up inside in the sitting room and bicycles leaned against the lobby wall so they wouldn't become flying projectiles outside. If they'd had more warning, the windows would have been boarded up in anticipation of the approaching storm. However, neither of the inn's handymen had been available to perform that task.

Bracing her body against the door, she closed her eyes and turned the knob but it didn't move. Her eyes flew open wide and she stubbornly tried again and again, shaking the knob and trying to force it to turn. "*No!*" She pounded her fists on the door. Locked out. Nowhere to go. In the midst of terrifying danger . . . she was going to die alone.

Turning away from the door, she pushed her back up against it, sliding down into a crouching position. Tears streamed down and melted into the rain drops already glistening on her cheeks. As she envisioned how it was all going to end for her, she began to sob. She rested her bottom on the welcome mat and hugged her legs. Her body shook uncontrollably. Slumping forward, she rested her forehead on her knees. This was it. Amid regrets crossing her mind, she wished she'd gone to the lighthouse one more time. She didn't get a chance to go back up into it after she was interrupted by Renard when she first arrived. How she loved that lighthouse, it always made her feel safe—

*The lighthouse!* Facing the stark reality there were no other options, it was her only hope. She'd have a treacherous climb down the cliff trail and a terrifying hike across the breakwater, but somehow she had to make it.

Gathering her courage, she dashed down the front steps and across the lawn. As she neared the trail through the woods, gusts blew in from the sea, nearly knocking her off balance. She didn't bother to take a last look at her car. In an irrational, twisted sort of way, she felt as though it had betrayed her.

Landing on the muddy, narrow path, she was relieved the trees provided some shelter against the strong wind. Moving only as swiftly as she dared, she took little steps in rapid succession, her feet slipping and sliding as she went. She was desperate to get to the lighthouse before the full force of the storm hit. When she reached the lookout on the bluff where the trail took a turn, Elizabeth slowed down to navigate the switchback. Just as she thought she was clear to speed up, her foot slipped out from underneath her. After some awkward acrobatic maneuvers with arms flailing, she caught herself and resumed her descent to the steeper part of the trail. Stronger winds smacked her face where the trees thinned. Clutching outstretched boughs, she struggled to keep her legs underneath her. Her thoughts returned to Nana, Rashelle, and Kurt, hoping they'd made it safely to the shelter. Lamenting she didn't have a way to get in touch with them, she hoped they weren't worrying about her.

After a precarious and long slog down the slippery path, hands stinging from slipping along tree branches, she reached the bottom, winds buffeting her body. Ahead of her, at the end of the rocky breakwater, stood the stalwart lighthouse, her refuge.

"Not much farther now. Almost there." She endeavored to convince herself with hollow words. There was no turning back.

Stopping first at the shed, she reached in, groping for the key hanging on the nail. Her hand kept missing the mark, swiping at the roughly hewn wall. Reaching in farther, expanding the circle she traced with the tips of her fingers, she finally hit the nail. . . . It was empty.

"Oh my God!" she screamed into the wind. Her words landed on no one else's ears. *Why wasn't the key there? What did it mean? Was there someone in the lighthouse? Did someone forget to hang it up after locking up?* Elizabeth had no idea what the answers were. As she watched the wind whipping the waves over the breakwater, her path to safety, she wondered if she should take the chance and try to cross it.

Out of options, she had to risk it. Girding herself for the perilous trek, she set out across the boulders, leaning forward to keep from being blown backward. Sleet stung. She tried to focus on each step, on her usual technique for crossing the jagged surface. One foot in front of the other, pushing through the wind, she felt a wave crash behind her but didn't dare look. Too close. *One step at a time.* Another wave crashed in front of her. Was the next one going to be over the top? She couldn't let the thought occupy her mind. *One step at a time. Can't be much farther.* Then she made the critical mistake of checking to see how close she was.

The wind caught her and pushed her onto her heels. Forced to take a few steps backward, her left foot missed its mark on the last one. Her shoe wedged down into a crevice between two large rocks. A sharp pain exploded in her ankle, now twisted at an awkward angle. As she let out a groan, a wave crashed over her. Her wedged foot kept her from getting knocked into the frigid water, but the wave pushed her onto her side. Landing hard, jarring her body, she lay on the jagged boulder with her hip throbbing, cold and soaking wet. Her body ached.

Another thunderous wave crashed on top of her. She held her breath until the water subsided. Helplessly pinned on the rocks, she wasn't winning the fight and didn't know how much more she had in her. Lying there with the storm thrashing all around her, fighting for air, she considered giving in and letting Mother Nature do her will.

*Elizabeth, you have to get up! Don't just lie there. Get up!*

It took everything she had left to pull herself into a sitting position. Grabbing onto both sides of her leg, she yanked on the foot stuck between the rocks. It wouldn't budge. If she couldn't move, it meant certain death. She didn't want to die out on the rocks, all alone. Her grandmother would be so sad when they found her . . . if they found her. She thought about her grandfather and how he had battled the storm and didn't win. She wondered if this was how he had felt. Another wave crashed, hitting her hard. Water slammed into her nose and mouth. Overwhelmed by the onslaught, she couldn't manage a cough at first. After a few seconds, her body went into panic mode and fought to get the water out of her nasal cavities. She coughed and choked and gasped.

*Lizzi, get up! Get out of there!*

Thankfully the waves subsided enough so she could catch her breath. Then another wave crashed. This one knocked her sideways again, but she kept herself from hitting the rocks, desperately trying to stay upright. In all her struggling, fighting the waves, her foot had gotten wedged deeper. Her life depended upon getting to the lighthouse. She had to get her foot dislodged—her foot, but not necessarily her shoe! With newfound hope, she loosened the ties enough to extricate her bare foot, leaving the shoe between the boulders. She was running out of time. The waves were getting higher and more violent. Bowing her head to the wind, she sprinted toward the beacon, eyes focused on her footfalls.

Reaching the large wooden door, she threw herself against it. Since it was on the side opposite the wind, it gave her a momentary reprieve. Shifting her feet apart for better leverage, she gripped the handle. Her eyes fell upon unfamiliar hands, scraped from her battle on the rocks. Despite her efforts to pull, the weighty door wouldn't budge. She tried again, this time using so much force her wet hands slipped off the handle and she catapulted backward, landing hard on her backside. Her body jolted on impact. *It can't be locked!* Picking herself up, she lunged at the door, banging on it with both fists. "God, please help me! You're my only—" It felt as though the door was moving toward her. *Could it be?* She stepped back but hung onto the handle for stability as it moved effortlessly in her grasp. Elizabeth was stunned by who came into view. In the open doorway, looking as stunned to see someone out on the breakwater, was none other than her sweet, elderly grandmother. Amelia grabbed hold of Elizabeth and firmly pulled her inside, slamming the door behind them.

"What are you doing here? For God's sake, Lizzi, you could have been killed trying to get down here," she scolded, nearly shouting. "Why didn't you leave when you could?" Reaching behind

Elizabeth, she turned the key in the lock on the old wooden door, securing them inside the lighthouse to ride out the storm together.

"Nana!" Elizabeth shouted over the driving wind and crashing waves just outside the wall. It sounded like the ocean was trying to swallow the lighthouse. "What are *you* doing here?" Her emotions overcame the shock of finding her grandmother there. "I'm so glad to see you!" She hugged her with all her might. Her love for her was boundless.

Finally Amelia pulled away, taking a step back. "Let's find a place to sit this one out." They headed to the wall on the far side, across from the door, the direction the wind was coming from. A couple of old blankets were already scrunched up in a loose pile on the floor. As they held each other and prayed, waves crashed relentlessly against the wall behind them. *Please hold strong. You've stood for all these years. Please protect us from the storm.* The century-old structure creaked and groaned as the wind and waves battered. Amelia and Elizabeth held onto the hope they would survive.

# CHAPTER TWENTY-SIX

As the winds died down a bit, with the eye of the storm approaching, they knew it would only be a brief respite. The tail end would soon follow, often more powerful than the initial assault. The Pennington ladies shifted in place, adjusting their position on the uncomfortable pile of lumpy blankets beneath them.

Amelia cleared her throat. "Lizzi, there's something I need to tell you, once and for all. You should have heard this long ago and if I don't tell you now . . . well, it's time you knew what happened to your parents."

Elizabeth took in a short breath. Finally, and in the middle of a major hurricane, she was going to hear what she'd been aching to know for years.

"We all have kept this from you, thinking we were protecting you from the pain. But I imagine not knowing was just as painful." She hesitated, appearing to gather her thoughts.

Elizabeth was anxious yet fearful to hear the truth.

"Your parents loved you so very much. I don't think I've ever seen two people who got as much joy from being with their child as your mother and father did with you. You meant the world to them. The three of you were inseparable. You did everything together. When one was helping to run the inn, the other was with you.

"Your mother was good at handling the day-to-day operations at Pennington Point. The guests and the staff loved her. She was so sweet. Your father was more of a "big picture" kind of guy who ran the operations from a back room. He grew up to be a lot like his father. He had a big heart and felt a tremendous responsibility to his family. He and your mom made a great team, and the inn was quite successful under their reign." She paused again, perhaps struggling to control her emotions, and then continued. "You were so happy while they were alive. You loved to be where your parents were. All of that changed one day."

Amelia's face fell as she averted her eyes. Elizabeth imagined it was difficult for her to talk about. She'd lost her son and daughter-in-law.

"You were little, about four years old. You and your father had taken a walk down to the lighthouse one afternoon, as you loved to do so often. It became dinnertime so your mother took a walk down to fetch the two of you. It had been particularly windy that day, the fringes of an offshore storm, so the water was unusually rough. No one could have predicted what happened next. Your mother had nearly reached where you and your father were sitting on the breakwater, and to her horror, she watched as a rogue wave crashed on top of you. She ran to try to help. When the water receded, your father was nowhere to be found, but she could see you clinging to the rocks at the water's edge. You were half submerged in the cold water. Frantically, she ran to pull you out. There was no one else around to help. She picked you up and carried you partway up the rocks when another wave knocked her down from behind—"

"She fell and the force of the wave knocked me out of her arms," Elizabeth continued.

Her grandmother's tired eyes squinted in disbelief.

"She was able to keep me from getting sucked in by the sea. But she wasn't so lucky. She was pulled into the water as my father had been."

"How did you know?" Her voice was breathless. "Who told you?"

"No one. I saw it in a dream." It was all coming back to her, crashing through her mind. "It was many years ago, and at the time I wasn't sure what to make of it. I will never forget it, though. So it was my parents . . ." Elizabeth slipped away in her thoughts. Her poor mother and father. Then she thought for a moment of Amelia's connection to the event. "But how did you know what happened to them?" She hadn't been there.

"I also had a dream. Could have been the same one as yours. I think it was your mother trying to show us what actually happened. She must have known we were agonizing over it. You know, loved ones who have passed on have different ways of communicating with us. One way is through dreams. It's their way of helping us deal with our grief."

Elizabeth listened to her with a degree of skepticism, yet deep down had a feeling she should believe her wise old grandmother.

"It's true, dear. If you can resist becoming frightened when these things happen, they can be quite comforting."

Elizabeth flashed back to the images on the rocks in her dream. What an awful way to die. . . . So the newspaper clippings she'd dug out of the old desk in Cecilia's room were about her parents. But one of the articles had a headline about three people being swept off the rocks, not two.

Amelia continued. "At first, we thought all three of you had perished off the breakwater. You evidently were a little dazed after the incident but somehow found your way back up to the inn. You slipped through the lobby unnoticed and went and hid in a closet in the rooms you shared with your parents. It took a while before anyone found you, so they were originally searching for three people. Someone from housekeeping eventually opened the closet and found you covered in blood from your head lacerations and in shock."

Elizabeth ran her fingers across the scars from three small slashes on the side of her chin. At least now she knew where she'd gotten them.

"After that day, you often hid in that closet. We never did figure out why." Amelia chuckled softly. "I thought it might somehow make you feel close to your parents. Do you remember doing that? Do you remember why?"

Elizabeth stared past her, fixated on a rung of the wooden circular staircase, trying to conceive the details her grandmother was sharing. "Aunt Cecilia."

"What?" Amelia arched her eyebrows.

"Aunt Cecilia." Her eyes filled with anger accumulated over the years. Her voice grew firm and loud. "I hid in there because I felt safe . . . safe from Aunt Cecilia. She was always yelling at me when I was little. I hated it. I tried to stay away from her, but she always seemed to find me. The closet was my refuge from her."

Amelia appeared as though she wasn't sure how to respond. "Lizzi, Cecilia is dead. She died before you were born."

Elizabeth tried to process her grandmother's words. "W-what?"

"Cecilia died a long time ago. She wasn't a very happy person to begin with, bitter at the world, self-conscious, suspicious of other people. Never married. She got sick one winter and got really ornery. Her body never recovered. She was gone before spring. It was probably pneumonia. We didn't have all the medical resources back then like we do now. That was back in 1969."

It wasn't making any sense to Elizabeth. "How can this be?"

"Well, some of the guests over the years have reported seeing a ghostly figure of a woman from time to time. I thought perhaps it was the young girl who died at the school. I suppose it could have been Cecilia."

Elizabeth's mind reeled. She struggled to grasp her grandmother's revelation. Her great-aunt was dead, nothing more than a spirit. Her parents died on the very rocks she crossed so many times as a child and, yet, she somehow survived? It didn't seem fair. But then again, so many things in life weren't.

"Elizabeth, I'm so sorry. This must be hard to hear. I never knew when the right moment would be to tell you, so I kept postponing it. I'm sorry."

Choked up, Elizabeth was finally able to speak. "Nana, I love you so much. I know it was difficult for you to tell me." She swallowed hard, caught up in her emotions. "It *was* a bit of a shock to hear." Taking hold of her grandmother's hands, she looked deeply into her gentle blue eyes. Her face appeared drawn and worried.

Wind howling outside the old lighthouse walls signaled an upswell in the hurricane's intensity. It was time to brace for the other half.

"Thanks for telling me, Nana." Reaching over, she pulled her grandmother close and wrapped her arms around her. Amelia hung on tightly as if she didn't want to let go.

Elizabeth's thoughts wandered, and she pulled away. "Nana, why did you come down to the lighthouse instead of going to the shelter?"

Amelia's arms dropped and she turned away. "Oh, Lizzi. You were supposed to go off to the shelter and not worry about me." She looked sideways at her granddaughter. "I couldn't imagine leaving the inn even with a hurricane coming. I thought I should stay with the ship, like your grandfather had done, and go down with it, if necessary. I've never abandoned it when adversity has struck. I've seen this place through good times and bad. And there have been a lot of bad. I told Kurt and Rashelle that I would get a ride from you—"

"And you told me you were going with them," she countered, growing angry with her grandmother for deliberately putting her life in danger.

"Precisely," she quipped as if she wasn't going to let her Lizzi give her a hard time. It was her decision. "I realized the safest place for me to ride it out would be here. So I managed to get down here before it got too rough." She thought for a moment and then admitted, "It was a little scary until you showed up." Winking, she patted her granddaughter's shoulder.

Elizabeth couldn't believe Amelia was willing to die with the inn. No sooner had she completed that thought than she felt hypocritical. It could have been certain death for her if her grandmother hadn't been at the lighthouse to open the door.

The Pennington ladies settled in again to weather the tail of the storm.

# CHAPTER TWENTY-SEVEN

As the wind howled outside, Elizabeth and Amelia huddled close together, nestled on the floor across from the old wooden door. Suddenly, a thunderous crash rocked the wall behind them, jolting them into each other's arms. They watched in horror as water seeped in under the door. Springing to their feet, they gathered the blankets and scrambled for the stairway. Elizabeth helped guide her nana up the first few steps. Amelia ascended slowly, careful not to lose her footing on the weathered steps.

Water rose quickly and covered the floor. Before Elizabeth could reach the first step, she was ankle deep, one sneakered foot and the other one bare. They climbed a dozen or so steps before they sat down on the wider end of the wooden planks a couple steps apart from each other. Huddling with the blankets around their shoulders, they watched the water slowly rise up the stairway. After a while, it seemed to be receding, but the next big wave against the fortress sent more water inside. How far would it rise? Would the lighthouse remain steadfast in the storm? Amelia and Elizabeth prayed it would.

Perched on the steps, listening to the wind howl, watching the water rise and recede, Amelia spoke again. "Lizzi, there is something else I need to tell you."

Elizabeth feared the next words out of her mouth. *What else could she have to say?*

"Lizzi, there may be a problem trying to hang on to this place."

"*What?*" Elizabeth's gasp was drowned out by the roar of the storm. Reeling backward, she banged the back of her head against the metal railing, re-awakening pain in the bloody knot she received earlier in the tunnel. It started to throb, so she rubbed near it to try to relieve the pressure.

"I may not actually be a Pennington." Amelia hung her head as if ashamed.

Elizabeth could scarcely comprehend what her grandmother was trying to tell her.

"You see, when I was little—and that was so many years ago—I was probably around six or seven . . ." She winced as if succumbing to a stabbing pain. "A little older than you were when you lost your parents."

Elizabeth felt a nasty tug in her abdomen. The pain was raw.

"My parents, evidently, were having trouble getting along. I don't remember much of it. I just remember a lot of yelling. They decided the three of us would be better off if they split up. I don't know if they ever got divorced. That wasn't very common back then. I imagine, they argued about who would have custody of me. In all their wisdom, they thought I should decide who I would live with. A tremendous burden to put onto a small child. To do this, they took me for a ride to the shore, to Pennington Point. Back then, the public could hike the trails to the lighthouse during the summer months. There were more trails, including one through the woods that brought you out farther down the access road.

"My parents decided to walk down to the bluff with me and leave me there. I was to decide who I was going to go home with. One waited at the top of the trail through the woods and the other waited at the top of the only trail that exists now. I was to decide and walk to the top of the trail where that parent was waiting. I must have agonized over the decision and took too long, because neither parent was there when I got there. I don't remember which one I tried first, but neither was waiting for me. Each must have figured I had chosen the other and given up."

"Nana, how awful." Elizabeth brushed away a small tear that had rolled down her grandmother's cheek.

She seemed to be lost in reliving her story, not acknowledging Elizabeth's touch. "I must have wandered the property searching for my parents. It got dark and I ended up spending the night in the woods. By morning, I was undoubtedly traumatized over the whole situation." Amelia's eyes filled with tears. "I've often wondered if they really just abandoned me."

"Oh, Nana. No!" Elizabeth jumped up and hugged her grandmother with all her might. "That can't be true." They embraced while the wind howled and the waves continued to crash outside.

Finally they pulled apart and Elizabeth sat down on a step above her, eyeing the water creeping up the steps. The tide was coming in.

Amelia pulled the blanket tighter around her shoulders and continued. "Evidently the couple who owned the school, the Penningtons, found me and took me in. I don't know if I even knew my last name. Evidently they pieced together my story from what I could tell them. They probably searched for my parents, but if they had gone their separate ways thinking I was with the other parent, they wouldn't have realized I was missing and wouldn't have looked."

Elizabeth's throat tightened at the thought.

Amelia appeared to let out an inaudible breath before continuing, "So when I say they took me in, that's what they did. They took care of me. I used the last name of Pennington because they never knew what my real name was. But they never officially adopted me." She let her last comment sink in for a moment.

As Elizabeth listened, the painful reality kicked her in the gut. If Amelia wasn't a Pennington, then neither was she. Perhaps neither of them possessed legal claim to the property. She felt as if the ground was collapsing beneath her. A twinge in her stomach forced her to shift her position on the step.

Amelia went on. "The Penningtons were such nice people. They had two children of their own. A boy and a girl, both were a few years older than me. After we were all grown, I grew very close to the Pennington boy."

Elizabeth had an inkling of where her story was going.

"Things ran their course and, eventually, we fell in love. He asked me to marry him. I couldn't imagine doing anything else. Of course, some people thought we were brother and sister when, in fact, we were no relation at all. We just happened to live under the same roof for many years. His sister was one of those people who opposed the marriage."

"Aunt Cecilia."

"Yes, Cecilia."

"But, Nana, if you were married to the Penningtons' son, then doesn't that make you a Pennington, at least by marriage?"

"In theory, yes. Unfortunately, I haven't been able to find our marriage license, and the files at town hall don't go back far enough. No one seems to be able to put their hands on a copy. This *was* an awful lot of years ago."

"So, why do you have to worry about that? You know you were married to him. Isn't that enough?"

"Not when this real estate attorney says he has proof I don't rightfully own it."

"*What!*" The thunderous winds and waves were taking a back seat to their conversation.

"He claims he has definitive proof and I would be better off selling the property to him at a reasonable price than to lose it outright."

"Nana, this guy sounds like an extortionist. He can't have anything on you. This is absolutely ridiculous!"

"I have no proof that I do own it." Her head hung low as if in defeat.

"Nana, don't you worry another minute about this. I'll figure out a way to get this guy off your back. You certainly *do* own this inn."

Amelia perked up, sitting a bit straighter. "Well, let's see if we even have one after this storm passes through." She managed a half-hearted chuckle.

Elizabeth imagined her grandmother felt as though everything was slipping through her aging, frail fingers. She watched as Amelia wiped away a tear, trying to remain strong, wrapping her arms around herself and closing her eyes. Scooting up as close as she could, Lizzi pulled her nana closer. She worried about how much she'd been carrying on her shoulders all her life, particularly lately. Squirming on her step with an uncomfortable twinge of guilt, Elizabeth was going to do whatever was necessary to help her straighten out the mess.

The two Penningtons stayed cuddled on the stairs for what seemed like an eternity, as if the clocks of the world had stopped, but the wind and the waves were going to go on forever.

With her arm around her grandmother's back, Elizabeth held on tightly. As Amelia's head slid onto Lizzi's shoulder, she vowed to take care of her nana. She would make it all better. She'd show her.

Amelia's eyes opened. "Lizzi, I love you. You've grown into a wonderful, beautiful person. Your parents would be so proud of you. *I'm* so proud of you."

Elizabeth strained to hear her grandmother's soft voice over the storm, gazing down on her like a parent looked upon her young child.

"Thank you for everything you've done . . . everything you will do."

Amelia's eyes got heavy and she fought to keep them open. The ordeal had clearly made her weary. As her eyes closed, her body grew heavier, making it more difficult for Lizzi to hold her perched on the step.

"No . . . Oh, Nana, no!" Elizabeth pleaded. "Nana, please no. Dear God, please don't take her."

Resting her cheek on top of her grandmother's head, her eyes filled with tears. Her heart sank. She didn't think she could feel any sadder. At that moment, she felt a gentle squeeze on her shoulder. Someone knew she needed shoring up. It was going to take all her strength to hold onto her grandmother through the rest of the storm.

# CHAPTER TWENTY-EIGHT

*S*unlight pierced through the small, rectangular windows that punctuated the walls. Elizabeth slowly opened her eyes to the stillness that filled the dimly lit lighthouse. The storm had passed. It was a new day. Glancing to the step below, she realized her grandmother wasn't there. Trying to hold onto her throughout the night had proven too difficult for Elizabeth. At some point, she must have let go when she lapsed into inevitable sleep. In the cruel reality of daylight, her eyes came to rest at the foot of the stairway. There was Amelia in a lifeless heap on the floor. Elizabeth leapt to her feet.

"*Nana!*" She stumbled down the stairs, landing awkwardly at the bottom, her legs stiff from perching on the steps all night. Her knees buckled so she gave into them and knelt next to her grandmother. Although the water had receded, the floor was still wet and slippery. "Nana. I'm so sorry I let you fall! I couldn't hold on. . . . I'm sorry." The horrific image of her grandmother rolling down the stairs started to form in her mind, so she shook her head to clear it before she actually saw her land at the bottom. Reaching out, she touched Amelia's arm, still struggling to believe she was gone. "I'm *so* sorry." Elizabeth pressed her eyes closed as a painful jab pierced her heart.

With her mind racing, Elizabeth tried to envision how to get her grandmother out of the lighthouse. Help was a long way away. Leaning over, she kissed Amelia on the cheek. It was not the soft, warm skin she was used to feeling when they embraced. It made her pause. Struggling to get up, she hobbled toward the door, leaning into it with the left side of her body. She rotated the key and pushed. At first it didn't give so she moved her feet farther away to give herself more leverage. Another heartier push and the door eased outward, letting sunlight flood in.

Turning for one last look at her grandmother, Elizabeth then slipped through the opening, squinting against the bright sun. As her hand brushed up against her leg, it caught an uncomfortable bulge in her pants. Curious if her cell phone could have survived her treacherous trip across the breakwater, she slid her fingers into her pocket, wriggling it out of the soggy fabric. It appeared unscathed. Willing it to work, she pushed the button to turn it on. Nothing. No lights. No sounds. It was dead. Elizabeth's spirit suffered another blow. Getting help was going to be more difficult than she had thought. Disgusted, she shoved the phone back into her pocket and set off on her trek to find help.

In sharp contrast with the tumultuous storm the night before, it was a remarkably beautiful day with a calm, clear blue sky. A pleasant breeze blowing in off the water played with her hair, tousled from a rough night spent on the lighthouse stairwell. Unsure of the hour, Elizabeth guessed mid-morning. The air was warm and the sun already strong. It felt good.

Reminding herself to watch her footfalls crossing the breakwater, she stepped methodically on each boulder as she traversed. Every wave that crashed nearby, no matter how gentle, froze her momentarily in place as she relived the fury Mother Nature unleashed the night before. After several steps, she was still not entirely used to the movement but kept going.

Finally reaching the shed at the other end, Elizabeth wondered what lay ahead on her climb up the hill, through the woods. She pressed on.

Not far onto the muddied, narrow path, she encountered extensive debris, which made the climb much more challenging than usual. She hung onto strong boughs to steady herself while stepping over small branches and climbing over larger ones. Winded, she didn't slow her pace. In spite of the impediments she reached the bluff in due time, stopping periodically to glance out to the lighthouse. It stood as it had for so many years, belying the fury of the storm it had endured and the sadness that remained within it. Elizabeth closed her eyes. A tear escaped and ran down her cheek. She turned away. There was no time to waste, so she continued up the hill.

The top half of the path was as cluttered as the bottom, forcing her to navigate through limbs littering the way, slipping in spots that were particularly wet. Huffing and puffing, Elizabeth reached the top but did not linger. Still standing proudly on the precipice, though bruised and battered, the main building had broken windows and shutters hanging by a thread. Her beloved childhood home had clearly taken the full force of the storm. She drew in a short breath, trying to quell the pain. Her car was nowhere in sight, clearly a victim of the storm's wrath as well. Probably lodged deep in the woods beyond the inn or floating somewhere out to sea. Unable to take in the devastation any longer, she walked toward the access road, trying to draw on her grandmother's strength and focus on what she needed to accomplish. Feeling achingly alone, it was as though she was the only survivor of the storm.

Surveying the extent of trees and branches strewn about, she acknowledged they would pose a challenge for an emergency vehicle to get through. Elizabeth searched her memory for the nearest place to find a working phone and remembered a couple of houses near the other end of the access road. She would start there.

Catching a glimpse at her feet, she laughed out loud. There was no point in having only one shoe on, so she yanked it off. Winding up like a baseball pitcher, she hurled the mud-soaked sneaker into the woods and listened for the soft thud when it landed. She managed a smirk and then set off down Pennington Road. She wasn't sure exactly how long it was, but if she were to take a guess, she would say it was about a mile. Maybe a mile and a half. But then again, she wasn't good at estimating distances. Or time for that matter. She blamed it on spending so much of her existence on the right side of her brain being creative. No matter. Any distance seemed much farther on foot. Especially barefoot.

The partially graveled dirt road proved painful to traverse, and she regretted discarding her only shoe. Too late. Refusing to turn back, especially for a shoe now lost in the woods, she kept walking.

Her bare feet made no sound on the road and the woods were eerily quiet. Her soles were becoming sore. The occasional rock protruding through the packed dirt cut into them and made her wince in pain. Thinking of her grandmother alone in the lighthouse, she kept walking, scanning the woods on both sides as she went.

After progressing several yards, she cast one more look back at the inn and didn't notice a particularly sharp object lodged in the road. It cut into the bottom of her foot, which absorbed the weight of her body. Too much for her to recover from, she yelled out for no one to hear and fell forward, landing hard on the dirt road. The fall cleared her lungs so she lay on the ground fighting for air. Panic crept in. Taking short puffs until she could catch her breath, her scare subsided. Picking herself up, she resumed her hike, oblivious to the cut in the bottom of her foot. Small tracks of blood staggered behind her.

After climbing over countless downed trees and negotiating through crisscrossed branches along the way, Elizabeth could see the end of the road where it met Route 72. There were no cars passing by. It was so still, even the birds remained silent. Not a usual day in Pennington Point. Turning onto the main road, she traipsed toward what she hoped would be civilization and help for her grandmother. The road transitioned from dirt and gravel to hot pavement. Elizabeth was relieved to have something smoother to walk on. After about fifty yards, she came upon a small cottage, and the sight made her heart flutter. It would be a relief to get off the hot pavement.

Crossing the cool grass of the shaded front lawn, she took note of the empty driveway but reasoned the cars were in the detached garage. Dispensing with formalities, she opened the door to the screened-in porch and took the few steps to the front door. It was quiet, but Elizabeth remained optimistic there was someone inside. She banged with the side of her fist. Silence. She listened for footsteps or hushed conversation. Nothing. She banged louder. Nothing. The owners either were at a local shelter or had closed up the cottage and headed back to Connecticut, or wherever they were from, and called it a season. Twisting the knob met with resistance. She considered breaking in, but figured even if she did, the phone probably wasn't working anyway.

Retracing her steps across the porch, she did her best to talk herself into believing she would find someone home at the next house. Letting the porch door slam behind her, she started off across the lawn.

Back on the hot pavement, her feet became so sore she began to limp. With the strong September sun directly above her, perspiration beaded up on her forehead. Her body was heating up, and she grew dizzy. She couldn't remember the last time she'd had anything to eat or drink. Fighting to stay focused, she persevered to get to the next house on the road, walking in the eerie silence until she noticed she was having trouble walking in a straight line.

The heat from the pavement became unbearable, though, so she moved over to the narrow swath of weeds next to the road. Not all that soft but certainly much cooler. As she plodded along, she admired yellow dandelion blossoms, delicate Queen Anne's lace, and light blue bachelor's buttons that dotted the embankment as it dropped down and away from the road.

Her legs grew weary and it became arduous to keep putting one foot in front of the other. Her parched throat made it difficult to swallow. She hesitated as dizziness overcame her. Her knees buckled, and the last thing she saw was the faded white line on the side of the road.

Her body dropped in the weeds, but gravity took over and forced it to roll down the embankment, landing with her arms and legs splayed at awkward angles. She lay at the bottom of the gully, out of view from passing motorists, in the hot, late summer sun.

# CHAPTER TWENTY-NINE

Darkness. *A muffled voice.* Elizabeth tried to open her eyes. Her lids were heavy. The voice again.

"Elizabeth."

It sounded familiar.

"Elizabeth. You have to wake up. Elizabeth!"

Managing to pry open her eyes, she moaned. The bright sunlight forced them closed again.

"Elizabeth! Stay with me."

Trying again, she got them open but her vision was blurry. Blinking and then squinting, she finally understood who was hovering over her, shielding her eyes from the sun.

"Kurt." Her voice was gravelly and barely audible. Her mouth felt like sandpaper.

Slipping his arm around her shoulders, he lifted her into a sitting position.

She groaned.

"Here. Drink this." He pressed a plastic water bottle to her lips and she drank, water dripping down her chin, onto her shirt. He pulled it back after she'd taken a couple of gulps. "Not too much at once," he cautioned. "We need to get you out of the sun. Let me help you up."

Without another word, he hoisted her to her feet. Still groggy, she couldn't support her own weight. He scooped her up in his arms, like a groom carrying his bride over the threshold, and climbed the embankment to where his car was parked on the road. Opening the passenger side door, he carefully placed her on the seat. Once he had secured her seatbelt, he closed the door and ran around to the driver's side. He jumped in, revved the car to life, and cranked the air conditioner to high. Turning to Elizabeth, he offered her more water.

As the fog in her head cleared, she looked to Mitchell to fill in some blanks. "How did you find me?" She remembered getting to the top of the trail from the lighthouse, but after that it was a bit fuzzy, particularly the part where she ended up in a ditch.

"Well, you didn't exactly make it easy for us."

"Us?"

"Yeah. When you didn't show up at the shelter yesterday, we were all worried about you. You and Amelia. Where were you?"

Suddenly, the events of the last several hours came flooding back to her. "Oh Kurt, Amelia is gone. She died in my arms last night." She burst into tears and relayed the story of how she got locked out of her car and the inn so she sought shelter at the lighthouse, only to find her grandmother when she got there. Wiping her tears with scraped and filthy hands left streaks of dirt on her sunburned cheeks.

Kurt seemed to fill in the rest of the details on his own. "All right." He glanced at the water bottle she clutched on her lap. "You stay put in the AC. I'm going to make a phone call."

Stepping out into the hot sun, he nudged the door closed and pulled out his cell phone. He leaned up against the car and used the back of his free hand to wipe sweat from his forehead. Suddenly, he stood up straight, like a soldier coming to attention. Elizabeth could just make out his muffled words.

"Lieutenant, we're going to need the medical examiner."

# CHAPTER THIRTY

A cool, *stiff breeze blew in* off the ocean, pushing Elizabeth's hair across her face. She watched as two men, with black, short-sleeved shirts stamped with MME on the back, loaded the stretcher into a white commercial van. Unable to take her eyes off the black plastic zippered bag containing Amelia's body, she struggled to keep from reaching out and unzipping it. She ached for her grandmother to be able to breathe again. A sharp pain stabbed at her stomach. Her eyes stung with brimming tears. She didn't think she had felt so miserable in her entire life. Amelia was gone. Forever. Elizabeth was alone for the first time. She felt forsaken, like the young girl who may not have been found before the hurricane hit. Surely she had perished. Or had they found her? Her mind raced with horrible images.

The back doors of the van banged shut in succession, rattling Elizabeth out of her thoughts and refocusing her on the pain of losing her dear grandmother. Dizziness crept in, causing her to take a step to the side to shore up her balance. As the van pulled away, her emotions completely took over. She hung her head and sobbed uncontrollably. Overcome by grief, she barely noticed the warm touch on her shoulder and then the tender, strong arms that wrapped around her, pulling her to his chest. She welcomed the refuge and put her arms around his waist. Her whole world had fallen apart. She was desperate to hang onto whatever was left. His hand traced the length of her spine and back up again. Completely lost in his embrace, not wanting it to end, she was glad Kurt was there. He was turning out to be one of the good guys.

With her sobbing under control, Elizabeth stepped back and his warm blue eyes drew her in. She whispered a grateful thank you.

He nodded. "You need some rest, Elizabeth. You've been through a lot, and not exactly unscathed." He eyes went to her scraped and battered legs. She was still barefoot. "We should get you checked out by a doctor, then let you get some much-needed sleep."

Detecting a look of bewilderment, Elizabeth surmised her appearance was nothing less than disheveled, perhaps bordering on pathetic.

"Oh, I'm all right. Don't worry about me. Really. I'm fine. . . . I might be a little tired," she conceded.

Allowing herself a glance toward the inn, Elizabeth was stunned by the devastation left in the wake of the hurricane. The mere thought of the necessary repairs was daunting. Nausea in her stomach returned. Not able to take in any more, she looked away.

"I'll give you a ride to the hotel where a bunch of us are staying in town. If there are no rooms left, you can have mine." Mitchell brought her back to more pressing matters.

"That's very nice of you, but you—"

"I insist."

She didn't protest any further.

Riding in silence for the ten-minute drive to a local chain hotel, Elizabeth watched as the pine trees along the road zipped past in a hypnotizing motion, making her feel dizzy again. She pulled her gaze away. With exhaustion washing over her, she fought it with everything she had left.

When they arrived, Kurt pulled the car into the circular drive, up to the double doors in front. Elizabeth decided to stay put. After the night she'd endured, she didn't have the energy to stand in line to check in. She watched as Kurt approached the entrance to the hotel where he grasped the door and then stepped back to hold it for a young mother struggling to steer a stroller through the doorway while hanging onto the upturned collar of a toddler. Elizabeth smiled. Someday.

Waiting in the quiet of his car, her eyelids grew heavy and her head bobbed in response to her body's yearning to rest. The sound of Kurt opening the passenger door startled her awake. In his extended hand was a card key. She took it from him, relieved to have a place to stay.

"I bumped into Rashelle in the lobby, and she's going to stop by your room to drop off some clean clothes for you."

Elizabeth nodded in acknowledgment. Clothes and a shower might go a long way to lift her spirits. Time would tell if any of her belongings were intact back at the inn. She would cross that bridge another time. Kurt took hold of her upper arm to help steady her out of the car, staying close to her side as they entered the hotel.

Crossing the lobby, she averted her gaze from the staff at the reception desk. If they were looking her way, she could imagine the expressions on their faces from the spectacle of her stumbling through. Better to avoid the situation altogether, so she set her sights, instead, on the elevators. The ride up to the seventh floor was quiet. Thankfully no one had joined them in the lobby, and they didn't have to stop on the way up to let in any other passengers. The doors opened to the antiseptic smell of cleaning supplies mixed with stale cigarettes. Holding onto Elizabeth's arm as they padded down the brightly carpeted hallway, Kurt guided her in a zigzag past two large housekeeping carts parked on opposite sides of the hall, a few feet away from each other, piled high with clean sheets and towels, boxes of tissues, and single-use toiletries.

Farther down the hall was a room service tray, left over from the night before, on the floor in front of a guest room door. Kurt yanked her arm just before she caught a toe on a half-full water glass. At the end of the hall on the right was the room they were looking for. An exit sign hung from the ceiling and pointed toward the doorway across from her room. She slid the card into the slot and a small red light came on. She sighed. All she wanted was to lie down for a while. Three more times she attempted, varying how fast she inserted the card and how long she left it in before removing it. The red light appeared and her patience waned with each attempt. Double-checking the room number listed on the small cardboard folder that came with the card, she verified the number on the door. With her fatigue, she wouldn't have been surprised if she was trying to open the wrong door. Before she could try the card again, Kurt spoke.

"Would you like me to give it a try?" he offered, sounding as though he was trying not to offend her.

Anxious to get inside, she accepted his offer. "Sure. Thanks."

Kurt slid the card in and the green light came on immediately. He stifled a grin.

Elizabeth shook her head, too exhausted to get annoyed. "Whatever." She took the card back from him and squeezed it. The hard edges pressed into her palm. "Damn card keys," she mumbled.

He pushed open the door and held it for her. "Give me a call once you've had a chance to get some sleep, and we'll grab a bite. I'm in room 321." He pulled the door closed behind her, leaving her to the stale smell inside the tidy room.

Her accommodations were set up as a modest two-room suite. She stood in the center of a sitting room with a pullout couch, a small desk across from it, a coffee table, two end tables, and a kitchenette opposite the windows. A flat screen TV was mounted on the wall to the left of the desk. The adjoining room held a small bathroom and a bed that seemed to completely fill the space. The décor was moderately tasteful, and the room was adequately functional.

Flopping onto the couch, she drifted off to sleep but was awakened by the sound of Rashelle's voice and pounding on the door. Straining to remember where she was, she dragged herself from the couch and staggered to the door, wincing at her sore feet. When she opened it, Rashelle had her arm raised, her hand formed into a fist as though her knocking had been interrupted.

"There you are. I've been knocking for a while. Are you all right?"

Rashelle's voice was a little too loud for Elizabeth's liking. Ignoring the question, she glanced down at the clothes tucked under her friend's arm and the shoes dangling from two fingers. "Thanks so much for letting me borrow more of your clothes. I really appreciate it."

"No problem. Hey, look, Lizzi. I'm sorry for everything you're going through. I'm so sorry about Amelia. . . . And sorry about the inn." She swatted at Elizabeth's arm in an awkward gesture of compassion. "Oh, and I thought you could use this, too." Bending down, she picked up a bottle of white wine she must have put down to pound on the door and proudly held it out.

"Thanks, kiddo. You know me too well." Elizabeth took the clothes and wine from her. "My cell phone isn't working." She patted a front pocket of her stained pants. "I'll catch up with you somehow. I'm just going to grab a little nap and get cleaned up," she explained, hoping her attempt to get rid of her friend wasn't too obvious.

"Sounds good. See you later." Rashelle left without another word.

Elizabeth let the door swing shut behind her and placed the bottle on the desk. Having every intention of grabbing a shower to wash off the travails of the past several hours, she put the borrowed clothes on the top of the toilet, dropped the shoes on the floor, but then had a change of heart about the wine. Returning to the sitting room, she decided a little Pinot would taste good. Grabbing the bottle by the neck, she rummaged through the drawers in the kitchenette for a corkscrew to no avail. In frustration she slammed it back onto the counter and then noticed the top. A screw-off. She laughed. "Good thinking, Shelle." Twisting it off, she looked around for a glass, figuring it would probably be cheap, opaque, and plastic. She was pleasantly surprised to see four water glasses and four wine glasses arranged upside down on the counter, each resting on a plain, white paper doily. As she raised a wine glass for inspection, she noted it was small in stature and certainly not the quality that would have been used at the inn, but it would do. She filled it as close to the brim as possible. After placing the open bottle on the counter next to its cap, she headed to the bathroom for a nice hot shower, taking sips from her glass as she walked.

Slipping out of her soiled clothing felt profoundly cathartic. She'd been in them far longer than any clothes were meant to be worn and through more than most would ever experience. Tattered and stained, the only option was going to be throwing them in the nearest trash can. Not even the local charity would be interested.

While the shower warmed up, Elizabeth continued to sip her wine. It swept away the chill in her bones as it trickled down. The reflection in the mirror made her recoil. She looked worse than she'd imagined. Leaning in, she examined the slash marks on her chin that now had new meaning. Leaving her glass on the sink, she slipped into the warmth of the pulsating water, wincing as it hit her cuts and scrapes.

Turning to stand with her back to the shower, Elizabeth embraced the invigorating sensation of the pulsating spray. She wished she could stand there forever, but the heat was making her feel sleepy. As she started to relax, her thoughts switched to her poor grandmother. Her stomach twinged uncomfortably as she grappled with the tragic images. Tears stung her tired eyes. Grabbing onto the stabilizer bar meant for handicapped guests, her whole body shook as she sobbed. Her knees buckled and she collapsed into the tub. The warm water continued to rain down on her while she cried until there were no more tears. Drawing in several deep breaths, she grabbed the bar and pulled herself up, hanging on until she felt comfortable standing on her own. She began to sob again but hung on until she could pull herself together.

Recognizing the need to get out before she drowned, she washed with the tiny bar of soap housekeeping had left in the dish, being careful to give gentle attention to the scrapes and deep cuts on her hands and legs as well as the bump on the back of her head. After drying off with a towel the staff at the inn wouldn't have called bath sized, she slipped into Rashelle's clothes, grateful for her friend's generosity.

Ignoring the shoes for the time being, she snatched her glass from the sink and drained the last couple of sips. Bypassing the steamed-up mirror, she returned to the sitting area and refilled her glass, drinking it halfway down before refilling it, trying to obliterate her pain and the horrific images. Heading for the king-sized bed, she drew the curtains to darken the room and ease her tired eyes. Taking another gulp from her glass, she noticed the clock on the table read 3:00. Her body felt as though it could easily have been a.m. Perched on the edge of the mattress, she threw back the rest of the Pinot and slipped under the covers, her wet hair dampening the pillowcase. In no time, she dropped off.

# CHAPTER THIRTY-ONE

Waking *from a fitful sleep* to a clamorous ringing, it took Elizabeth a few seconds to recognize the sound. The room was so dark she had to fumble to find the phone, knocking the receiver onto the bedside table. Before she managed to get it to her ear she could hear Kurt's voice.

"Elizabeth? Are you okay?"

"I was until the phone rang." She regretted her words as soon as they left her mouth.

"I'm sorry, Liz. It's been several hours and I thought you could use—"

"What time is it?" she interrupted, her voice rough and uneven.

"It's a little after nine."

"P.m.?" She struggled to make sense of it, her head still hazy from being awakened.

"Yes, p.m. I thought you could use a little food."

Elizabeth's body was awake enough to send hunger pangs at the suggestion. "Yeah, I could eat," she admitted. "Give me a couple minutes and I'll meet you in the lobby." She rubbed the sleep out of her eyes.

"See you then."

Groping in the dark, she found the lamp on the bedside table. Closing her eyes tightly, she turned the switch and slowly reopened them. She let out a grunt, replaced the phone receiver, and started for the bathroom. Avoiding the mirror, she went straight to the task of splashing water on her face. Then she realized she had no make-up to use and had no idea what room Rashelle was staying in. She wouldn't be able to borrow from her this time. She also didn't have a comb or brush, so she wet her fingers at the sink and ran them through her hair, hoping to improve her appearance as much as she could so it wouldn't be so obvious she'd just rolled out of bed. Unable to ignore the mirror, she groaned. Hopefully he had a sense of humor. There wasn't much else she could do. She slipped on Rashelle's shoes that resembled black ballet slippers, noting they weren't anywhere close to her taste, and headed downstairs.

When the elevator doors opened, she had a clear view across the lobby and into the bar. Kurt with his blond, wavy hair was perched sideways on a stool so, she imagined, he could easily watch the big screen TV and glance to the elevators from time to time. She got about halfway across before he swiveled on his stool and beamed. He stood up and walked toward her.

"Hey, Elizabeth. Good to see you. The restaurant has closed for the night, but we can grab a bite at the bar if you don't mind."

He didn't seem to notice how horrible she looked. She figured he must have taken a few thespian classes while at Colby. Either that or he was just being compassionate. For that possibility, she was grateful.

"That's fine with me." Then it occurred to her she didn't have her purse. Everything was back at the inn. . . . At least she hoped she would find it when she got back there. "Uh, Kurt, I don't have any cash on me, or credit cards for that matter."

"Oh, hey, don't worry about it. I've got it covered." Leading her by the arm, he motioned for her to take the stool next to the one he'd been sitting on. The bartender dropped a couple of menus in front of them without a word and then returned to restocking glasses in the overhead rack. The short glass in front of Kurt held an amber colored liquid on ice. Jack Daniels, she guessed. The two sat in silence as they perused the short bar menu. When the bartender returned, they both ordered burgers, hers medium and his medium rare. Elizabeth also asked for a glass of white wine, which he poured right away and delivered to her before putting in the food order. *Did she look like she needed it that badly?* She supposed she did.

After a few minutes of sipping drinks and listening to the din of the bar, Elizabeth spoke. "So, can you fill me in on what happened back at the inn?"

"There's really no rush, and there's not a lot I can tell you at this point."

"Yes, there is a rush. I need to get back to work at some point, that is, if my boss hasn't fired me already. The last time she called,

I hung up on her." A knot formed in her stomach at the thought of what she would have to return to.

Ignoring her last comment, Mitchell kept their conversation on the events at the inn. "The investigation is ongoing, but I can tell you what they know so far." His gaze softened toward Elizabeth.

She blushed, wondering if he was hiding underlying feelings. "Oh, go ahead and spill it. How much worse can it be after the last couple of days?" Elizabeth grabbed her glass and took a swig.

Kurt tilted his head as if he knew with certainty it would, in fact, get worse, but he chose not to answer her question directly. "Let's start with the Hutchins. The piece of the puzzle solved before the evacuation was that the Hutchins had given false names when they checked in and are actually the Rizzos. Why they chose to do that is unclear at this point, but they're in custody and have a lot of explaining to do. The poor gentleman you found on the kitchen floor, Joseph Stevens, the accountant, seems to be connected with Hutchins because of the numbers he punched into his cell phone before he died. 2, 1, 0, 1 are the numbers you came up with when you translated from the cell phone keypad to the calculator. Two is the building number for Acadia House and 101 is the room number—the Hutchins' room. Mr. Stevens would have dialed 2101 to reach him on a room phone."

"You mean Rizzo."

"Ah, yes. Rizzo. At this point it looks like he was Rizzo's accountant, but there is no obvious motive for murdering him, so the investigation continues."

Mitchell turned his head to acknowledge Rashelle approaching them.

"Hey, guys. How's it going?" The lilt in her voice seemed forced, and the sigh at the end gave her away.

Elizabeth spun around, eager to greet her. With a tired smile, she stood and hugged her good friend who was now an unemployed inn manager. "So good to see you." She stepped back slightly to include Kurt in the conversation.

"Hey, Mitchell."

"Rashelle."

"Kurt was explaining what they've figured out so far in the investigation before the hurricane hit." Images of the inn's devastation caught her for a moment.

"Mind if I sit?"

"Of course not. Pull up a seat." Elizabeth reached out, gave her arm an affectionate squeeze.

Rashelle grabbed the stool next to hers and pulled it closer. "Okay, so go on." Their focus was back on Kurt.

Before he could get started, Elizabeth jumped in, "I have a question. How is it that you got so involved in the investigation and know so much about what went on? Was that in your job description as the tennis pro?" She could feel the twinkle in her eyes and didn't try to hide it.

At that untimely moment, the bartender appeared to take Rashelle's order. She went for a lobster roll and her usual glass of Chardonnay. He returned to deliver her wine on a small, white cocktail napkin. She took a sip and turned to Kurt to acknowledge she was listening.

"Good question." He swallowed the last of his drink and seemed to enjoy the suspense he was creating. "I was hired by your esteemed general manager," he nodded toward Rashelle, "upon the urging of your grandmother."

They waited to hear something they didn't already know.

"I actually work for the FBI."

Elizabeth's and Rashelle's jaws dropped. Kurt seemed amused with their reaction.

Liz spoke first. "What?" She hadn't seen that coming.

He chuckled. "Well, I'm glad to hear I didn't blow my cover."

"So why were you there?" Shelle didn't see the connection.

"I'm sorry, ladies, it's an ongoing investigation. There isn't anything more I can tell you at this point. But as soon as it's complete, you'll be the first to get briefed on the outcome."

"What about the girl who was missing? . . . Kelsey."

"I'm sorry, Liz. I can't."

Sorely disappointed in his response, it was unbearable not knowing the fate of the young girl. Perhaps Mitchell was trying to spare her more pain, but instead he unknowingly angered her. It was difficult to suppress it. Desperately needing answers, she was furious he wasn't willing to reveal anything.

"But, hey. I owe you an apology." He reached over, and she felt the light touch of his warm hand on her forearm. "I'm sorry you ended up getting shut in the tunnels."

"Yeah, what was that all about?"

"I went back a couple minutes later and opened the hatchway, but you were nowhere in sight."

He held his gaze steady as she glared at him. "I have *you* to thank for this nice little bump." She reached up and winced when she located the partially healed wound.

"Liz, I didn't have much choice. Perkins suddenly appeared around the corner, and if he'd seen you, he would have taken you into custody and it would have gotten ugly. Real quick. Escaping custody is a pretty serious offense, you know."

So is aiding and abetting a criminal, she thought, and had to ask, "So why did you do it? That was a huge risk for you."

"It was a risk I was willing to take . . . for you." His fingers slipped away, leaving a cold spot on her arm. Hurt lingered in his eyes that she didn't comprehend at first.

As his words hit her, Elizabeth reeled from the realization she'd misread him. She had spent so much time questioning his motives—perhaps rightfully so under the circumstances—that she couldn't recognize he was on her side. One of the good guys. And it seemed he had an interest in her that went beyond his professional responsibilities. Hopefully she hadn't done irreparable damage to their relationship.

At that moment, their burgers arrived and the bartender assured Rashelle her order was on the way. The girls exchanged glances and then turned away, gazing lazily toward the big screen TV. The three grew silent as Kurt and Elizabeth started in on their late dinners. Soon after, Rashelle's lobster roll arrived and they all ordered another round. They ate without exchanging words. Only the sounds of the bar's televisions and the loud chatter of patrons filled their ears. Elizabeth longed for a quiet corner—for two.

# CHAPTER THIRTY-TWO

I n the days after the hurricane, while authorities performed an autopsy on Amelia's body, Elizabeth and the staff did their best to clean up at the inn. Lizzi also kept busy making phone calls, determining priorities, and coordinating outside contractors to perform the repairs necessary to make the inn and outbuildings watertight. One of her calls was to her boss to let her know she wouldn't be back to work right away. Since she no longer had a cell, she placed the call from her hotel room late one evening when she could be fairly certain Vera would not be in the office. There was something quite liberating about leaving a message for her, knowing Vera had no way to return her call directly. At some point, she would need to see about getting another cell.

Elizabeth thought her grandmother would have liked the idea of having her memorial service at the inn, next to her garden. Although it was a beautiful, sunny September afternoon, the inn seemed so sad. Plywood covered the broken windows until

Elizabeth could have a chance to decide what her long-term plans were for the property. The front of the main building had suffered extensive damage—there wasn't much of a porch left. Acadia House was so heavily damaged there was talk it should be leveled and rebuilt. Moosehead Lodge seemed to be in much better shape. Some minor repairs should put it back into working order. All of those decisions would be made in time. At the moment, the focus was on saying good-bye to beloved Amelia.

One by one, staff and local neighbors stopped on their way out to speak to Elizabeth as she stood like a sentry at the gate to her grandmother's garden. Everyone had warm, comforting words to share with her. They all seemed to love Amelia. She would be sorely missed. The inn wouldn't be the same, physically because of the storm, but also the ambiance would suffer without Amelia at the helm. Its future hung in a delicate balance.

After the last mourner had passed by, Mitchell approached her tentatively. "Elizabeth, I'm so sorry about your grandmother." She looked into his eyes and could only shake her head. No tears came. Apparently she had used them all up. He wrapped one of his long arms around her shoulders and pulled her close. No words were spoken. Giving in to what she needed, she appreciated his thoughtful touch. When they stepped awkwardly apart, she felt instantly cold. Shaking off a chill, she wanted to grab hold of him again but didn't want to appear as lost and desperate as she felt.

Kurt acknowledged Chief Austin making his way toward them. "Hello, Chief."

"Hello, Mitchell. Miss Pennington." He tipped his hat, appearing more humble than usual. "Sorry to interrupt." The chief extended his hand to Elizabeth. "I just wanted to offer my condolences to you."

"Thank you very much." As they shook, he pressed his other hand on top of hers in a compassionate gesture.

"Elizabeth, you should know that Chief Austin was instrumental in identifying the Hutchins as the Rizzos. He made a huge discovery when he did a search of their room and uncovered a magazine that had their correct name on it. It was the break we needed in the case. After that, it was relatively easy to put the pieces together."

Elizabeth considered Mitchell's words for a moment and then realized what he was trying to do for the chief. Kurt must have seen her going in the Rizzo's room with Rashelle to snoop around.

"Chief, nice work."

"Just doing my job, ma'am."

"Well, we certainly appreciate it. Nice job."

"You're welcome, Elizabeth. I'm sorry that it all turned out the way it did. You and your grandmother didn't deserve any of it."

"Thank you." She averted her gaze, trying to hold herself together.

"And there is some good news in all of this," the chief continued.

Elizabeth looked back, eager for him to continue.

"The lobsterman, Slater, and his passengers were rescued not far off the coast well before the hurricane hit. We may never know if there was a connection with that mishap and the mess at the inn. Either way, none of the passengers were guests of the inn. But at least that part had a happy ending."

Relieved to hear, Elizabeth forced a smile at the news. "That's wonderful. Thank you."

"Well, I'll leave you to carry on. I must get back to the station to see if the state boys need any more assistance." He gave a quick tug at the waist of his pants, as if to ensure it was secure, and then tipped his hat as he turned to take his leave.

"Thanks again, Chief."

After nods and a wave, he strode toward his squad car, a little more spring in his step than he'd had lately. Elizabeth was impressed Kurt had returned the chief's self-esteem to him. What a thoughtful and sweet gesture.

Mitchell gazed into her eyes. "There's something else I need to talk to you about, Liz." He hesitated as if trying to decide how to proceed, pointed to a garden bench for them to sit on, and then continued. "The medical examiner released your grandmother's autopsy report." Their eyes met as they sat down. "It showed she had a high level of a drug called Zoloft in her blood stream when she passed away that suggests ingestion over an extended period of time. Zoloft is an anti-anxiety drug with side effects that include drowsiness. Her doctor told us he'd never prescribed it or any other similar drug for her. Do you have any idea where she might have gotten something like that?"

Confused by the revelation, she shook her head. Her grandmother never liked to take any kind of drugs, over-the-counter or prescription. That certainly didn't sound like something she would have done on her own.

"The fatigue she was experiencing from the drug put an additional burden on her body that was hard for her to handle. With everything going on, she didn't have time to slow down and rest. The ME concluded that the Zoloft contributed to her passing." He allowed her a moment to process that information.

Tears welled up. The evening in the lighthouse came rushing back. Her poor grandmother had been through so much before she arrived on the scene to help. Elizabeth feared that having to shoulder the burden of running the inn on her own also contributed to her passing. Her guilt resurfaced. Asking herself what kind of granddaughter let that happen, she reprimanded herself for not checking in with her more often.

Kurt stood up as Rashelle neared. She approached Elizabeth's side of the bench and put her hand on her friend's shoulder, her face drawn. She pulled away before Elizabeth could reach up and connect with her.

The sad cries of gulls riding the current above them seemed to underscore the mood.

"What does all this mean? Was my grandmother . . . murdered?" she demanded.

Rashelle looked from Elizabeth to Kurt.

"It's possible. We can't be sure. Hopefully we'll have more answers soon."

His response didn't help. She needed to know. The conversation stalled as they considered the questions left unanswered.

Perking up, Elizabeth threw out a random thought. "I wonder what happened to my drawings. My portfolio."

"One of the officers may have picked it up. I don't know what shape it might be in after the storm. But we can certainly look."

Mitchell examined her face closely as if surprised she was at all concerned about something that seemed so trivial.

"It's not that big of a deal. I just thought perhaps I could get it back. Artists can be quite possessive of their work, you know."

"We'll certainly try," he assured her, pressing on to the next topic. "The room the Hutchins requested happened to be the same location the missing student had disappeared from years ago. This was either a tremendous coincidence, or somehow someone knew."

Elizabeth was skeptical. "I don't see how."

"Well, anyway, Renard's confession does fit if we put it into the right time frame. Looks like we solved that age-old mystery of the student's disappearance. Of course, now he's facing prison time. Apparently, the situation of the missing guest brought back too many memories, ones he'd tried to suppress. With them came a flood of emotions, including tremendous guilt. Unfortunately, before he decided to confess, he was afraid his brother would snitch on him and felt compelled to silence him."

"He killed Gerard?" Elizabeth asked.

"Yeah."

"So Gerard wasn't off searching for parts for the lawn mower. The creep killed his own brother."

"He agreed to show us where he buried both bodies so we could exhume them. There won't be much left to the girl, but if we can contact the parents or someone in her extended family, I'm sure they would want some closure."

Elizabeth had a good idea of where at least one of the bodies was. Things were not right in the section of the woods where

Mitchell had caught up to her after she escaped the Lieutenant's squad car. It was too quiet there. Eerie.

"And that's about the long and short of it at this point. That's certainly enough for now." Kurt looked at Elizabeth, who held her gaze just beyond him.

"So, what happened down in the tunnel . . . to me? I know there was a cave-in, but was it caused by human intervention?"

"It would take an engineer to determine if it happened naturally or if someone's deliberate actions caused it. Apparently you got grazed on the back of the head by a support beam. Fortunately, you didn't receive the brunt of the force. A couple seconds difference and you might not have been sitting here right now."

Elizabeth rubbed the back of her wound, which was healing nicely. Someone had saved her life. Remembering the voice in the tunnel, she wondered if it had been her mother. Her gut told her it was. "I guess I've lived to design another day." She allowed herself a little humor.

Looking awkward, with her hands stuffed in her pockets, Rashelle chimed in at last. "Lizzi." She bit the edge of her lip. "I need to apologize. I haven't been completely honest with you, and I'm very sorry."

Elizabeth wasn't sure she wanted her dear friend to continue. Whatever had she done?

"Before all the craziness around here, I had a little affair of my own."

Elizabeth raised her eyebrows.

"I'm so sorry, Liz. I guess I wasn't prepared for the abrupt change in lifestyle coming here from the city. It's so quiet, especially at night. After a while I couldn't stand it anymore. There was nothing to do. I needed a little excitement in my life, and I certainly wasn't going to find it at the inn. So I went into town on my nights off to do the bar circuit, meet new people, maybe find a guy. Well, I did meet a guy who I was absolutely crazy about. Once he knew where I worked, he was straight up with me and told me he'd been fired as the tennis pro not too long ago."

Rashelle seemed to take no notice of Elizabeth's tsk and continued. "At first, I was shocked and disappointed. I wasn't sure what to do. I felt like I was cheating. Unfortunately, that made our relationship that much more exciting. I know that probably sounds silly . . . immature. Because of the excitement, I kept it going even though I knew we shouldn't. I had no right to do that. I know Aaron wasn't supposed to be anywhere near this place. Then I wrecked my car, though, so he had to pick me up. I think it was fun for him, too. I'm sorry, Liz."

Her friend's behavior was trivial in comparison to the big picture, and Elizabeth had already put the pieces together, yet part of her still felt betrayed. She was at a loss for words.

Rashelle backed away from the bench. "We'll talk later when everything else is all sorted out. I'm sorry to have added to your burden. Not a very nice thing for a friend to do, I know. I'm truly sorry." Uncharacteristically somber, she walked to where a rental car was parked on the drive, a dark four-door sedan of some sort. Elizabeth couldn't bear to watch as she drove away, down the access road away from the inn. Her heart ached.

Mitchell seemed anxious to wrap up the conversation and picked up where Rashelle left off. "The state police have Aaron

Gabeau in custody and are interviewing him to see if he has any connection to all of this. They will also be speaking with Rashelle." Silence hung in the air to signal the topic was officially over. "Liz, why don't we get out of here? I imagine you could use a change of scenery about now."

Although a few of the loyal staff were still cleaning up from the service, stacking chairs salvaged from the tunnel, the last of the mourners had paid their respects and taken their leave. "Well, I'm at your mercy until I can get another car. I guess I'll have to pick up a rental somewhere. I've got to return to the city and see if I can pick up the pieces of my career."

The sound of a truck engine with its wheels crunching on gravel made their heads turn. It was a flatbed with a delivery. It was her beautiful silver Z4.

"What the—?"

Kurt beamed at her reaction. "Your car suffered some body damage, but it looked fixable. The wind had pushed it up against the bushes along the woods, which may have served as a cushion for it. It must have been out of sight from you when you returned to the inn after the storm. I'm sure there were much more pressing priorities at that point so you overlooked it. We scooted it out to a local auto body shop and asked if they could put a rush on it."

Elizabeth allowed herself a genuine smile. The driver had left the truck idling on the circle and trudged toward them, a key fob dangling from two extended fingers. Mitchell took it and handed it to her.

The lump in her throat made it difficult to speak. "Thanks, Kurt. This means so much to me. I can't thank you enough." She threw her arms out and hugged him tightly. As he hugged her back, she could feel her heart starting to mend. With time, everything would be all right again. She had to believe it.

As the delivery guy swiftly rolled the car from the tilted flatbed and landed it on the driveway, she didn't try to suppress a grin. She turned back to Kurt with a glint in her eye. "Would you like to take a ride with me?"

He seemed tickled she'd asked. "Of course, let's go." Slipping his arm around her, they started across the lawn to the driveway.

Thrilled to be taking him for a spin before she hit the highway back to the city, she felt as if she was melting. It had been too long since she'd felt this good.

Climbing in, she was pleased to see it was incredibly clean. A new lavender air freshener dangled from the rearview mirror. "Cute." She punched the ignition button and the engine sprang to life, sounding like a cat purring in her ears. Pushing the gearshift into first, she eased off the clutch and crunched across the gravel drive.

Elizabeth slowed down long enough to glance back. It looked like her great-aunt was standing in the window of one of the front rooms, her room, watching her niece go. She was sure Cecilia would always be watching over the inn. It pained Elizabeth that she'd been unable to deliver on her promise to her. They'd saved the inn from the attorney getting his greedy hands on it, but were powerless against Mother Nature's wrath.

# CHAPTER THIRTY-THREE

*Moving a little more slowly* than usual, Elizabeth slapped at the snooze button to give herself a few more blissful minutes of sleep. She'd driven straight through without stopping the night before and had arrived at her apartment late in the evening. As difficult as it was to leave behind her childhood home in such a deplorable condition, she also carried with her the raw pain from the unspeakable human tragedy. She didn't think she would ever recover from the heartbreak of losing her grandmother, and it bothered her she didn't know if the young girl had been found. All she could do was remain optimistic and believe they were doing everything they could.

Already missing the inn—the comfortable familiarity of it, the salty sea air, and the warmth of her grandmother's hugs—the corners of her mouth curled down into a pout when she realized she was going to miss seeing Kurt as well. She hoped he would get back to her soon and fill in the missing pieces.

Mentally and physically drained, she dragged herself out of bed and set out on her usual commute to Loran Design. She had no idea what was in store for her or what mood Vera was going to be in. A second cup of caffeine seemed like a good idea, so she stopped into her favorite coffee shop on the walk from the parking garage.

Taking in the pungent aroma as she entered, Elizabeth was comforted by the familiarity of it. It was a local, family-owned shop, not a high-priced national chain, and she felt good about giving them her business. The husband and wife owners were a cute couple who looked like they might be Italian, maybe Greek. It was hard to place their accents. Exchanges were brief. Always working side-by-side behind the counter, they swiftly filled coffee orders while offering fresh-from-the-oven, homemade pastries and muffins. Elizabeth was one of the regulars, and they always acknowledged her when she approached the counter.

With a hot coffee in hand, she continued her pedestrian commute in the morning sunshine, content to be walking next to and through groups of people she'd never met before. She slowed her pace to take in the sights and sounds of the city, which she never wanted to take for granted, and to postpone the inevitable. Seeing Vera face-to-face.

Rewinding the video in her head to the part where she hung up on her boss, Elizabeth feared Vera would fire her on the spot for insubordination, but held out hope she needed her and could possibly forgive her. Eventually, she reached the revolving doors of her building, slowing from the last person who had entered, and pushed the nearest glass panel. Starting through the half-circle motion, it crossed her mind to keep going all the way around and jump back out onto the street again. She rolled her eyes and groaned. *Just do it, Elizabeth. Get it over with.* She exited and crossed the lobby.

Ascending to the twenty-second floor, alone with her thoughts, she ran through a couple possible scenarios of her inevitable meeting with Vera. Neither was pleasant. The doors opened into the lobby of Loran Design. No one was at the front desk and no one sat in the waiting area furnished in ultra-modern, off-white leather seating. Elizabeth took in the familiarity of it all and turned right toward her office. Fortunately, she didn't have to pass Vera's on the way. A few minutes to herself would be ideal to gather her thoughts and finish her coffee. Her boss could wait. She'd waited this long.

As Elizabeth approached the conference room on the left, she could hear a male voice. Recognizing it was Drescher, she slowed her pace. Her heart sank when she realized she didn't have her portfolio and had nothing to show him. Nothing to prove she'd been working hard on his new project while she was away. Although the portfolio had somehow made it back to the inn, the damage from the storm destroyed the drawings. She'd have to start over again. Panic rose inside her. As she quickened her pace to slip past, she heard him say, "You and I both know this is going to happen the way I want it to. We also both know there will be serious consequences if it does not."

Unsure she wanted to know what he'd referred to, Elizabeth kept walking with her eyes forward, anxious to be out of range of the rest of the conversation. Once in the privacy of her office, she focused her attention on settling back in.

Her space was decorated with a modern, updated feel. Since it was an inside office, there were no windows, but it was still bright and airy with light-colored grasscloth wallpaper. A light wood desk and credenza with sleek lines took up most of the space. There was also a small round work table framed by two ghost chairs in one corner. Abstract prints were tastefully hung on three of the walls. An open-concept shelving unit occupied the fourth.

Once her laptop booted up, she busied herself with checking emails. As she scrolled through the long list of unopened mail, it dawned on her that one of her first priorities needed to be replacing her cell phone. It had been a welcome relief not having one since the hurricane. No calls from a persistent client and, better yet, no calls from her obnoxious boss. But she needed to get one now that she was in the city and back to work.

A nagging feeling tugged at her gut that she was keeping Vera waiting. As if on cue, Sara stuck her head in the doorway.

"Elizabeth, so glad to see you're back, and I was sorry to hear about your grandmother. Not what you were expecting from a weekend away, I'm sure. Listen, I can't hold her off any longer. When you get a chance—well as soon as you can, Vera would like to see you in her office."

Squinting her eyes in disbelief, Elizabeth asked, "How did she know I was here already?" She didn't expect an answer. They both knew Vera had this uncanny sense of what went on at Loran Design. It was almost creepy. Elizabeth's stomach clenched tighter. She couldn't procrastinate any longer. Swallowing hard, she nodded to Sara. "Okay, I understand. I'll be right there."

Striding down the hall as confidently as she could pull off, she tiptoed past the conference room Drescher occupied and then made her way through the lobby. Throwing back her shoulders, she stepped into Vera's doorway, raising her fist to knock lightly on her open door. To Elizabeth's surprise and partial relief, Vera was not at her desk, but she decided to wait for her, anyway. After all, she'd garnered the courage to approach her, so she wasn't going to waste the energy that had taken.

Vera's office was decidedly dark and bordering on depressing. Venetian blinds were open but turned upward, minimizing the amount of outside light that entered the room. Her oversized mahogany desk faced the door and had a masculine feel to it. A matching credenza was pushed up against the wall behind it. A pair of post-impressionistic prints hung on the far wall, and a small sculpture adorned a pedestal between the two windows that looked out onto the streets of Manhattan. Elizabeth noticed one of Vera's skinny, brown cigarettes smoldering in a cheap black plastic ashtray on her desk. A wisp of smoke snaked its way upward, disappearing five or six inches above its source. Clearly she hadn't been gone long.

On the credenza sat Vera's purse, a signature satchel bag by Louis Vuitton splayed open. A small brown container sat next to it. Elizabeth's eyes grew wide. Throwing caution aside, she rounded Vera's desk and snatched up the prescription bottle with a small white childproof twist-off cap. Her heart beat faster as she turned it over to read the label. Zoloft. She jumped when she heard Vera's voice.

"Hello, Elizabeth. So good to see you. I was so sorry to hear about your grandmother." Vera was sporting a mauve-colored suit in raw silk, matching two-toned stilettos, and the customary bulges in the jacket pockets.

Elizabeth glared at her boss.

Vera's eyes moved to the bottle in her employee's hand. Her eyes narrowed and deep lines creased her forehead. "Can I help you with some—?"

"It was you!" Elizabeth couldn't believe her boss was involved with the events at the inn. But why?

Vera took a step back. "Whatever are you talking about, Elizabeth?"

"You know exactly what I mean!" she asserted, disgusted her boss was denying her involvement. Elizabeth clamped her jaw as she marched toward Vera, holding the prescription bottle out in front of her. "How could you? What the *hell* was in it for you?" Her voice grew louder with each sentence. "You murdered my grandmother." Elizabeth's face was so close to her boss', she looked uncomfortable. For once, their roles were reversed.

Vera's mouth fell open. If she was feigning surprise, she was a very good actress.

"Elizabeth, I can assure you I have no idea what you're talking about." Her voice matched the volume of Elizabeth's but then quieted. "Think about what you're saying." Her sudden, gentle demeanor was uncharacteristic of Vera. "I know you must be very upset about your grandmother, and I'm so sorry that it happened. Truly I am. But I don't think you really know what you're saying. Maybe you came back to work too soon. If you need to take more time, take it. We'll just forget this whole conversation happened." She paused and gazed upon Elizabeth, perhaps searching for a clue to what she was thinking. Vera's face twisted into a piteous sneer.

Stepping back, away from her boss, Elizabeth needed to run from her. The situation had turned surreal. She'd made an incredible, unthinkable accusation. Without another word, she placed the prescription bottle on Vera's desk and strode to the door, brushing past her boss as she went. Her eyes were glazed and fixed on the door. Staggering slightly, she put a hand out to steady herself in the doorway. Painfully aware of Vera's silence behind her, Elizabeth gathered herself and stormed out.

Her head pounded as she staggered down the hall, needing to put as much distance between her and her boss as possible. In her haste, she didn't notice if Drescher was still in the conference room when she passed. Once inside her office, she closed the door, wishing it had a lock. Her mind raced. What had she done?

The sudden clanging of her desk phone jarred her from her thoughts, and she slammed her back against the door. When the ringing stopped, it hit her. In the quiet of the small space, she realized her office phone was her only means of communication with anyone, particularly outside of Loran Design.

The clock on her credenza ticked loudly, echoing in the silent room. Frightened by the encounter with her boss, her survival instincts kicked in. Opening the door slightly, she flipped the light switch off and then walked around to the other side of her desk. Pulling her chair partway out, she slid into place under the desk and then pulled the chair back in as far as it would go. She settled in with her back up against one side, her legs pulled up to her chest and arms wrapped around them. It was a dark, but familiar place.

After no answer at the other end, Kurt ended the call. Fearing she had walked straight into the face of danger, he tossed his phone onto the passenger seat and climbed in behind the wheel.

# CHAPTER THIRTY-FOUR

*Struggling to keep her* breathing steady and quiet, Elizabeth didn't know how long she could stay tucked out of sight, but she needed time to think. The confrontation in her boss' office seemed more like a nightmare than anything real.

Suddenly the light turned on. She flinched but held still, listening for footsteps. Someone walked around her office, treading softly on the carpet. Elizabeth watched to see if anyone came into view from her perspective down under. Finally she saw a shoe. A man's black shoe. Then the second one moved next to the first. They were pointing toward her credenza. Having a feeling she knew who the shoes belonged to, she placed her hand over her mouth and nose to stifle any possible sounds from escaping. She hoped he would just leave. Then came the voice from the doorway.

"That's Elizabeth and her grandmother." It was Vera. Elizabeth surmised the male she was talking to must be pawing through her photos on the credenza. The subtle rattle of the frame being returned to its original location made her uncomfortable he was handling something so personal. The photo had been taken years earlier when her grandmother attended her college graduation, a very special occasion Elizabeth felt so fortunate to have been able to share with her.

Then came the second voice. "Very sweet." He made no attempt to hide his insincerity.

This confirmed her suspicion it was Drescher.

The shoes left her field of vision and made their way back to her office door.

"I'm sure she hasn't gone far." Vera sounded smug.

"Well, her office was dark, so maybe she's already left."

"She just got here! She better not have left. Especially if she didn't tell *me* first!"

Elizabeth cringed at Vera's loud, grating voice. Apparently her suggestion to take off more time was disingenuous. Starting to perspire, her back and legs stiffening, she felt trapped.

The light in her office went out and their voices continued down the hall out of range.

She waited and listened. No discernable sounds. No lights. No voices.

The still of the office rang in her ears. *Where had everyone gone?* Finally brave enough to scoot out from under the desk, she grabbed hold of the arms on the chair and peered over her desk into the hall. Nothing. Crawling back under, she waited some more. No one knew she was there, so she felt safe. The only sound was the clock on her credenza. *Tick. Tock.* The ticking echoed in her head. She wished it would stop.

# CHAPTER THIRTY-FIVE

W*aking to darkness*, drenched in sweat, she had no idea how long she'd remained hidden. Even if she could see the clock on her credenza from where she was, it was too dark to make out the time. Listening intently to her surroundings, she felt the need to escape her close quarters. She wanted out of Loran Design. Without knowing if anyone was still there, the safest way to exit would be down the back stairs used only for fire drills.

Slipping down the hall, she reached the door and pushed the horizontal bar. This wasn't the circular staircase at Pennington Point Lighthouse with only a few flights to descend, there were twenty-two floors. Elizabeth hung onto the railing. Her shoes clicked noisily, echoing in the stairwell. Signs on the doors displayed floor number . . . 21, 20, 19 . . . Although gravity was in her favor, her legs grew sore. She ignored them and kept moving . . . 15, 14, 13 . . . At twelve, she had to stop briefly. Her legs felt wobbly. They were starting to burn. Time to make the gym a priority.

Elizabeth pressed on . . . 10, 9, 8 . . . Stopping again to give her legs a break, she listened for a moment. *Was that the sound of a door closing?* All was quiet. Nothing. Then footsteps above her. She drew in a quick breath and set off again. Eight stories to get down as fast as possible. She didn't want to find out who was closing in on her . . . 5, 4, 3 . . . She was close to the bottom but the footsteps were louder. *Who was in the stairwell with her?* Forcing her legs to keep moving on to the second floor and finally the first, she pushed open the exit and burst into the alley but eased the door closed. Scanning the space between the buildings, she saw no one. Dumpsters were scattered throughout the narrow passage. Frantically trying to get her bearings, she needed to head toward Lexington. Turning right, she ran as fast as her legs would carry her. Halfway up the alley her left foot landed in a pothole and her ankle rolled. Pulling up on her other foot enough to catch herself, she resumed running, but with a noticeable limp in her step. The exit door behind her slammed shut, but she didn't look back.

When she hit the plaza in front of the building, she surveyed the street as she ran to the curb, waving her arm and whistling. A yellow cab pulled up. A light rain was falling but she barely noticed. Opening the back door, she started to climb in, but a hand grabbed her from behind.

A familiar voice assured her, "Elizabeth, it's me."

Pivoting away from his voice, her back slammed against the side of the taxi.

"Kurt!" It took her a second. "What are you doing here? You're a long way from Maine." She smiled with relief.

"I thought you might want to hear the results of our investigation . . . and I wanted to make sure you're okay." Genuine concern filled his eyes.

Suddenly she became aware her suit was rain-drenched and her hair was tousled from her run down the stairs.

He appeared amused by her unkempt appearance, a state she had been in far too often lately. At least she had make-up on this time.

Becoming self-conscious, she ran her fingers through her hair to try to put it back into some sort of mediocre coiffure.

As Mitchell's amusement turned to concern, he offered her his jacket. Elizabeth tried to convince him she was fine. In spite of her objections, he insisted.

They crossed the street to a neighborhood bar, one that Vera and Elizabeth had visited on a few occasions. STIR had an uptown, metro feel with contemporary lighting and seating, most of which were unoccupied. The air was stale, but tolerable, and the canned music had an elevator montage flavor to it, which wasn't her taste, but she could ignore it. They found a quiet corner and ordered a round of drinks. Although the bar was known for its martini menu, they stuck with their usuals—Pinot Grigio for her, Jack Daniels on the rocks for him. As the standard basket of pretzels and dipping sauces arrived along with the drinks, Elizabeth stole a glance across the table, thrilled to see Kurt and relieved to leave behind whomever was in the stairwell with her.

They shared small talk between sips, but Elizabeth was anxious for him to get started. She pulled the lapels of his jacket up closer around her shoulders and looked to him to begin the debriefing.

"Elizabeth, you may find this hard to believe . . ."

"Go on," she implored, not understanding his hesitation.

"Your client . . ." He hesitated again, perhaps buying himself time to choose his words carefully. "Your client, Jack Drescher, was involved in all of this." He let that sink in.

She sat back to put distance between her and something she couldn't wrap her mind around. "What? Kurt, what are you talking about?"

"Evidently he had some business dealings that had gone sour recently and was not doing well financially. Actually, that's an incredible understatement. Apparently, he was so over-leveraged he was desperate. His accountant, who was the now-deceased Joseph Stevens, had refused to sign off on a set of financials Drescher had prepared in the hopes of securing additional financing. Stevens refused to have his name associated with the statements because they were not only misleading, but downright false. Completely fabricated. So, without the CPA's blessing, the bank refused Drescher any additional credit. As a result, he was becoming insolvent. He had dwindling liquid assets to work with on a day-to-day basis, and it looked like his business was coming to a grinding halt. In his mind, the inn was his last hope, so he began several months ago harassing poor Amelia about selling the place."

"So he was the real estate attorney who wouldn't leave her alone?" Elizabeth followed along, but was incredulous.

"Yes. He pretended to be an attorney in the hopes of coercing her to sell the inn for next to nothing. The place could have meant millions to him. A prime piece of coastal Maine real estate. We think initially his plans were to build luxury condos. But when cash became more of a problem, he switched his plans to buying it cheap and selling it quickly to the highest bidder. That could have solved his financial problems in one transaction."

"Oh my God! But how would he have known about our inn? I know he and I never talked about it. Our discussions were always strictly professional." She looked at Kurt and furrowed her brow. "Vera."

He shrugged his shoulders in a gesture of "could be."

Elizabeth imagined Vera chatting away with Drescher over drinks and inadvertently passing on personal information about her. Perhaps it hadn't been so inadvertent.

"Right. Well, most of the harassment came in the form of phone calls, but then he took it up a couple notches and started sending letters, very professional-looking letters as this fictional attorney he was portraying. . . . Your poor grandmother."

Elizabeth squirmed from the weight of her guilt. Had she been there sooner, maybe she could have been more helpful. She wished her nana had called earlier or, better yet, wished *she* had thought to call her grandmother. Unfortunately, she'd have to live with that.

"We had been tracking Drescher's movements in his business dealings throughout New England when we made the connection between him and Pennington Point Inn. As the tennis pro there, I was able to maintain a good cover while I kept an eye on things up close. We knew it was a matter of time before he slipped up and we could nail him. He's now facing a long list of charges, including extortion and murder. Ironically, the financial problems that prompted all this were so trivial in comparison."

"Yeah. Seems like it really got out of control." A client she had respected on a professional level had done the unthinkable.

"I'll say. He thought he could convince Amelia she didn't rightfully own the property."

"Yes!" Elizabeth recalled their conversation in the lighthouse. "My grandmother told me she couldn't find her copy of their marriage license and had no luck at town hall."

"Well, we didn't give up on that. We put someone on it. I think the town clerk was too lazy to go into storage when Amelia asked. But it's amazing how motivated she became when we flashed an FBI badge. The oldest records had never been put on microfiche or into any other type of long-term storage. They were carelessly thrown into boxes and stored off-site when they moved into the new town hall. It was a minor miracle they still existed and could be read. We located a copy of Amelia's marriage certificate and the deed to the inn. Case closed on those questions."

"Thank God." Her relief was palpable. "If only she were around to hear this."

"Oh, I think she knows." He reached over and touched her hand.

Elizabeth allowed her gaze to fall on a distant point across the room. Trying to process what Kurt was saying, she couldn't help but wonder if this had anything to do with all the times she had rejected Drescher. Was this payback? Part vengeance, part greed? Dirty son of a bitch.

Mitchell continued. "Evidently Amelia wasn't caving in like he wanted her to. So he decided to pump up the pressure by making things miserable on a daily basis for her and the staff, to the point that no one would want to stay or work at the inn. Apparently his brother-in-law owed him a favor or two, so Drescher coerced him into checking into the inn for the weekend to fan the flames."

"Hutchins—or Rizzo." Elizabeth was keeping up.

"Exactly. Bill and Lisa Hutchins were really James Rizzo, Jack's brother-in-law, and his wife, Ann, Drescher's sister."

Elizabeth fought back her rage toward the Dreschers and Rizzos, every last one of them.

"The Rizzos pretended to have a daughter who went missing."

"So there was never a Kelsey Hutchins who was feared dead?" Her teeth clenched in anger.

"No. That was merely an elaborate distraction for us and another black mark on the inn to dissuade potential guests from booking reservations there."

"They had half the Maine State Police out searching for that girl."

"Don't worry. The Rizzos, too, will be prosecuted to the fullest extent of the law. They have racked up filing a false police report, obstruction of justice, interfering with a police officer, aiding and abetting a felon. The list goes on.

"On top of it all, Drescher lured his accountant, who wouldn't sign off on his financials, to Pennington Point under the pretense of burying the hatchet, so to speak. Instead, Drescher buried the hatchet in him, probably thinking he could pin it on Tony, if he used his knife, or you and Rashelle by filming you finding the body, which we think he accomplished by hiding in the wine cellar. It looks like he didn't stay long. Just long enough to take care of his accountant. Probably hung out in the Rizzos' room. He could slip in and out pretty easily with its location at the far end of the compound.

"The package we found in your car, that supposedly contained the missing girl's necklace, was actually from Drescher. We think it was originally supposed to be a token of his affection for you, but when you left unexpectedly for the weekend in Maine, it suddenly took on a whole new purpose."

Staring intently at the floor, Elizabeth couldn't ignore the reference to Drescher's feelings for her. "Somehow, whatever they get doesn't seem like it's enough for what they've done."

"I know. But they all will certainly see prison time. Drescher also had his nephew involved in this mess, too."

"Jimmy."

Mitchell raised his eyebrows, clearly impressed. "Yes, again. He got himself hired as an all-around handy guy, helping in all areas of the inn's operations, wherever he was needed. He got his foot in the door by first befriending Slater."

Elizabeth felt her face flush with mounting anger.

"He asked Slater to recommend him for the job. So since his various and sundry duties took him all over the inn, he was able to slip in and out without anyone getting suspicious or asking questions. Drescher had him distributing those handwritten notes asking about the missing girl. His intention was to further stir up the pot and to legitimize the search."

Elizabeth realized she wasn't the only one receiving the mysterious notes. "I never thought I could feel this much hatred toward someone."

"I understand. But that wasn't all he was distributing." He paused again.

Narrowing her eyes, she dreaded what he was going to say next.

"From what we can tell, Jimmy was also the one who was delivering Zoloft to Amelia."

Elizabeth's nostrils flared and her fists clenched tightly.

"He apparently brought drinks to Amelia under the guise of delivering refreshments from the kitchen, and they were laced with the drug."

Elizabeth jumped up, slamming her palms on the table. "*That bastard!*"

Skirting around to her side, Kurt grabbed onto her shoulders. As she burst into tears, he pulled her into his arms. She cried softly with her face buried in his chest. After a while, she lifted her head, having trouble accepting the revelation. It was bad enough when it looked like someone might be slipping her grandmother the drug. But somehow, it was so much worse hearing who actually did the dirty deed.

Suddenly, her knees buckled. Kurt grabbed her more tightly around the torso, easing her back into her chair, propping her upright. "Breathe, Elizabeth, breathe." His face inches from hers, he watched her closely.

Blinking to stay focused, her head bobbed for a moment and then stabilized. He kept his arm around her back to support her. When she raised her hand to indicate she was all right, he pulled away but kept within a safe distance.

"Sorry. I don't know what came over me."

"Oh, Elizabeth, no worries. This is a lot to take in."

Gazing through her tear-filled eyes, she was so glad to see him again, even if he was the bearer of bad news. "So Vera was never involved?" Elizabeth cringed when she thought back to her accusation in her boss' office that morning. "I found a bottle of Zoloft on her earlier."

"It doesn't appear so. Zoloft is a pretty common drug. Readily available. We have agents tailing Jimmy and should have him in custody shortly."

Even so, she didn't know if she could ever trust Vera again. She was so connected to Drescher and determined to keep him happy, no telling what she was capable of doing for him or any other client. She'd told him about the inn. Elizabeth was sure of it.

"God, it's incredible how screwed up things can get, especially when you have no control over them."

It would take time, but she knew eventually she would be able to accept what had happened at the inn recently and so many years earlier with Renard and the missing student. She needed to move on. And maybe that meant moving on from Vera as well.

Glancing down, Mitchell's fingers punched at his cell. Looking up with a smile, he announced, "We just took Drescher into custody."

Elizabeth considered the news for a moment, then stood up, leaned over and kissed him on one side of his face, brushing the other with her hand. "Kurt, I hope to see you again. Thank you for everything you've done. I really appreciate it. I know my grandmother would, too." She pulled his jacket off her shoulders and draped it over the chair she had vacated then turned away, leaving a half glass of wine on the table.

"Elizabeth, are you okay?"

Lowering her head for a moment, she turned back and one side of her mouth curled upward. "I'll be fine."

Leaving Mitchell behind, she walked to the door, out onto the streets of Manhattan.

Glancing across to her building, she got a glimpse of Drescher being led out the front door with his hands in cuffs behind him. He appeared rather humble between two uniformed New York City police officers. Half a dozen plain-clothed men wearing black windbreakers followed behind. Three unmarked black Suburbans with lights flashing on the dashboards waited at the curb, along with two New York City patrol cars.

Drescher jerked his head toward her and they locked eyes. His held the unmistakable look of defeat.

Turning away, Elizabeth sauntered in the opposite direction down Lexington Avenue in the light rain.

# ABOUT THE AUTHOR

*O**ften writing late* into the night, transfixed by the allure of flickering candlelight, national award winning author Penny Goetjen embraces the writing process, unaware what will confront her at the next turn. Riding the journey with her characters, she's often as surprised as her readers to see how the story unfolds.

Ms. Goetjen fell in love with Maine at a young age, spending a childhood of glorious summer vacations there visiting her maternal grandmother, the inspiration for her loveable character, Amelia. It was her grandmother's creaky old house where she experienced her first paranormal encounter.

Always drawn to the breathtaking, raw beauty of the shore, she brought her own children to Maine so they could learn to appreciate the state as well. She and her husband, Kent, are the proud parents of three grown children and split their time between Connecticut and South Carolina.